Introduc...

Moonlight and Mistletoe by Carrie Tu......

Professional organizer Sarah Montgomery is hired to organize her elderly neighbor's cluttered apartment by Justin Latimer, her neighbor's grandson. Sarah believes free-spirited Justin is a lazy, unemployed poet who is taking advantage of his grandmother's generosity. Though attracted to him, she guards her heart against her growing feelings. As Sarah and Justin work together and enjoy Christmas events in New York City, romantic sparks fly—but will new revelations douse them?

Shopping for Love by Gail Sattler

Emily Jones has good reason for wanting to get lost as a tourist in the crowded shopping districts of New York City. But when Bryan Evans literally knocks her off her feet, her heart is spun even more off balance. When Christmas comes, will she go back home to life as normal, or will a piece of her heart always stay in the Big Apple?

Where the Love Light Gleams by Lynette Sowell

When the spruce tree in widow Gwynn Michaud's New Hampshire front yard is chosen for Rockefeller Center, her grown children send her to the Big Apple to see the tree lighting. Her host, Theophilus Stellakis, enjoys his ordered life and clockwork schedule as a professor in Manhattan. Will this Christmas bring change for both of them?

Gifts from the Magi by Vasthi Reyes Acosta

Cecilia Montes, a busy Latina grad student, buries herself under piles of work to keep her loneliness away. Then Elias Perez, a childhood friend, returns to the city as the youth pastor at her church. She is surprised to discover that the formerly sickly boy is now a strong, vibrant man of God. As Cecilia helps Elias with the youth, their friendship is renewed. But only when Cecilia learns to trust the Lord in new and deeper ways is she ready to receive gifts of love.

A *Big Apple* CHRISTMAS

*Love Unites Four Couples
During the Christmas Season in New York City*

VASTHI REYES ACOSTA || GAIL SATTLER
LYNETTE SOWELL || CARRIE TURANSKY

BARBOUR
PUBLISHING

MOONLIGHT AND MISTLETOE

by Carrie Turansky

Dedication

To my daughter Melissa, who shared her love
for New York City with me.
I treasure the wonderful memories we've made together.

The LORD is my light and my salvation—
whom shall I fear?
The LORD is the stronghold of my life—
of whom shall I be afraid?
PSALM 27:1

Chapter 1

The wailing siren of an approaching ambulance penetrated the walls of Sarah Montgomery's fourth-floor Manhattan apartment. A shiver raced up her back. The sound grew louder, then stopped abruptly on the street below. Her stomach tensed, and she glanced out her window. She hoped there wasn't a serious accident nearby.

Sarah slipped on her black wool coat, and her mind shifted to her schedule for the day. Ten o'clock: Meet with a new client, Harriet Hartman, to discuss organizing her cluttered Upper East Side apartment. Twelve o'clock: Have lunch with Catherine Meyers to give her the bid for reorganizing her dental office. Two o'clock: Return home to work on her Web site, answer e-mails and phone calls, and schedule her appointments for next week. Though it was still early November, everything would get busier as the holidays approached. Five o'clock: Work on the speech she'd be giving next Monday evening—"Ten Tips to Save Time and Streamline Your Life."

Sarah glanced at her watch, picked up her briefcase and

keys, and stepped out the door. She had a subway train to catch, and she couldn't be late. After all, it wouldn't make a very good impression if a professional organizer couldn't get to an appointment on time.

Down the hall on the left, the elevator doors opened. Three people dressed in rescue squad uniforms stepped out, maneuvering a rolling gurney with them.

Sarah's steps stalled as they hustled toward her.

A tall, silver-haired paramedic strode ahead, checking apartment numbers. The other two guided the gurney from the side and back. The lead paramedic stopped in front of her neighbor's door and knocked. "This is the rescue squad. Can you come to the door?"

Lillian Latimer's little dog barked frantically inside the apartment. Fear twisted around Sarah's heart as she considered the possibilities.

The paramedic knocked again and exchanged an anxious glance with one of his partners. "We'll have to get the building manager up here."

"I have a key!" Sarah dropped her briefcase and dashed back to her apartment. Thankfully, Lillian had given her a spare key last month after she'd locked herself out. She snatched it out of the drawer and hurried back to the hallway.

Seconds later, the lead paramedic opened Lillian's door. "Mrs. Latimer?" He stopped just inside the apartment. Holding the dog back, he turned to his partners. "Leave the gurney. Let's find her first and see what we're dealing with."

They hustled into the apartment, leaving Sarah in the hall. She bit her lip and took a step closer, peeking around the door.

Lillian's West Highland terrier rushed back into the living room and out the door past Sarah, dragging her red leather leash behind her.

"Molly, wait!" Sarah lunged for the wrist loop and snagged it just before it trailed out of reach. "Where do you think you're going?"

The Westie whined and then twirled in a circle, her little body quivering with emotion. She stopped and looked up at Sarah with a wide-eyed, worried expression.

Sarah bent down and gave the dog a reassuring pat on the head. Her white fur was warm and strangely comforting. "It's okay, Molly. Everything's going to be all right."

The little dog tugged her toward the apartment door, and Sarah followed. As she stepped inside, surprise rippled through her. Her neighbor had lovely drapes and expensive furniture, but Sarah could barely see them past all the clutter. Stacks of magazines and newspapers took up much of the floor space. Piles of mail and miscellaneous papers covered the couch and coffee table.

The silver-haired paramedic stepped into the living room. "Mrs. Latimer is worried about her dog. Would you take her to the bedroom and let her see the dog's okay? That should help her calm down." He glanced around the messy room. "It's going to take a few minutes to clear a path and get the gurney in here."

"What happened? Is she going to be all right?"

"She fell and hit her head pretty hard. She'll need some X-rays. We're taking her to emergency at St. Luke's."

Sarah nodded and made her way down the hall. Lillian's injuries sounded painful, but at least they weren't life threatening.

Molly jerked on the leash and led the way to the back bedroom, where Sarah found Lillian lying on her bed. Her curly white hair looked like a halo against the pink pillowcase. The woman's faded blue eyes lit up when she saw Sarah with her dog. "Oh, thank goodness you have Molly. I was worried she'd run out the door."

"No, she's fine, just anxious to see you." Sarah stood by Lillian's side and watched one of the paramedics hold the stethoscope to Lillian's arm as he pumped the blood pressure cuff and checked the reading.

"I'm so sorry you fell. Is there anything I can do to help you?"

Molly whined and stood on her hind feet, clawing the side of the mattress.

"They say I have to go to the emergency room, but I shouldn't be gone too long. Could you take care of Molly until I get back?" Lillian reached out and tenderly touched the dog's head. "She's not much trouble."

Uneasiness prickled through Sarah. Growing up, she'd never had a dog. Her parents wouldn't allow it. But it couldn't be that hard. She'd just give Molly a bowl of water and some doggy treats, and Lillian would be home in a few hours. Sarah smiled. "Of course. I'd be glad to watch her for you."

"Thank you, dear." Her neighbor closed her eyes, looking pale and weary.

Sarah bit her lip as she watched Lillian. She hated to think of her going to the ER with no one there to comfort her or bring her home. "Do you want me to call someone to meet you at the hospital?"

Lillian touched her forehead, looking confused. "Well, I suppose you should call my grandson, Justin. His number is on the refrigerator."

Sarah nodded. "I'll take care of it. Anyone else?"

"No. Justin will know what to do and who else to call."

"All right. You just rest. I'll call him and watch Molly. Don't worry about a thing."

Lillian grasped her hand tightly. "Thank you, Sarah. You're an angel."

"I'm glad I can help." Sarah smiled and squeezed Lillian's hand. "It's no trouble at all." She glanced down at Molly and swallowed, hoping that was the truth.

❄

Later that afternoon, Sarah sat at the desk in her apartment. She glanced at the calendar on her BlackBerry, mentally calculating the time she'd need to leave for her first appointment tomorrow morning.

Molly whined and nudged Sarah's leg.

"You don't have to go outside again, do you?" She felt a little strange talking to a dog, but Molly seemed to understand. When she heard the word "outside," the dog's ears stood up, she barked once, and the expression on her face looked like a doggy smile.

Sarah laughed and picked up the leash. "Okay, come on." Molly dashed to the door, dancing with excitement. As Sarah clipped the leash on Molly's collar, the doorbell rang.

She looked through the peephole and saw the back of someone's head. The person had shoulder-length, wavy, light brown hair. With the distorted view, she couldn't tell whether the person was a man or a woman. A ripple of apprehension traveled up her back.

She opened the door but left the chain lock in place. Better safe than sorry in this city.

The person turned around. Sarah immediately realized he was a man—a very good-looking man with a long, straight nose, strong chin, and golden brown eyes. He looked about thirty. She glanced at his clothes, and her eyebrows rose. He wore a baggy dark green sweatshirt with a torn neck, worn black jeans, and slip-on leather loafers with no socks. She kept the chain in place and stood back a little.

He smiled, and a deep dimple creased his left cheek. "Hi. I'm Justin Latimer."

Surprise rippled through her. She'd pictured Lillian's grandson a little differently when they'd talked on the phone earlier.

He lifted his brows, reflecting her hesitant expression.

Heat radiated into her face. "Oh. . .yes. I'm sorry." She unlatched the chain and opened the door wider. "I'm Sarah Montgomery."

Molly lunged past her and leaped at Justin. Sarah hung on to the leash.

Laughing, he squatted to greet the dog. "Hey there, Miss Molly. What've you been up to? Giving this lady a hard time?" He scratched behind the Westie's raised ears and let her lick his cheek.

"How's Lillian?" Sarah glanced down the hall toward her neighbor's door.

He stood to face Sarah, and a serious expression replaced

his smile. "She sprained her wrist, and they think she has a concussion." He frowned and glanced away. "Her blood work came back with some strange results, so the doctor wants to run some more tests. They're keeping her overnight."

"I hope she's not too upset. I know she thought she'd be coming home today." Sarah glanced down at Molly. Keeping the dog for one day had been a challenge. She wasn't sure how she'd manage working and watching her tomorrow.

Justin held his hand out for the leash. "Don't worry. I'll take Molly."

Sarah dipped her chin, surprised he'd read her thoughts, but she didn't release Molly to him.

"It's okay." Amusement shone in his eyes. "I stay with Molly whenever my grandmother goes out of town. That was part of the deal we made when I got Molly for her."

"You bought Molly for Lillian?"

Grinning, he nodded. "Yes, I'm the guilty party." He leaned down and ruffled the hair on the dog's head, his expression growing pensive. "She was lonely after my grandfather died. I thought a dog would be a good companion for her."

Sarah's heart warmed as she watched him. "That was thoughtful."

"Well, I'm glad it worked. Now Molly is one of the most pampered pooches in Manhattan." He gazed at the dog with affection. "And my grandma has someone who needs her and a reason to get up in the morning."

Sarah nodded and studied him. Even though he needed a good haircut and new wardrobe, a man who cared that much about his grandmother deserved a measure of trust. "Why don't you come in, and I'll collect Molly's things." She opened the door even wider.

"Thanks." He followed her into the apartment. His gaze traveled around the living room and dining room. "Wow, this is nice." He hesitated and glanced at her. "Spacious and very. . . neat."

She smiled. "You sound surprised."

"It looks like the same floor plan as my grandmother's apartment, but it's a shocking contrast to her. . .housekeeping style."

Sarah held back a chuckle. "Yes, I saw her apartment for the first time this morning."

He lifted his hands. "She wasn't always like this, but since my grandfather died, things have gotten out of hand. Hopefully, I can sort through some things and clean up while she's at the hospital."

Sarah tipped her head, considering the possibilities. "Maybe I could help you."

His dark brows rose. "You want to help me clean out her apartment?"

"That's what I do."

"You're a cleaning lady?"

She pulled in a deep breath and stifled her initial response. "No, I'm a professional organizer." She reached in her suit jacket pocket and handed him a business card.

He took the card and read it, but his expression told Sarah he could use a little more explanation.

"I help my clients develop and implement plans to simplify and organize their lives, homes, and offices."

He nodded but still looked uncertain.

"I help them discover why they struggle with disorganization. Then I teach them how to overcome clutter, get organized, and realize their dreams."

His eyes lit up. "That's exactly what my grandma needs." He rubbed his hands together. "When could you start?"

"I'm glad you're interested, but Lillian would have to be the one to hire me. As I said, I'm not a cleaning service. I work with my clients and help them learn the skills they need to not only get organized, but stay organized."

"I've tried to help my grandmother clean up several times, but we never get very far. She has a hard time making decisions, and she doesn't want to throw anything away."

Sarah nodded. "That's a common problem, but it's not impossible to overcome." She sent him a confident smile. "I'm sure I could help her. I deal with people like that all the time."

"It might be a lot easier just to go in there while she's away, throw out all the extra stuff, and clean everything up. She might not like it at first, but she'd eventually forgive us and appreciate what we did."

Sarah cringed. His sneak-attack strategy was not the best way to handle this. She would only agree to such a plan in the most desperate situations. If he wanted lasting results, he'd have to trust her and let her do the job her way. "The first step is discussing this with Lillian. I need to understand her unique situation, then set objectives and goals with her. And of course we'd have to agree on a time frame and fee for the job."

"Of course." He nodded.

"Your grandmother's apartment needs a lot of work. I'll have to bring in some other people to help with the initial phase. It could be costly."

"Money is not an issue. My grandmother's safety and peace of mind are what's most important."

Sarah nodded, impressed by his caring attitude and commitment to help his grandmother. For someone who dressed so casually, he certainly was decisive. Of course, he was offering to spend his grandmother's money, not his own. Sarah recalled the beautiful furniture buried under the clutter in Lillian's apartment. Her neighbor obviously could afford to hire a professional organizer, and she certainly needed one. Now all they had to do was convince Lillian that Sarah was the one she could trust.

Chapter 2

Justin pushed the up button to call the hospital elevator and took a quick side-glance at Sarah. She was pretty in a sophisticated, designer kind of way with her long, dark blond hair twisted up in a sleek knot. And those blue-green eyes of hers would make any guy take a second look. They reminded him of a tropical ocean, shimmering with life and color. He smiled and tucked his hands in his jacket pockets. He wasn't usually attracted to nine-to-five professional types, but there was something different about Sarah, a softness behind the starched exterior that intrigued him.

He shook off that thought. Sarah was here because she had the skills they needed to get his grandmother's apartment in order. Their relationship was professional, not personal. But while he was staying at his grandmother's, they were also neighbors. Didn't the Bible say you were supposed to love your neighbor? Inwardly chuckling, he reminded himself he needed to stay focused and stop letting his mind wander.

The elevator doors opened. "After you." He held the door for her.

She stepped in and returned his smile. "Thanks."

He followed her and pushed the button for the seventh floor. "I think it would be best if I suggest the idea of cleaning my grandmother's apartment."

"Why's that?"

"If you bring it up, she's going to be embarrassed about the mess and not want to discuss it."

Sarah's eyebrows arched. "I'm very sensitive to my clients' feelings. I know how to handle this."

He pulled in a deep breath, surprised that someone who looked so soft and pretty one minute could be so cool and prickly the next. "I'm sure you do, but I know my grandmother, and if we aren't careful, she's going to get stubborn and resist the idea."

Sarah lifted her chin and looked him in the eyes. "I'm here to help her, and I know how to communicate that in a non-threatening and caring way."

"Okay, but I'd still like to be the one to bring it up. Then you can go ahead and explain what's involved."

Sarah hesitated a moment longer, finally conceding with a brief nod.

The elevator doors opened, and they stepped out. Justin led the way to his grandmother's room. He knocked softly, listened for her response, then pushed the door open.

His grandmother smiled when she saw them, but she looked tired and frail with the sling around her neck and her left wrist wrapped in bandages. Rather than the regular hospital garb, she wore the blue flowered nightgown he'd brought her yesterday.

The arrangement of pink roses he'd ordered had arrived and now sat on the windowsill, brightening the room. He bent and kissed his grandmother's forehead. "How are you feeling today?"

"Much better. I don't understand why the doctor won't let me go home."

"He wants to do a few more tests to be sure everything's okay. He explained that to you earlier this morning, remember?" She'd called him on his cell phone a little after eight to recount the doctor's visit and instructions.

"Of course I remember, but I feel fine as long as I don't use my wrist." She shifted her gaze to Sarah. "It's good to see you, dear. Thank you for coming. How is Molly doing?"

Sarah exchanged a glance with Justin. "Molly's fine. We had a good day yesterday, and then Justin came and took her to your apartment last night."

She settled back on the pillows and closed her eyes. "Oh yes, that's right. Justin is staying there with Molly." She rested for a moment, then opened her eyes and looked at him. "Did you walk her this morning?"

"Yes. We had a nice jog around the neighborhood right after you called." He sent up a silent prayer, hoping his grandmother was ready to switch topics. "There's something we need to talk about. I've wanted to suggest this for a long time, but I've been putting it off because I didn't want to upset—"

Sarah's eyes widened, and she shook her head. But when his grandmother turned her way, her expression quickly changed to a gentle smile. "What Justin means is that we'd like to get your apartment ready for you to come home, and we wanted to make a list of things you'd like us to do for you."

She looked back and forth between them. "A list?"

Sarah smiled. "Yes. You see, I'm a professional organizer. I help people get their homes and offices in order so they can feel comfortable and enjoy them. And Justin and I thought you might like me to do a little organizing while you're here. That way, when you come home, you can just rest and relax."

Justin nodded. "We don't want you to fall again, and everything is so. . ."

Sarah pressed her lips together and gave her head a little shake, squelching him a second time.

He stared back at her, trying to figure out why she wasn't letting him finish a sentence.

"Well, I'm not sure." His grandmother's eyes clouded, and she smoothed the sheet on her lap. "I don't like it so cluttered, but when I try to clean up, it just seems like the piles get deeper, and then I get discouraged and give up."

"Oh, I understand," Sarah said gently. "It can feel very overwhelming. That's why it's a good idea to hire someone to come in and help you. I can sort and organize things, label them, set up a filing system for bills and papers, and when you're ready, I can teach you how to stay on top of things." She smiled and laid her hand over Lillian's. "I'd love to help you."

Tears glistened in Lillian's faded blue eyes. "I'm sorry I've made such a mess of things, but after Andrew died, I just lost heart, and I haven't been able to keep things up since then." She raised a trembling hand to her forehead, shielding her eyes from them.

Justin clenched his jaw, and his throat ached. "It's all right. We don't need to talk about this right now. I'll just clean up a few things—"

His grandmother lowered her hand and looked at him with a perturbed expression. "No, Sarah's right. My apartment needs a good cleaning, and I have to get things sorted out first. I just wish I wasn't stuck in this hospital so we could get started today."

Justin held back a surprised chuckle.

"There's no reason we can't start now." Sarah beamed a triumphant smile and took a notepad and pen from her purse. "I'll just ask you a few simple questions, and that will show us exactly where to begin."

His grandmother nodded, looking relieved. "All right. That sounds easy enough." She pushed the button to raise the head of her bed and looked at Justin. "Would you mind getting me some coffee?"

He stared at her. "Coffee?"

"Yes, and none of that awful vending machine brew. I want the real thing." She turned to Sarah. "How about you, dear? Would you like some, too?"

Sarah smiled, her eyes shining. "Yes, thanks. That would be great."

"But are you supposed to have coffee? What would the doctor say?"

"For goodness' sake, Justin. I didn't have a heart attack or a stroke. I just sprained my wrist. Now run along and see if you can find a coffee shop." She shooed him toward the door. "And don't forget the cream and sugar."

Justin raised his gaze to the ceiling and shook his head. "Okay, two coffees coming up." He turned and headed out the door in search of some hot java that would meet his grandmother's approval and hopefully garner another enchanting smile from Sarah.

❄

Sarah knocked on Lillian's apartment door and waited for Justin to answer. She heard Molly barking inside. She hoped he was up and ready to let her get started. She had two other people coming to work with her this afternoon. Before they arrived, she needed to survey each room and make a step-by-step plan.

The door opened, and Justin smiled out at her. "Good morning." His hair looked clean and damp from the shower, and he wore a brown corduroy shirt and well-worn blue jeans. Though she didn't always like such casual clothes, she had to admit that on Justin they looked comfortable and even appealing.

Sarah squelched that thought, greeted him, and squeezed through the doorway before Molly could get away. She set down her tote of cleaning products and organizational supplies. Molly trotted over and sniffed the containers.

Justin grinned. "Well, I'm ready to get started. What do we do first?"

Sarah looked up at him. "Thanks, but don't you have to go to work?"

"Not really. I'm taking some time off right now."

"What do you do?" She'd been curious about his occupation since they'd met, but this was the first time it seemed appropriate to ask.

"I'm a writer."

"Oh. . .what do you write?"

He scratched his jaw, looking a little embarrassed. "I've written some plays and songs. But mostly I write poetry."

Sarah nodded and tried to keep an open expression on her face, but Justin's answer squelched her thoughts of having a relationship with him. Though she admired his kindness to his grandmother and would even admit she felt attracted to him, she'd never date someone seriously unless he had a strong work ethic and a respectable, well-established career, because someday she'd like to get married and have a family. Maybe she'd continue working part-time when the kids were in school, but she wanted the freedom to choose to work or stay home, and she definitely didn't want to spend her life supporting some free-spirit, starving-artist type who didn't have a dime and couldn't provide a decent living for himself or his family.

"Sarah?"

"Oh, sorry." Her face grew warm as she realized where her thoughts had taken her. "Guess I got distracted for a minute."

He chuckled. "That's okay. I do that all the time."

She sent him a quizzical look. "You get distracted?"

"Yeah, sometimes I see something that sparks an idea, and off I go." He waved his hand in the air. "Some days I have a hard time keeping up with my imagination. I even wake up at night with words to a song or poem running through my head."

"They just come to you at night?" Sarah couldn't imagine that happening to her.

"Yeah, so now I keep a flashlight and notepad on my nightstand."

"You actually wake up in the middle of the night and write things down?"

"Sure. That's when I get some of my best ideas." He looked at her as if that was the most logical thing in the world.

She couldn't keep a straight face any longer. Laughter bubbled up and overflowed. "I'm sorry. That just seems so. . .strange."

"What's strange about it? Don't you ever wake up with a great idea?"

"No. I fall asleep right away, and I don't wake up until morning."

He studied her for a moment, looking disappointed. "Too bad. If you listen, God speaks to you in the night."

This conversation was getting stranger by the moment. "He speaks to you?"

"Yes. That's what David says in the psalms: 'On my bed I remember you; I think of you through the watches of the night. Because you are my help, I sing in the shadow of your wings.'" He smiled. "So it's not so strange. I'm in good company."

"You mean you and King David?"

"Yes, we have a lot in common. He was a songwriter and a poet, too."

Sarah nodded, still trying to make sense of the man and the conversation. Justin obviously knew his Bible. He even memorized verses. She hadn't met many other people who took their faith that seriously. Maybe she shouldn't equate free-spirited and creative with lazy and unproductive. But she couldn't imagine someone spending his life writing songs and poems and not having a real job.

Sarah pushed those confusing thoughts away. It didn't matter what she thought of him. She was here to organize Lillian's apartment, not get involved with a song-writing, Bible-quoting poet!

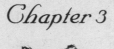

Chapter 3

Sarah pulled three more books from Lillian's shelf and stacked them on the floor at her feet. Her neighbor obviously loved to read and had a wonderful collection. The temptation to browse through the European history book tugged at her, but she laid it on the pile. This was crunch time. Lillian would be coming home tomorrow morning, and Sarah needed to finish up the living room tonight.

The grandfather clock in the corner struck seven as Justin strode into the room toting two heavy-duty trash bags. "I cleared out all those broken appliances and old take-out containers from that lower cabinet by the refrigerator."

"Great. Did you get those out-of-date medications from the bathroom?"

He nodded, concern shadowing his eyes. "I'm glad you had me check. Some of them were really old."

"I'm sure it's hard for her to read those tiny expiration dates." Sarah took two children's poetry books from the shelf and added them to the stack on the floor. "It would probably be a good idea to take a look in her medicine cabinet every few months. Expired medications can be dangerous."

Justin set down the trash bags and walked over to look at the pile of books. A frown creased his forehead as he picked up the top two. "You're not thinking of throwing these away, are you?"

"Not yet."

He narrowed his eyes. "Then why did you take them off the shelf?"

"I'm boxing them up and putting them in the guest room for now. Hopefully, by the time Lillian and I go through them, she'll be ready to donate some to the library book sale."

His eyes flashed, and he held the books to his chest. "These are first editions, signed by the author. I'm sure she doesn't want to get rid of them."

"Okay." Sarah shrugged. "If you think they're important to her, we can keep them." She pulled out a book about dog breeds and another about touring Italy to make room for the poetry books. "Mind if I put these in the guest room?"

"That's fine," he muttered and tucked the poetry books in the empty places. Then he turned and studied her with a serious expression. "You're not a fan of poetry?"

Surprise rippled through her at his tone. "I like poetry as much as the next person. But we're not talking about what I like or what you like. We're trying to understand what's important to your grandmother and help her get organized and simplify her life."

"Right." Justin blew out a deep breath. "Sorry. Guess I'm taking all this clearing out a little too personally." He walked over and picked up the bulging trash bags again.

Sarah watched him, thinking how nice it was to have someone strong to help. Over the last three days, he'd climbed ladders, lifted heavy boxes, and moved bookshelves to retrieve things that had fallen behind. And he'd done it all under her direction without complaining. Sarah took one more appreciative glance at Justin as he disappeared out the door. She reminded herself she should focus on the task at hand, but her thoughts drifted back to Justin.

She couldn't deny her attraction, but no matter how strong, handsome, or helpful he was, she wasn't going to get involved with him. It would never work. He was a late-night person, and she loved early mornings. He liked jazz, and she favored classical. He was impulsive and fun loving, and she was cautious and serious. But most important, she had goals and a productive career, and he seemed to have nothing to do but take care of his grandmother and her dog.

Sarah put the last book into the box and tucked in the flaps. How did he have enough money to live in the city? He hadn't mentioned exactly where his apartment was located, but it was probably in one of the poorer areas. She shivered and rubbed her upper arms at that thought.

❄

Justin unlocked the apartment door and let himself back inside. He glanced around his grandmother's living room, and a warm sense of satisfaction flowed through him. It looked like a different place. Sarah had done an amazing job of sorting through everything. He hoped his grandmother would appreciate it.

His stomach growled as he glanced in the dining room, searching for Sarah. It was time to quit and get something to eat. He hoped he could convince Sarah to come along with him tonight. She'd made an excuse the last time he'd asked. He'd teased her about having a boyfriend to see if that was the problem. She'd blushed and tried to pretend the question didn't fluster her. Finally, she admitted she was single and not dating anyone special at the moment.

That boosted Justin's confidence, and he decided to keep asking.

He checked the guest room, but Sarah wasn't there. Walking down the hall, he pondered the mixed signals she'd been sending him. They had a great time working together, laughing and talking as they sorted and cleaned. He sensed a special connection growing between them. But sometimes, when they were having fun, she'd suddenly grow cool and detached as though she was afraid to let him get too close. He frowned, wondering what that was about.

Rounding the corner, he spotted Sarah smoothing out the comforter on his grandmother's bed. He stood in the doorway, watching while she adjusted the two decorative pillows. He smiled, thankfulness rising in his heart. They'd faced piles of clutter in every room, but Sarah had patiently worked through it all, one step at a time, always careful to save anything she thought would be important to his grandmother.

"Everything looks great. Thank you, Sarah."

She looked up and smiled. "You're welcome. I hope Lillian likes it."

"I'm sure she will." He noticed the tired look in her eyes.

She'd worked long and hard to finish by tonight. "How about we go get some dinner and celebrate?"

She sent him a wary glance. "Thanks, but I still need to—"

"Please, I'm starving. You've got to be hungry, too."

"But what about—"

He shook his head. "Whatever it is, it can wait until tomorrow. We need to eat dinner, and I have the perfect solution."

"What's that?" A small smile lifted the corners of her mouth as they made their way down the hall and into the living room.

"I have a friend who opened a new restaurant this week." He raised his eyebrows and grinned. "And he gave me a coupon for two free dinners."

"Really?" She sent him an odd look he couldn't quite read.

"Yeah. I hear the food's great."

She hesitated, but he could see her weakening. "Okay. I suppose I can finish in the morning before Lillian comes home."

"Great! Let's go." He took her arm and led her out the door before she had time to change her mind.

Chapter 4

Sarah clutched her coat around her, trying to keep the cold wind from rushing down her neck. "What's the name of this restaurant?" She glanced at Justin and noticed his nose and ears had taken on a rosy glow.

"The Golden Door. It's not much farther." He pointed up the street. "Sorry, I should've suggested a taxi."

She wished he had, but she suspected he didn't have the money to pay for one, and she didn't want to embarrass him by offering to take care of it. "It's okay." She forced a smile and tried to keep her teeth from chattering.

He guided her past three older women wearing heavy wool coats. They pointed and stared up at the tall buildings, talking excitedly among themselves as they shuffled along. Sarah decided they must be tourists.

Her heart warmed as she watched them. Yes, New York was noisy, busy, and sometimes harsh, but she loved it. Moving here two years ago and starting her own business had been a risk, but she was glad she'd come.

"Here we go." Justin pulled open the restaurant door and waited for her to enter first.

The strong smell of curry and incense greeted Sarah as she stepped inside. She held her breath for a moment, fighting off her rising apprehension. She'd only eaten at two Indian restaurants, and both times she'd been miserable. Hot, spicy ethnic food had never been her favorite.

"Wow, this looks great." He motioned toward the dining room.

Sarah swallowed and nodded. The unusual Indian music pulsed through her, reminding her she had a slight headache. Maybe she was just hungry, but she wasn't sure what she could eat here that would take care of that problem.

"Justin!" A young Indian woman stepped out from the hostess podium. "It's good to see you. Ravi will be so glad you're here." Her exotic dark eyes glowed as she spoke, and a little diamond sparkled on the side of her nose.

A tall Indian man dressed in a blue shirt and black slacks stepped into the foyer, grinning broadly as he approached.

Justin laughed and grabbed him in a bear hug. "Hey, Ravi, how's business?"

"Very fine." He nodded toward the dining room. "You have come at a good time. We can seat you now."

"Thanks. But first I want you to meet Sarah." Justin placed his hand on Sarah's lower back. "These are my good friends, Ravi Guptava and his sister Asha. Ravi and I went to college together at Columbia."

Sarah smiled and held out her hand. "Hi, I'm Sarah Montgomery."

"Ah, Sarah, welcome to the Golden Door." Ravi grasped her hand and shook it vigorously. "I did not know Justin had such a fine friend. Where has he been keeping you?"

Sarah's face warmed as she searched for an answer.

Asha smiled and reached for her hands. "Don't worry about my brother. He loves to tease."

"Yes, I'm sorry." Ravi nodded, his large dark eyes reflecting his sincerity. "We just met, and already I've offended you."

"No, it's okay." Sarah glanced at Justin, hoping he would say something.

His eyes twinkled as he shifted his attention to Ravi. "I've heard great things about the Golden Door."

"Ah, good! Come, let me show you to your table." He led them past the colorful buffet and reeled off the names of several exotic dishes.

Justin nodded and smiled. "This looks fantastic."

Sarah didn't recognize any of it except the rice and the flat tortilla-like bread called *chapati*.

Ravi seated them at a table for two by the front window. "Would you like the dinner buffet, or would you prefer to see the menu?" He glanced back and forth between them. "Please, you may have whatever you wish tonight."

Justin smiled at her. "Sarah?"

"Uh. . .the buffet sounds good." At least she could see the food and try to guess what it was before she put it on her plate.

Ravi bowed slightly. "Very good. Help yourselves and enjoy!"

Justin led the way to the buffet and invited Sarah to go first.

She glanced at the overflowing platters surrounded by tropical fruits and flowers. "I don't know much about Indian food. Maybe you should go ahead and interpret."

Justin chuckled. "Okay. I'll try."

A few minutes later they were seated at their table again with full plates. Justin smiled and slid his hand across the table toward her. "Would you like to pray with me?"

She wasn't used to praying aloud in restaurants, but she liked that he'd asked. She took his hand and bowed her head.

"Father, thank You for providing this dinner for us tonight. We ask You to watch over Ravi and his family and make his restaurant successful. Please be with my grandma and help her continue to heal as she comes home tomorrow." He hesitated for a second, and his voice grew softer. "Thank You for Sarah and all the gifts and talents You've given her. Please bless her for her kindness to my grandma. Most of all, we thank You for loving us and making us part of Your family. In Jesus' name we pray, amen." He squeezed her hand and then let go.

She'd never expected to be included in his prayer, and it softened her heart and drew her to him in ways she hadn't anticipated.

"Man, my mouth is watering." Justin picked up the chapatti, dipped it in the meat sauce, and lifted it to his mouth. No fork, no spoon, just his hands.

Sarah watched, uncertain if she should follow his lead or use her silverware.

He grinned. "Come on, try the lamb. It looks great." He took a big bite and moaned with delight as he chewed.

She pulled in a deep breath and scooped up a little meat

sauce with her chapatti. Leaning over her plate, she took a small bite. The chewy chapatti tasted buttery and delicious, and the lamb was so tender it practically melted in her mouth. As she swallowed the spicy sauce, her mouth began to burn. "Wow, it's hot!" She reached for her water glass.

Justin shook his head. "Eat some of the *raita*." He pointed to the cucumbers in yogurt sauce. "It'll cool you off better than the water."

She quickly spooned a big bite into her mouth and let the cool sauce bathe her throat.

Concern creased his forehead. "I'm sorry. I should've warned you it was spicy."

Now her cheeks felt hotter than her mouth. She lifted her hand and fanned her face. "I'm fine, really." But she could barely croak out the words.

He looked down at his plate, trying to hide his grin.

Watching him, a giggle rose in her throat. She tried to hold it back, but it soon made her shoulders shake and brought tears to her eyes. She reached up and covered her mouth. But it was too late. Cucumber sauce dripped down her chin.

Dimples creased his cheeks as he joined in with her laughter. "Here, let me give you a hand." He reached across the table and gently wiped her chin with his napkin.

She pulled in a calming breath and pressed her lips together. "Sorry about that. I'm so embarrassed." But when he grinned at her with that twinkle in his eyes, she giggled again. "Stop, we're making a scene."

He glanced around, nodded to the man at the next table, and turned back to her. "Ah, don't worry. They just wish they were having as much fun as we are."

Sarah shook her head and smiled. He was right. She hadn't laughed so hard in a long time, and it felt wonderful.

She glanced across the table at Justin. With his long hair and casual clothes, he certainly didn't look like your typical Manhattan businessman. But there was nothing false or pretentious about him. He seemed perfectly content with himself and his life. And his easygoing attitude made her feel comfortable, as though she could relax and be herself. But it was more than that. He made her feel special and appreciated. And that was something she hadn't experienced in a very long time.

As soon as that thought settled in her heart, reality broke through and burst her bubble. No matter how wonderful he made her feel, she was not going to give her heart away to a man who couldn't give her a secure future.

❄

Justin tightened his hold on his grandmother's arm as he pushed open her apartment door. "Welcome home."

She stopped in the doorway, her eyes wide as she surveyed her neat living room. A bronze mum plant in a rustic basket graced the coffee table, and three gold pillar candles flickered on the mantel. The aroma of apples and cinnamon floated in the air.

Sarah appeared from the kitchen, a warm smile lighting her face. "Lillian, I'm so glad you're home." She crossed the living room to meet them. "Here, let me take your coat for you." Sarah's voice sounded a little higher than normal, and a small line creased the area between her eyebrows. She glanced up at

Justin, a question in her eyes.

Lillian's chin began to tremble, and she reached for Sarah. "Thank you, dear. Everything looks wonderful."

Justin released the breath he'd been holding and smiled at Sarah.

"You're welcome." Sarah returned his smile as she hugged his grandmother.

Lillian pulled back and scanned the room again. "I can hardly believe it's the same place. Where did you put it all?"

"Don't worry. Sarah has a great system for everything. We stored several boxes in the guest room for now, and when you're ready, she'll help you go through them and set up files for your mail and important papers."

Sarah nodded. "Justin also put a new set of bookshelves in there so you'll have room for all your books and magazines."

His grandmother turned and embraced him. "Thank you, Justin. I don't know what to say."

He closed his eyes and held her close for a moment, thankful she was safely home again. All of his life she had been there for him, and now it was his turn to show her how much she meant to him. "You don't need to thank me. I could never repay you for everything."

His grandmother stepped back. "Nonsense! You don't owe me anything. We're family, and that's all there is to it." She patted his chest affectionately, then turned and looked around. "Say, where's Molly?"

Sarah headed down the hall. "I think she's in the bedroom. I'll get her."

Justin helped his grandmother take off her coat and hung

it in the front closet.

Molly trotted into the living room and made a beeline for her mistress, her tail waving like a flag.

"Oh, hello, my little darling. Did you miss me?" Lillian lowered herself into the navy blue recliner and lifted Molly onto her lap. The dog squirmed and licked her chin.

Justin grinned as he watched their reunion. Buying Molly had been one of his better ideas. It ranked right up there next to hiring Sarah to organize his grandmother's apartment.

Sarah joined them in the living room. "Would you like me to make some coffee?"

Lillian looked up from petting Molly. "Coffee would be lovely, dear. And what's that wonderful smell?"

"I'm warming an apple pie in the oven. I thought you might like a little treat to celebrate your homecoming."

Justin pulled in a deep, cinnamon-scented breath, and his mouth began to water.

"I only had a light lunch at the hospital. Pie would be wonderful. Let's all have some. Then we can sit down and visit."

"Sounds like a good idea to me." Justin followed Sarah into the kitchen. "Well, that went better than I expected," he said quietly. He took a tray down from the top of the refrigerator and set it on the counter.

Sarah glanced at him as she filled the coffeepot. "She's happy. That's what's most important."

"And you're very clever to bring an apple pie. That's her favorite."

Sarah laughed softly. "I know."

"How did you figure that out?"

"I did a little detective work when I visited her at the hospital the other day."

Justin's heart warmed as he thought of all she'd done for his grandmother. He moved closer and slipped his arm around her shoulder. "Thank you, Sarah, for everything. It means a lot to me." He wanted to say more, but she stepped away.

"I'm glad she can rest and focus on getting her strength back." Sarah's cheeks glowed pink as she took the coffee from the cabinet.

He leaned back against the counter, watching her. Why did she pull away like that? Was she sending a message that she wanted him to back off? He quickly dismissed that idea. She was probably just shy and needed more time to warm up to him.

That was all right. He wouldn't rush her. He knew she wasn't impressed that he was a writer. For a moment, he considered telling her about the four volumes of children's poetry he'd had published in the last six years and all of the recognition and awards he'd received for them. But trying to sway her with his fame or his bank account didn't seem right. He wanted her to respect him for who he was, not for his bio on the back of the book jacket.

He'd have to find another way to reach her heart.

Chapter 5

Sarah set three coffee cups on the tray, then added the sugar bowl and cream pitcher. She tried to ignore the way Justin's gaze followed her as she crossed the kitchen and retrieved the steaming coffeepot.

Why had he put his arm around her shoulder? As she recalled his tender touch and the look in his eyes, she sensed he had more than friendship on his mind. Excitement tingled through her, but a tremor of apprehension quickly followed.

"Sarah?" Justin's voice sounded soft and appealing as he stepped up next to her.

She lifted her gaze to meet his, and her heartbeat sped up.

Warmth and affection glowed in his golden brown eyes. "I hope you know that I—"

"How's that coffee coming?" Lillian asked, walking into the kitchen.

Sarah jerked, and coffee splashed on the tray, just missing her fingers.

"Sorry, I didn't mean to startle you." Lillian watched them

with a curious smile.

Justin grabbed a paper towel and wiped up the spill. "Did it burn you?"

"No, I'm fine." She pulled in a calming breath and smiled at Lillian. "The coffee's ready." She filled three cups, then grabbed a pot holder and took the apple pie from the oven.

Lillian glanced around her spotless kitchen. "I think we should have Thanksgiving here this year."

Justin frowned. "Cooking a big meal like that would be a lot of work for you."

"Who said anything about cooking? I'm sure your mother would bring the food. Although I'd dearly love to roast a turkey."

"But I thought the plan was to go to my parents' house."

"It would be much easier for me if they'd come here. Then I wouldn't have to put Molly in a kennel or make that long drive over to Jersey in all that traffic."

"I suppose that's true, but the doctor said you should rest."

Lillian waved away his concern. "All I'd have to do is set the table and roast the turkey. And you could help me with that." She smiled at Justin. "You are going to stay for a few more days, aren't you?"

He nodded. "I'm planning on it."

"Good!" Lillian gestured toward the dining room. "We could put in the extra leaf and use the ivory damask tablecloth. And with all those boxes cleared out of the dining room, I'll be able to open the china cabinet and get out my special dishes and silverware."

Contentment flowed through Sarah as she listened to her

neighbor's growing excitement. Knowing Lillian would be able to enjoy her home and have her family over for a holiday meal meant more to Sarah than receiving a paycheck for organizing the apartment.

"I don't think we'd need the extra leaf." Justin glanced at the dining room. "It would be just Mom and Dad, you, me, and Jared."

Lillian sat down on the kitchen stool and tapped her fingers on the counter. "Well, maybe Sarah can join us."

Sarah almost dropped the pie server. "Oh no, I wouldn't want to intrude on your family time."

"Nonsense! You wouldn't be intruding." Then Lillian clicked her tongue. "What am I thinking? You're probably going home to be with your own family."

Sarah lowered her gaze. "My parents are in Europe right now. They aren't planning to be home for Thanksgiving." The words felt like a heavy weight on her shoulders.

Justin set some forks on the tray. "Are they there for work or vacation?"

"Both." Sarah cut a piece of pie. "My father has business meetings in Switzerland, then they're joining friends and touring Germany, Austria, and Italy."

He crossed his arms and leaned against the counter. "What does your father do?"

"Oh. . .he's in international banking."

Justin's eyebrows rose. "I see."

Her heart felt like a deflated balloon. No matter how much money her parents earned, it hadn't brought their family closer or strengthened their relationships. Their decision to tour

Europe over Thanksgiving was another painful reminder of the low priority they placed on spending time with Sarah, and that hurt more than she liked to admit.

"I'm sorry you won't be able to spend the holiday with them." Lillian gave the counter a brisk tap. "But that just means we can steal you for our celebration." She looked up at Sarah with a hopeful expression. "You will come, won't you? I could never enjoy the day knowing you were next door all alone."

Sarah glanced from Lillian to Justin, trying to gauge how he felt about his grandmother's invitation.

He smiled. "I'm sure my family would love to have you come. And I can guarantee the food will be good."

Lillian laughed. "Especially since Justin and I are roasting the turkey!"

Happy anticipation washed over Sarah. "Okay. It sounds great. What can I bring?"

"Whatever you like, dear. Maybe something that's traditional for your family."

That suggestion drew a blank. Sarah thought for a moment. "I could make an apple pie, or I have a great recipe for carrot cake."

Justin's eyes lit up. "Does it have cream cheese frosting?"

"Absolutely, and lots of carrots, raisins, pineapple, and walnuts."

He sighed with delight. "Please, make the cake."

Chapter 6

Sarah carefully balanced the tray with one hand as she knocked on Lillian's apartment door. She glanced down at the round, two-layer carrot cake. Creamy white frosting covered the top, and chopped walnuts decorated the sides. It looked perfect, but she wasn't sure how it tasted. And that was the problem. You couldn't cut a cake and take a bite before you served it. You just had to follow the recipe and go by faith.

And faith had never been her strong point.

She smoothed the bottom hem of her sweater. Why was she feeling so fidgety? She wasn't on trial. She was here today as Lillian's guest. It didn't matter what Justin's family thought of her.

But for some reason it did matter—very much.

The door swung open, and Justin smiled out at her. "Hi, come on in."

His warm response eased some of her nervousness. For a second, it looked as if he wanted to hug her, but she raised the tray between them. "I brought the carrot cake."

"Wow, that looks great. I think I'll eat dessert first."

She sent him a teasing smile. "Sorry, you have to wait just like everyone else."

They walked into the living room, and Justin introduced her to his father and brother.

Justin's father, Paul, stood. "So you're the one who cleaned out the apartment?"

Concern flashed in Justin's eyes. "Sarah's a professional organizer, Dad."

"Of course, that's what I meant. You did a great job. Mom can't stop talking about it."

Justin's brother, Jared, glanced up from the football game he was watching. "Hey, Sarah, you want me to take that cake off your hands?"

Before she could answer, Justin placed his hand on her lower back and guided her toward the kitchen. "No way. We're going to give it to Mom for safekeeping."

"Keep your eye on him, Sarah," Jared called. "He loves carrot cake, and he's not above sticking his fingers in the frosting."

Justin looked over his shoulder. "Hah! I think that's more your style."

Sarah smiled at the brothers' playful banter.

The wonderful aroma of roasting turkey floated toward Sarah as they passed through the dining room. She glanced at the table set with Lillian's wheat-patterned china and sparkling water glasses. She and Justin had spent most of Wednesday afternoon helping Lillian get everything ready.

Justin led the way into the kitchen. "Mom, where do you

want Sarah to put this cake?"

His mother turned to face them, a warm smile filling her pleasant face. "Sarah, I'm so happy to finally meet you. Please, call me June. And look at the beautiful cake! Did you make this?"

Sarah nodded, suddenly feeling shy.

"It looks delicious. Let's put it on the counter for now."

Lillian waved a pot holder. "You're just in time, Sarah. We're going to take the turkey out of the oven any minute. Oh, I'd better get the camera." Lillian tossed the pot holder aside and scurried out of the kitchen.

June took Sarah's hand. "I can't tell you how much I appreciate what you've done for Lillian. Since Paul's father died, she let everything go. But now. . .it's like she's finally coming out of her grief and is ready to live again." Tears misted her eyes, and she hugged Sarah. "Thank you so much."

June's embrace tightened Sarah's throat. "Lillian's an amazing lady," she said as she stepped back. "I've enjoyed getting to know her."

"I still can't believe she agreed to let you help. Every time I suggested cleaning up, she got so emotional I had to drop it."

Sarah nodded. "Sometimes when a loved one dies, people don't want to change anything. So they just create another layer of life on top of the old. It can be a subconscious way they try to hold on to the one they lost."

June's eyes widened. "I never thought of it like that, but it makes sense." She smiled at Sarah. "There's obviously more to what you do than just throwing out junk and labeling everything." She turned to her son. "You're right about her,

Justin. She's just as smart as she is pretty."

Justin rubbed his forehead, looking embarrassed.

June laughed and patted his cheek. "It's okay, honey. Sarah doesn't mind hearing a compliment."

Lillian returned to the kitchen and began snapping pictures, including one of Sarah and Justin together. Soon they were all seated around the table, and Justin's father offered a beautiful prayer to begin the meal. Seated between Lillian and Justin, Sarah enjoyed the delicious food, lively conversation, and heartfelt laughter.

As the meal drew to a close, June looked across at Sarah. "We have a tradition of sharing special Thanksgiving memories."

Sarah nodded and forced a smile, hoping they didn't expect her to go first.

June glanced expectantly around the table. "Okay. I'll start. The first time I hosted Thanksgiving, I was a young bride of twenty-two. Of course we roasted a big turkey. Lillian helped me with that." She smiled at her mother-in-law. "And I made a beautiful blueberry pie from scratch. But as I carried it across the kitchen, I tripped and it landed upside down on my shoe."

Paul chuckled. "I came in the kitchen and found you crying. But we couldn't let that pie go to waste. So we flipped it over, brushed it off, and served it with vanilla ice cream. We called it blueberry crumble, and everyone loved it!"

Jared leaned forward. "You served a pie after you dropped it on the floor?"

"Not the part that touched the tile!" June said. "Just the good part underneath."

Sarah glanced at Justin, watching his response before she

joined in with everyone's laughter. She wasn't used to being with a close-knit family, and it awoke a longing in her heart she hadn't known was there.

Jared cleared his throat. "Okay, my turn. Remember that year we all came into the city to watch the Macy's Thanksgiving Day Parade? It snowed about twelve inches the night before, and we had to stand in knee-deep slushy snow. You all wanted to leave early, but I insisted we had to stay until the end to see Santa Claus."

Justin grinned. "Yeah, I was ten and you were seven. We about froze to death, but we had a great time."

Jared settled back in his chair. "Okay, big brother, your turn."

Justin nodded and looked down at his plate. "Four years ago Jared was in the middle of chemo treatments, and we weren't sure if we should celebrate Thanksgiving."

June's face grew pale as she glanced at her husband and then her sons.

"We don't usually like to remember that year." Justin raised his gaze and looked around the table. "But it was a turning point for me." He focused on his brother. "Jared showed more courage and faith in God than anyone I've ever known, and he loved me enough to challenge my lack of faith, and that changed me forever." Justin reached over and clamped his hand on his brother's shoulder. "Thanks, bro. I owe you big-time."

Jared's eyes glistened. "I'd go through it again if that's what it took to see you walking with the Lord."

June lifted her hand to her mouth. "Oh, I think I'm going to cry."

Paul patted his wife's shoulder. "It's all right, dear."

"Yes, it is. The Lord answered our prayers for both our boys." June wiped her eyes with her napkin and sniffed. "How about you, Sarah? Do you have a special Thanksgiving memory you can share?"

Sarah tried to swallow past the huge lump in her throat. "Well, I don't have anything nearly as special as what you all shared."

"That's okay, dear. Just tell us one of your memories."

Sarah smoothed out the napkin in her lap. "Well, we usually go out to dinner on Thanksgiving." She hesitated when she saw the surprised expression on everyone's face. "My mother works full-time and doesn't like to cook, so my parents have a housekeeper. They give her the day off on Thanksgiving so she can spend time with her family. . .and we eat at a restaurant."

"Do you have any brothers or sisters?" June asked.

"No, I'm an only child. Both sets of grandparents passed away when I was young, so it's just my parents and me on Thanksgiving."

Understanding filled Justin's eyes.

"Well, I'm glad you could be with us today." June patted her hand. "Okay. Who's ready for dessert and coffee?"

"What do you have, June bug?" Paul winked at his wife.

She stood and laid her hand on his shoulder. "We have pumpkin pie and Sarah's homemade carrot cake."

Paul grinned. "I think I'd like to try them both."

A few minutes later, Sarah's stomach tensed as she watched June serve her carrot cake to everyone. She pressed her lips together, praying they liked it.

"Mmm, this is heavenly," Lillian said after her first bite. "Can I have the recipe?"

Sarah released the breath she'd been holding. "Sure. I'd be glad to copy it for you."

After they'd finished dessert, June exhaled a contented sigh. "Well, this has been lovely, but I suppose it's time to clean up."

Justin pushed his chair back. "You and Grandma did all the cooking. I'll handle the cleanup."

Jared stretched. "Great! Then Dad and I can finish the game."

Sarah stood up. "I'll help."

Justin sent her a warm smile. "Thanks."

She followed him into the kitchen carrying a stack of plates. His family carried in the rest and returned to the living room.

Justin ran water into the sink, squirted in some lemon dish soap, and reached for one of Lillian's aprons.

Sarah couldn't hold back a giggle as she watched him tie it around his waist

"Hey, don't laugh. I like this outfit. I don't want to wreck it."

"Sorry, you look"—she wanted to say "adorable" but quickly swallowed the word—"like a chef."

Laughing, he shook his head. "I'm a terrible cook, but I can wash pots and pans with the best of them."

As he stood there with that playful look in his eyes, Sarah knew he could do much more than that—he could steal her heart if she let him.

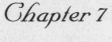

Chapter 7

Justin dunked his hands into the hot, soapy water and scrubbed the corner of the sticky casserole dish. Sarah stood next to him drying the heavy turkey platter. She'd tucked her blond hair behind her ears, giving him a great view of her softly rounded cheeks and pretty blue-green eyes.

"Today was nice." A small smile played at the corners of her mouth. "Thanks for inviting me. I mean, I know Lillian is the one who asked me, but—"

"You're welcome."

She carefully set aside the platter. "I've never been—I mean my family isn't. . ."

"Isn't what?"

"My family's not close like yours."

He thought about that for a moment. "We've been through a lot, and I guess our faith keeps us close, too."

Sarah bit her lip as she dried the crystal butter dish. "My parents aren't believers yet. I've shared with them a few times, but they don't see the need."

Justin nodded and realized he'd always taken his parents' faith and the stability it provided for granted. "How did you come to know the Lord?"

"In college I had a roommate named Amy. She talked about the Lord all the time. It drove me crazy at first. I asked her lots of questions, and she'd pull out her Bible and do her best to explain. It took me awhile to come around, but she never stopped loving me even when I didn't want to listen."

"How long ago was that?"

"Seven years."

"So you've been a believer longer than I have."

Surprise flashed in her eyes. "Yes, I suppose that's true, but you were raised in the church, right?"

"Yes. My parents took me every Sunday since I was a baby, but I never let it sink into my heart. Finally, when Jared got sick, I realized how little control I had and how much I needed God. I wanted Him to heal Jared, but I needed Him for so much more than that." He narrowed his eyes, remembering the painful storm that had crashed through his life four years earlier. But God had spoken into that storm and changed everything, giving him a new life. "I'm glad my family didn't give up on me."

"You're blessed to have them." She sounded wistful.

He nodded, watching her. "I can tell they like you."

Her face brightened as she looked up at him. "You really think so?"

"Sure." He dunked the roasting pan into the soapy water and grinned. "Of course, that's only because of your carrot cake."

She gasped and flicked him with the towel.

"Hey, you'd better watch it." He grabbed the sink sprayer and squirted her.

She squealed and jumped back, but the water hit her shoulder. "You soaked me!" She lunged for the spray nozzle and tried to turn it back on him.

He easily kept control of the sprayer, reached around behind with his other hand, and tickled her waist.

Gasping and giggling, she let go of the sprayer and tried to squirm away. He dropped the sprayer into the water, sending a wave of suds over the side of the sink.

She swatted a handful of soapsuds at him. They splattered his chin. He tried to wipe them off with his shoulder, but that just smeared them around.

"You look like Santa," she said between giggles.

"Is that right?" His arms encircled her waist, and his laughter faded as he looked into her sparkling eyes. His gaze dropped to her lips, and his heartbeat sped up.

Her lips parted as she tried to catch her breath, and fear flickered in her eyes.

He pulled in a slow, deep breath and dropped his hands from her waist, but he held her with his gaze. "You don't have to be afraid of me, Sarah. I'd never take what you don't want to give."

Her cheeks flamed. She lowered her gaze, but she didn't move away.

He gently lifted her chin until she looked into his eyes. "You're safe with me. I promise."

❄

Sarah glanced out the taxi window at the Christmas lights

decorating the front of Lord & Taylor. Raindrops on the glass turned the shimmering lights into sparkling diamonds. She smiled and sat back in the seat. Her meeting with a new client had run late, and she'd decided to splurge on a taxi ride home rather than fighting the rush-hour crowds in the subway. This wasn't much quicker, but at least it gave her door-to-door service and a way to avoid the icy cold rain.

The driver changed the radio station to Christmas music, and Sarah found herself humming along with the strains of "The First Noel." She glanced out the window again at the crowded sidewalk.

Thousands of visitors came to the city each year seeking that special New York Christmas experience—the hustle and bustle of shopping on Fifth Avenue, the beautiful tree at Rockefeller Center, the holiday concerts at Carnegie Hall, and everywhere the elegant evergreen wreaths and garlands decorating businesses, stores, and restaurants. The city was dressed in its best and ready to greet its guests.

Sarah hoped she could schedule in some free time to enjoy those sights. The idea of seeing them with Justin crossed her mind, but she quickly pushed that thought away. It had been four days since Thanksgiving. He hadn't called, and she'd only seen him once, when she stopped in to help Lillian find her Christmas decorations among the boxes they'd stored in the guest room.

Justin had been on his way out as she was coming in. He seemed happy to see her and said he wished he had time to talk, but he was on the way to meet a friend for lunch.

Her smile faded as she remembered watching him turn and

walk away without looking back. That was what she thought she wanted...but now she wasn't so sure. After spending Thanksgiving with him and his family, she was beginning to think she might have misjudged him. Not everyone could be a successful businessman like her father, but that didn't mean he wasn't worthy of respect and friendship. His strong faith and loving relationships with his family were something money could never buy.

She sighed and told herself none of that mattered if Justin wasn't interested in her, and apparently he wasn't since he hadn't called. But she was certain he'd wanted to kiss her when they were washing dishes.

She took her cell phone from her purse, turned on the ringer, and pressed speed dial to check her messages. The automated voice told her she had one new message. She pressed the button and held the phone to her ear.

"Hi, Sarah. It's Justin. Sorry I missed you."

She smiled, her heart lifting at the sound of his voice.

"Something's come up, and I have to go up to Toronto for a few days. I was wondering if you could do me a favor and check on my grandma for me."

Sarah's hopes deflated. She didn't mind helping Lillian, but she wished he'd called for another reason.

"She seems to be doing well," Justin continued, "but if it gets icy, she could probably use some help taking Molly out. If she needs more than that, you can call her friend Jean or my parents or her pastor. The numbers are on the emergency list by the phone." She could hear the smile in his voice. "I guess you know that since you set it up for her." He paused. "I don't think my cell phone will work in Canada, so I'll talk to you when I get back. I appreciate your help. Thanks."

The automated voice returned with instructions about deleting or saving the message. Sarah hesitated a moment, then pressed the button to save it. She felt silly, but it might be nice to play it again later and hear his voice when she was all alone and wishing he was there.

❄

"Where do I put this bank statement?" Lillian squinted at the piles of paper spread out on the dining room table.

"Is it savings or checking?" Sarah waited, giving Lillian time to figure that out. She knew how difficult this was for her friend. Her late husband had always handled the finances, and now Lillian needed to learn how to take care of them herself. Today she'd asked Sarah to help her straighten out over a year's worth of receipts, bills, and statements.

Lillian pushed her silver-framed glasses up on her nose. "Savings, I believe."

Sarah smiled and nodded, feeling as if they'd scored a point. "It goes right here."

Lillian placed it on the pile. "What do we do now that they're all separated?"

"We put them in labeled file folders and then alphabetize them in the file drawers in your desk. When tax time comes, you'll be ready to visit your accountant."

Lillian exhaled a heavy sigh. "Well, I need a cup of coffee before we tackle that job. How about you, dear? Can I make you one?"

"Thanks, that sounds great."

Lillian headed for the kitchen, and Sarah picked up the stack of savings account statements. She wanted to be sure Lillian hadn't mixed in any checking statements. They looked similar, and it would be an easy mistake to make.

Sarah flipped through the pile, her gaze taking in the same three transactions on each statement—a large deposit at the beginning of the month, a smaller deposit mid-month, and a surprisingly large withdrawal near the end of the month. These transactions kept the account almost level with several thousand dollars in reserve.

Sarah frowned as she studied the large monthly withdrawal. It seemed like a lot of cash for Lillian to carry, especially since she wrote checks for most of her monthly bills and used credit cards for shopping.

As Sarah stared at the numbers, a question formed in her mind. Did Lillian give that money to Justin? Was that how he paid for his apartment and living expenses? His comment about owing his grandmother more than he could ever repay flashed through her mind. She'd thought he was talking about an intangible debt of love, but could he have meant a generous monthly allowance that covered his expenses so he didn't have to work?

"Here you go, dear." Lillian crossed the dining room and handed her the cup and saucer. "I'll get mine and be right back."

Too late, Sarah remembered Lillian could only carry one cup at a time with her arm still in a sling. "I'm sorry. I should've helped you."

"Oh, it's no problem. I'm fine," Lillian called from the kitchen. She returned with her steaming cup and sat at the table.

Sarah forced herself to focus. "I think we should file these statements by date."

Lillian nodded and took a sip of coffee. "Good idea."

"You'll get an annual giving report from your church in January. Put it in the file labeled CHARITABLE GIVING." Sarah hesitated, unable to keep her doubts quiet. "Do you give to anything or anyone else?"

Lillian tapped her cheek for a moment. "I support a young woman who is a missionary nurse in Tanzania. She's doing a wonderful work there."

"You write checks for that, right?"

"Yes, and they send me a receipt each month." Lillian pointed to the stack on the corner of the table.

"Anyone else?" Sarah's stomach knotted as she waited for Lillian's answer.

Lillian hesitated.

Sarah swallowed and pressed on. "I noticed you make a pretty large withdrawal each month from your savings."

Lillian glanced at her, looking embarrassed. "I give that to someone who needs a little extra help right now."

"That's a lot of money. Are you sure you can afford to do that every month?"

"Oh, it's not that much. The Lord has blessed me and taken care of my needs. Why shouldn't I help others in return?"

Sarah gripped her cup, searching for the right words. "Giving someone a handout may not be the best way to help them.

In fact, you might be short-circuiting what God wants to do. Maybe they need to get a job to support themselves."

Confusion filled Lillian's eyes. "He has a job, but the cost of living is so high here that he can't pay for all of his expenses."

"If you continue giving him money, he may never be motivated to find a better job and improve his situation." Sarah felt as if she were climbing a steep hill and would never reach the top. "And if you give away cash like that, you don't get a receipt or any kind of tax break."

Lillian looked at her with a sympathetic smile. "I appreciate what you're saying, dear, but I've prayed about it, and I believe this is what the Lord wants me to do. Treasure in heaven is much more valuable than any tax advantage I could have down here. I'll keep giving until the Lord tells me to stop."

Sarah pressed her lips together and glanced away. Lillian had made up her mind, and there was nothing she could do about it.

Was this really what the Lord had directed Lillian to do? Or was her generosity preventing Justin from taking responsibility for himself? Sarah wasn't sure, but she was glad he was out of town. She didn't know what she would say if he walked in today.

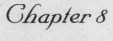

Chapter 8

Sarah settled back in her cozy overstuffed chair and propped her feet up on the footstool. Opening the Saturday morning paper, she perused the living section, checking the Christmas cookie recipes. With only two weeks until Christmas, she still had several things on her to-do list, and baking cookies was one of them.

She glanced at her six-foot Christmas tree in the corner of the living room. Getting it up to her apartment in the elevator had been an adventure. Thankfully, the building manager had seen her struggling and had come to her rescue. After she finally got it in the stand, she'd added white lights, red velvet bows, and treasured ornaments. She wished Justin had been here to help her decorate the tree, but he hadn't returned from Toronto, or if he had, he hadn't called.

A strange mixture of relief and sadness swirled through her. She missed him, his kindness, his warm sense of humor; but knowing he accepted so much money from Lillian bothered her. She just couldn't imagine building a future with someone who would take advantage of his grandmother's kindness like that. Of course, Lillian didn't see it that way. She seemed to think supporting Justin was a God-given calling. Sarah sighed and shook her head, still uncertain how she felt about that money.

The phone rang, and she decided to let the machine pick it up.

"Hey, Sarah, it's Justin."

Her heartbeat jumped to double time.

"Are you sleeping in?" He laughed. "Nah, I can't picture you doing that. Not on a beautiful day like this."

She glanced out the window at the clear, cold sky.

"I got home from Toronto last night, and I'm headed out to do a little Christmas shopping. I thought you might like to come along." He waited a second. "I missed you. But I guess if you're not there, you can't come. So. . ."

She leaped from the chair and grabbed the phone. "I'm here. Sorry, I was just. . .reading the paper."

"I'm headed over to the Fêtes de Noël at Bryant Park. Would you like to come?"

"What's that?"

"It's an outdoor holiday market with lots of funky, hand-made crafts and gifts." When she hesitated, he added, "You could finish up all your Christmas shopping."

"I finished in October." She felt a little embarrassed by her compulsion to organize everything, even her Christmas gift giving, but she might as well be honest.

"I should've guessed," he said, a smile in his voice. "But if you finished in October, we hadn't met, so you must not have a gift for me yet."

She sucked in a surprised breath and laughed. "What makes you think I'm buying you a gift?"

"Well, you'd better, because I have something really great for you."

His answer stole her breath for a second. "You do?"

"Yep. I got it while I was up in Toronto, but I might have to hold on to it if you're not going to reciprocate."

His teasing tone made her laugh.

"So do you want to come with me?"

She bit her lip. Spending the day with Justin sounded wonderful, but she wasn't sure it was wise. The debate lasted only about two seconds. "Okay."

"Great. When can you be ready?"

She glanced at the clock. "Where are you now?"

"Standing outside your door."

She almost dropped the phone. "What?"

"I'm in the hall, and I wish you'd let me in so I don't have to keep talking to you through the wall like this."

"You are so funny." She hung up the phone and hurried to let him in. Before she unlocked the door, she glanced down at her navy velour pants and matching hooded top. This was a cozy outfit for lounging around the house but not warm enough for outdoor shopping. She pulled the door open.

He smiled and held out a little poinsettia plant with a single bright red bloom. "Merry Christmas."

She resisted the urge to hug him. "Thanks. Come in. I just need a few minutes to change."

He looked her over with an appreciative glance. "Why

would you change? You look great."

She swallowed and tried to think straight. "Thanks, but I'd freeze in this outfit." She motioned toward the living room. "Make yourself at home. I'll be right back."

"Take your time. We're not in a hurry." He picked up the newspaper and sat in her favorite chair.

She headed toward the hall, trying to act as though everything was cool, but when she rounded the corner, she leaned against the wall and fanned her face. She was in so much trouble. What was she thinking? Thirty seconds with the man and she was acting like a love-struck teenager. Pulling in a deep breath, she straightened her shoulders. She could handle this. They were simply friends going out to do a little Christmas shopping. Rolling her eyes toward the ceiling, she shook her head and groaned.

❄

Forty-five minutes later, Justin took Sarah's hand and they climbed the steps to Bryant Park. She didn't pull her hand away, and that raised his hopes. He'd thought about her every day when he was in Toronto, and he couldn't wait to get back to see her. But he sensed a little more distance on her part than he'd expected. He hoped spending today together would draw them closer again.

Justin stopped and turned to her. "So what would you like to do first, ice-skate or shop?"

Sarah's eyes widened. "I haven't skated in years."

"That's okay. Once you get out there, it'll all come back to you."

She tucked her hands into her coat pockets, looking uncertain. "I don't want to risk breaking something."

Maybe she just needed a little coaxing. He turned her around to face the pond, where throngs of skaters glided across the ice. "Come on, doesn't it look fun?" With his hands on her shoulders, he leaned closer. "And unlike Rockefeller Center, it's free."

She shot him a piercing look over her shoulder. "I'd rather go shopping."

He guessed she didn't like skating. "Okay." With a slight bow, he gestured toward the tents. "After you."

They wandered from booth to booth, admiring beautifully carved wooden bowls, hand-painted silk scarves, framed fine art prints, and unique sterling silver jewelry. Sarah lingered at a booth displaying hand-knit hats, scarves, and gloves. She fingered a soft red wool hat and matching scarf with black beaded fringe.

"That would be a great color on you. Why don't you try them on?"

Sarah shook her head. "I never wear red."

"Why not? It would be perfect with your eyes and hair."

She smiled and touched the scarf again. "You think so?"

"Sure." He took the matching set off the display and handed it to her. "See how it looks, and if you like it, I'll buy it for you for Christmas."

She sent him a teasing look. "I thought you said you already have a present for me."

"You have a problem with me giving you two gifts?"

"I guess not." Her eyes glowed as she stepped in front of the mirror and tried on the hat. She wrapped the scarf around her neck and turned to the right and left, checking her reflection. "It's so soft and warm." She ran her hand down the scarf, stopping when she touched the small price tag at the bottom. She flipped it over, and her eyes widened. "Oh, I should've looked at this first."

He stepped closer and glanced at the tag. It was more than he'd expected but not unreasonable. "Seems like a fair price for a one-of-a-kind design like this."

She shook her head and took the hat and scarf off. "I don't want you to spend that much on me."

He touched her coat sleeve. "Sarah, please, it's not a problem. I'd like to buy them for you." He reached for his wallet, but his hand froze as he felt his flat back pocket.

Sarah frowned. "What is it?"

"My wallet's missing."

"Did someone steal it?"

He closed his eyes, replaying the events of the morning, trying to picture the last time he'd seen the wallet. He remembered getting dressed but didn't recall putting it in his pocket. "I must've left it at the apartment. Let me call and be sure."

Sarah nodded slowly, a doubtful look in her eyes.

That surprised him. Why was she bothered? He hadn't left it behind on purpose. At least he'd remembered his phone. He flipped it open and called his grandmother. She checked the guest room and found the wallet on the dresser. Justin thanked her and hung up.

Sarah crossed her arms and studied him. "It's at Lillian's?"

He nodded and stuffed his phone in his jacket pocket. "I'm sorry. I got in late last night. I guess I was tired from the trip and not thinking very clearly this morning." He knew it was more than that. "The truth is, I was so eager to see you, I must've just walked off without it." He smiled at her. "I'm lucky I remembered to put my shoes on."

Her expression softened, erasing the line between her brows. "It's okay. It doesn't cost anything to walk around and look. And I have money for lunch or whatever we want."

"Thanks. I'll pay you back. I'm not the kind of guy who invites a girl out and then expects her to pay for everything."

"Don't worry about it." She squeezed his hand. "Let's go."

Around two they ate lunch at a small café overlooking the park. Sarah ordered French onion soup with bubbly Swiss cheese melting on top, and Justin enjoyed a delicious Reuben sandwich. Sarah paid the bill, and they headed back outside to look at the rest of the booths.

Dusk began to settle over the park around four thirty, and the air grew cooler.

The white lights in the trees came on, and Sarah stopped to watch. "Oh, look. It's so pretty." Her face glowed, and her eyes sparkled, reflecting the twinkling lights.

"Yes, it's beautiful." But his gaze rested on her rather than the sparkling trees. He took her hand, and they walked back toward the ice rink, where they stood close together and watched the skaters. A cold wind whistled around them. Sarah shivered.

"Maybe we should go. I don't want you to freeze solid. Then I'd have to pick you up and carry you home."

She laughed. "I am getting a little cold. But I think I can still walk."

Only a few people strolled along the path as he led her

across the park. A brass quartet played carols near the steps, and they stopped to listen. Justin stepped behind Sarah and wrapped his arms around her to keep her warm. She melted back against him, swaying slightly to the music.

His heart felt full as he thought back through the day they'd shared. "Thanks for spending today with me," he said softly. "I'm sorry you had to pay for everything. I promise I'll pay—"

She turned and lifted her finger to his lips. "Let's not talk about money right now."

He wrapped his arms around her. "Then what shall we talk about?"

She smiled up at him, her gaze warming. "We could talk about how pretty the moon is tonight." She glanced off to the left.

He followed her gaze and saw the silver half-moon rising just above the twinkling trees. "Mmm, that's very nice, but that's not what I had in mind."

"What then?" She looked up at him with sweet openness.

His gaze traveled over her face, taking in the dark sweep of her lashes and the gentle curve of her lips. "I was thinking how beautiful you look in the moonlight."

She smiled, inviting him closer. He lowered his head. Her eyes slid closed as she lifted her lips to meet his.

He kissed her gently at first, then as she responded, he deepened the kiss, losing himself in the magic of the moment. Finally, he eased back and ran his finger down the side of her face. "Thank you."

She glanced away at the musicians, looking flushed and uncomfortable.

For a second, he wondered if he'd misread the invitation in her eyes, then he replayed the lingering sweetness of her kiss, and he knew he had not been mistaken.

But something had broken the spell.

"We'd better go," she said, stepping away. "I have an early appointment tomorrow."

Justin glanced at his watch. It was only a little after five, so her comment didn't make sense. But he understood what she meant. The evening was over. And for some reason he couldn't fathom, the kiss had ended it all.

Chapter 9

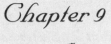

Sarah's hand shook as she downed the last of her morning coffee and set the cup in the sink. Closing her eyes, she pinched the bridge of her nose, willing away the headache beginning to build there. Too many anxious thoughts and too little sleep—that was the price she'd paid for kissing Justin.

With a soft moan, she flipped off the kitchen light and headed toward the front door. She had to pull herself together. She had an important meeting across town in forty minutes. This was no time to try to sort out her mixed-up feelings.

She grabbed her coat and picked up her purse and brief-case. As she stepped out the door, her foot kicked something. Glancing down, she spotted a small silver gift bag stuffed with red tissue. Her stomach tensed as she reached down and picked it up. Pushing the tissue aside, she peeked in and found a white envelope with her name on it.

She felt obliged to follow the rules even when no one was looking, so she opened the card first without searching through the bag. Inside the envelope she found a single sheet of white stationery. Unfolding it, she saw a handwritten poem from Justin. Her heart clutched as she read the words.

Bryant Park with Sarah

A warm and comforting hand to hold,
Laughter and smiles that will never grow old,
Eyes reflecting the sparkling sights,
A sweet kiss shared in the silver moonlight.

Thinking of you,
Justin

A light-headed feeling washed over her. He'd written her a poem? This was too much. She'd never intended to let things go this far. With trembling fingers, she pulled back the tissue and found a package of chocolate kisses. Her face flamed. This was not good. Not good at all.

She stuffed the gift bag in her briefcase and tiptoed past Lillian's door, praying Justin was not waiting behind it to see her reaction to his gift. She couldn't deal with it right now. She'd think about it later, when she recovered her sanity and good sense.

❄

Justin paced across his living room and stared out at the twinkling city lights. It had been three days since he'd moved back to his own apartment. He hadn't seen Sarah, and she hadn't returned any of his calls. He shouldn't have kissed her.

That's when the trouble had started. He'd tried to smooth things over with the gift he left by her door. But she obviously didn't appreciate the gesture. Maybe he'd blown her away with that sentimental poem. It certainly wasn't one of his best. The chocolate kisses were probably a mistake, too. She was more the Godiva chocolate type.

No, that wasn't the problem.

He stopped pacing and closed his eyes. Quieting his heart, he tried to form a prayer, but the words wouldn't come. He pulled in a slow, deep breath, allowing himself to relax and listen. Within seconds, a strong impression washed over him. God was doing an important work in Sarah's heart, and it had very little to do with him. That seemed like an odd answer to his wordless prayer, but he focused again, opening his heart and waiting for direction. Seconds ticked by. Finally, a firm conviction filled his mind. He should not give up on Sarah. She was a treasure worth seeking. He needed her as much as she needed him.

He whispered his thanks, pulled his phone from his pocket, and punched in Sarah's number. It rang five times, then clicked over to voice mail. He almost hung up, but a quiet prompting made him wait.

"Sarah, it's Justin. Listen, I'm sorry for whatever I said or did that upset you. I know we can work it out if you'll just talk to me. I miss you. I'll be up till midnight. Please call." He lowered the phone, preparing to push the END button.

"Justin?"

He yanked the phone to his ear. "Sarah? Man, you had me worried. Are you okay?"

"Yes, I'm all right." Her voice sounded strained and weary.

"Are you sure?"

She sighed. "I'm sorry, Justin. This just isn't going to work. I can't see you anymore. Please don't call me again."

He clutched the phone. "Sarah, wait. When two people care about each other and they have a problem in their relationship, they don't just give up and walk away. They talk it over and work it out." He held his breath in the silence, counting the beats of his heart.

"We're just so different." Sad resignation filled her voice. "That's fun and exciting now, but eventually it would wear us both down and make us miserable."

He suspected this was only the surface issue, but at least she was talking to him. "Okay, I see what you mean, but differences aren't necessarily bad. I love it that you're organized and efficient, and I like the way you use your gifts to help people." He rubbed his forehead, praying for the right words. "Differences keep life from getting boring. I don't want to be with someone who's just like me. That wouldn't be fun at all."

"Life is more than fun, Justin."

"I know. But I don't think it honors God to walk around all serious and stressed, never having a good time or enjoying life."

"You think I don't know how to have fun?"

"No, that's not what I meant." He rubbed the back of his neck. "I have a great time with you. You're a lot of fun." He waited, praying she would remember all of the special times they'd shared. "We may be different in some ways, but we have a lot in common—like our faith, our love for people, and our desire to make a difference in the world. Those are the kinds of things that hold two people together."

"Those are important. . .but I want to be with someone who's thinking more than two days ahead."

Her words stung. He'd never been the kind of guy to make a five-year plan, but he didn't think of himself as being irresponsible or shortsighted.

"I like my job," she said, her voice softening. "But someday I want to have a family, and I'd like to have choices about working or staying home. So I'm looking for someone who has a career and a plan for the future, someone who could take care of me and a family."

"That makes sense. And I'm that kind of guy."

An uncomfortable silence stretched between them.

"I know about the arrangement you have with Lillian."

He frowned. "What arrangement?"

"I saw her bank statements when I helped her set up her files."

His mind spun, trying to guess what she meant. "Okay. . . and?"

She exhaled. "Justin, I just explained it. Dating someone who is supported by his grandmother is not going to work for me. I know that's between you and Lillian. But how long do you think she can keep doing this? I don't know where she gets all her money, but what will you do when it's used up or she's gone?"

"Wait, you think my grandmother supports me?" The idea was so absurd he laughed.

"Yes! And what is so funny? This is breaking my heart, and

you're over there laughing?"

"I'm sorry. I'm just trying to figure out how you came up with that idea."

"So. . .you're saying Lillian doesn't support you?"

"No, I make more than enough to support myself."

Sarah exhaled a shaky breath. "I don't know what to say. I thought—"

"It's okay. I'm the one who should apologize. This is partly my fault. I haven't been totally up front with you about who I am or what I do, so I can see how you—"

"What do you mean?" Painful suspicion returned to her voice.

He grimaced, regretting that he'd ever kept his writing a secret from her. "I'm sorry. I can explain everything, but I'd like to do it face-to-face." He glanced at the clock. It was already after eleven, and it would take him at least a half hour to get to her apartment. "Can you meet me for breakfast tomorrow?"

"I have appointments all morning. I won't be done until one."

Remembering his afternoon plans, he smiled. This would be perfect. "How about meeting me at the café in Carter & Norton Books on West 43rd at one?"

"Okay. On one condition."

"What's that?" He'd agree to just about anything to see her again.

"Promise me that your job is nothing illegal, immoral, or dangerous."

He grinned, his hopes soaring. "I promise."

❄

Sarah walked through the front door of Carter & Norton and past the colorful book display. She would have loved to stop and browse, but she was already twenty minutes late. That hadn't been the plan, but she'd gotten off at the wrong subway station and then run into a barricade blocking off 42nd because of a fire.

She hurried through the store, looking for the café. There seemed to be a lot of mothers with young children and strollers in the aisles today, slowing her progress. She guessed Christmas vacation had begun for many families.

Finally, she spotted the café. On first glance, she didn't see Justin, and her heart sank. Had he given up and left? Circling around, she found him seated at a small table in the back, hovering over a yellow legal pad, writing furiously.

He looked up, and a smile flashed across his face. "Sarah." He said her name softly with a touch of awe.

"Sorry I'm late." She explained her delay as she took off her coat and sat across from him.

He reached for her hand. "I couldn't sleep much last night."

She noticed the tired lines around his eyes, and guilt washed over her. This mix-up was her fault. She wasn't good at relationships. She never had been. "I'm sorry."

He squeezed her hand. "It's okay. I was just wound up, so I spent some time praying, and then I was just lying there thinking about seeing you today." He smiled, waiting.

She swallowed, uncertain what to say. She'd been exhausted

and confused last night, but at least she'd been able to sleep. Today her emotions felt like a jumbled mess. She still didn't understand how he could support himself when he never seemed to work. It didn't make sense. But he'd promised her an explanation, and she'd decided to hear him out.

"Listen, we don't have much time." He glanced over his shoulder. "I have to meet some people in a few minutes, but I want to show you something."

Confusion swirled through her. "Meet some people? I thought you were going to explain. . .everything."

He rose from his chair. "I am. Come on." He took her hand and led her out of the café and across the store. When they reached a large display of children's books, he stopped and turned to her. "Look up there." He pointed to a large poster hanging from the ceiling over the display.

Sarah focused on the larger-than-life photo of a man who looked a lot like Justin. Realization flashed through her, and her heart thudded in her chest. "That's you," she whispered.

He laughed. "That's me all right. And this is my newest book." He handed her a copy of *Catching Snowflakes on My Tongue*.

"Newest," she croaked. "You have others?"

"Yes. Four more to be exact."

"You write books?" She blinked and tried to clear the foggy feeling in her head.

"I told you I was a poet."

"But I never imagined that someone actually bought your poems."

"Oh, they buy them all right." He pointed to the stack of

books. "They sell out almost as fast as the stores can bring them in. I sort of have a corner on the children's poetry market right now."

"You write children's poetry?" She flipped through the pages of Justin's book and saw clever ink drawings accompanying many of the poems. "Are these your drawings?"

"Yeah." He nodded, looking a little embarrassed. "I never considered myself much of an artist, but they used them in the first book, *Blue Jeans and Jelly Beans*, and it was a hit, so—"

"Mr. Latimer!" A plump woman with blond hair and a beaming smile approached. "I'm Connie Stanton, community relations manager."

"Hi." Justin smiled and shook her hand.

"We've got quite a crowd gathered already. I know it's a few minutes early, but I'd like to get started before the children get restless." She gestured past the display.

Justin nodded. "I'll be with you in just a minute." He turned to Sarah. "I'm doing a reading and then signing books."

Sarah looked from Justin's expectant face to the book in her hand. Her stomach tightened, and she felt a wave of uncertainty wash over her. This was all so. . .unreal.

Justin leaned closer. "I know this is a lot to take in, but I'd like you to stay and see what I do."

She swallowed and nodded. She owed him that much.

❄

An hour later, as the crowd cleared out of the children's department, Justin scanned the room looking for Sarah. He spotted her off to the left, sitting in a folding chair flipping through

Swinging on the Garden Gate, his second collection of poems. He thanked the community relations manager and the children's book buyer, then walked over to meet Sarah.

She looked up as he approached, her expression unreadable.

"So what do you think?" He smiled, hoping she felt as pumped as he did after interacting with the group of excited children and parents.

She closed the book and stood to face him. "You mean about the book signing?"

"My poetry, the signing, all of it."

"Well, it's certainly a surprise." Pressing her lips together, she laid the book aside and crossed her arms.

Frustration rose and tightened his chest. He'd hoped the enthusiastic crowd would impress her. He'd imagined she might even be a little in awe of his status as a famous author.

She lifted her gaze to meet his, accusation in her eyes. "Why didn't you tell me the truth from the beginning?"

Her words felt like a slap in the face. He pulled in a sharp breath. "You tried to throw out my books when we cleaned the apartment. That didn't give me much hope that you'd understand or appreciate what I do."

Her mouth dropped open. "Those were your books?"

He nodded, his anger cooling when he saw the regret in her eyes. "I thought it would be better for us to get to know each other first before I dropped all this on you."

She shook her head. "But it's just not right. You should've told me who you were."

"Come on, Sarah. You're not being fair."

She lifted her chin. "So you think it's fair for you to keep this a secret and then spring it on me? You expect me to be happy about that?"

He huffed out a frustrated breath. "You weren't happy when you thought I was a poor, aspiring poet, and you're not happy now that you know I'm a successful author. I don't think there's anything I could do that would make you happy."

Tears and confusion clouded her eyes. "That's not true."

"This isn't really about me and my career, is it?"

"What do you mean?"

"There's something else going on. What is it, Sarah? What are you afraid of?"

"I'm not afraid of anything!"

He narrowed his eyes, studying her for a moment. "I think you're scared to death to take a risk and fall in love."

She straightened her shoulders. "You fall down stairs, and you fall in ditches. You should plan your love life."

"Who told you that?"

"My pastor in my old church, and he's a very wise man." The look in her eye and the tilt of her chin told him how important this was to her.

"I suppose that's true. You shouldn't just fall for someone without getting to know them. But when you spend time together and discover you share a common faith, and there's that connection. . .then you shouldn't be afraid to test the waters and see what happens." He reached for her hand and softened his voice. "Love's not really as scary as it sounds."

She pulled away. "I'm not afraid of love!"

"Then what are you afraid of? Me?" Heat flashed up his neck, and his pulse pounded in his ears. "I've done everything

I can to show you how I feel about you. What else do you want?"

She lifted her hand and covered her eyes. "I don't know. But I just can't do this anymore."

Her words cut like a knife. He clamped his jaw, trying to hold on to his last shred of self-respect. "Okay. Fine. I won't bother you anymore."

She dropped her hand. Anguish filled her eyes. "Justin, wait."

"No, Sarah, you've made it clear how you feel." With painful resolve, he turned and walked away.

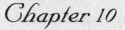

Chapter 10

"I have a little gift for you, dear." Lillian reached under her Christmas tree and retrieved the small package wrapped with shiny red paper and topped with a frilly gold bow.

Sarah smiled, her heart lifting. "That's so sweet. Thank you." As she held Lillian's gift, she remembered the card and check she'd received from her parents two days earlier. Their note said they would be spending Christmas in Rome with friends. That had been a blow, especially after everything that had happened with Justin. But she couldn't do anything about either situation, so she'd tried to keep busy and not think about spending Christmas alone this year.

"I loved the photo album you gave me." Lillian sat next to Sarah on the couch. "Those before and after pictures of the apartment are very motivating. Every time I'm the least bit tempted to let things pile up, I glance at them, and it does the trick." Lillian smiled. "Well, aren't you going to open your gift? It's Christmas Eve. There's no need to wait."

It was only a little after noon, but Sarah guessed it was Christmas Eve all day, so she carefully unwrapped the gift. Inside two layers of tissue, she found a wooden frame. She turned it over, and her hand froze. Her own face smiled back at her from the photo Lillian had taken on Thanksgiving. Justin stood next to her, his arm draped around her shoulder, a broad smile creasing his handsome face. Sarah's chest tightened as she tried to pull in a breath. Tears misted her vision.

"Oh, dear, I'm sorry. I thought you—"

Sarah swallowed. "No, it's all right. It's a great picture, really." Her voice cracked, and she tried to blink away her tears.

Lillian bit her lip. "I should've guessed something was wrong the way Justin was acting before he left for Jersey. Did you have a quarrel?"

Sarah nodded and grabbed a tissue from the box on the end table. "It's my fault. I've made a huge mess of everything." She wiped her nose and poured out the story.

Lillian listened with sympathy in her eyes. "I'm sorry for the misunderstanding about the money. I wish I would've explained who I was helping when you asked."

"I shouldn't have assumed it was Justin."

"Well, I don't mind telling you who I give it to. He's a wonderful young man from Poland who attends my church. He has a degree in architecture, but he's still learning English, so he works in a restaurant for minimum wage."

"I'm sure he appreciates your help."

Lillian smiled. "He does. But I'm more concerned about you and that dear grandson of mine." She patted Sarah's knee. "Problems come in every relationship, but they can bring you closer if you let them. Why don't you just call Justin and talk things over?"

Sarah sniffed. "We already talked. He took me to a book signing and showed me his books. I was upset that he hadn't told me sooner, and I didn't handle it very well."

"So he explained everything, you know all about his poetry, but you're still upset because. . ." Lillian lifted her silver brows.

Sarah shrugged, feeling more miserable than ever. "I know, it sounds crazy. Justin is wonderful. He has a growing faith and a promising career. He's kind and generous. We have a great time together, and when he's away, I miss him terribly." Sarah replayed what she'd just said, and the truth stole her breath. Justin was exactly the kind of man she'd always hoped to find. And she'd thrown it all away.

"It sounds like you care for him deeply."

"I do. But every time I think about calling him and working this out, a huge wave of fear rolls over my heart, and it about crushes me."

Lillian fixed her eyes on Sarah. "Are you more afraid that he loves you or that he doesn't?"

Sarah stared at her for a moment. "I don't know."

"Well, either way, there's only one cure for fear, and that's faith."

"Faith?" Sarah tried to imagine a life without anxious thoughts and feelings overshadowing her heart. "You mean I should just believe in myself and say I can do it?"

Lillian chuckled. "No, dear, not that kind of mumbo jumbo. The real thing. Faith based on knowing God loves you deeply and has a plan for your life that gives you a hope and a future."

Sarah pondered that statement for a moment. "I do have faith in God. I've been a believer since college."

"Yes, but applying your faith to your relationship with Justin seems to be the issue right now." Lillian settled back on the couch and gazed at the manger scene under her Christmas tree. Seconds ticked by. "You know, I'd dearly love to go to the Christmas Eve service tonight, but I don't want to go alone." She turned to Sarah. "Would you come with me?"

The shift in topics surprised Sarah. She glanced at Lillian and noticed the slight smile lifting the corners of her mouth.

"What time is the service?"

"Seven o'clock."

The idea touched a chord in Sarah's heart. She might not be able to spend Christmas with her parents or share it with the man she was almost certain she loved, but she could help her neighbor and bring her gift of worship to the newborn King.

❄

The scent of pine boughs and lemon oil drifted toward Sarah as she glanced around the sanctuary. Lillian's beautiful old stone church with its arched ceiling and polished wooden pews was the perfect setting for a candlelight Christmas Eve service.

The burgundy-robed choir stood and sang the first carol. The familiar words made Sarah's heart swell and brought tears to her eyes. When the choir finished three songs and returned to their seats, the pastor walked to the pulpit and opened his Bible. "We gather tonight to consider the gift of love God sent down to earth over two thousand years ago."

Sarah gazed at the glowing candles and bright poinsettias

lining the altar, and her thoughts drifted. What was Justin doing tonight? They would probably be celebrating Christmas Eve together if her suspicion and fear hadn't driven him away. Her heart ached. The pastor's words caught her attention, and she shifted in the pew so she could see his face.

"We don't often think of fear playing a part in the Christmas story, but the angel's announcement to Mary was initially frightening and confusing to her. Joseph also found himself in a painful and unsettling position when he learned Mary was pregnant. No doubt the young couple was misunderstood, ridiculed, and possibly rejected by family and friends.

"Can you imagine the courage it took for them to trust God and say yes to His plan? How did they find the strength to follow Him in the face of all their questions and uncertainties? They overcame their fears by believing God and trusting in His plan and His promises.

"And that's a message we still need today. Each one of us faces challenges that test our faith, perhaps even frightening situations that seem overwhelming to us. But God asks us to trust Him and walk by faith, believing in His love for us and holding on to His promises."

Sarah's heartbeat quickened as she listened. Faith that overcame fear. . .faith in God and in His love for her. Faith in His plans and promises for the future. That was the kind of faith she needed, the same kind of trust and dependence Mary and Joseph had so long ago as they faced the life-altering events leading up to that first Christmas.

Bowing her head, she breathed in deeply, allowing those thoughts to penetrate her heart. *Father, help me have faith like that, to know You more and trust You with every area of my life.* Slowly, a sense of peace settled over her spirit.

The choir rose to sing their final song, and the congregation joined them. *Silent night, holy night, all is calm, all is bright.*

Sarah smiled through her tears, new hope rising in her heart.

❄

Sarah grasped the leash tightly as Molly tugged her down the sidewalk toward the small park at the end of the block. She smiled, remembering the events of the last hour. She'd awakened that Christmas morning to a surprise gift—feathery flakes drifting down from the sky, lightly covering everything like powdered sugar sprinkled on gingerbread.

Though it was early, she'd called Lillian and offered to take Molly out for a walk. The temperature hovered just below freezing, and Sarah knew it might be too slippery for Lillian. When she stopped by for Molly, Lillian promised to cook a special holiday breakfast and have it ready when she returned.

Molly stopped and sniffed the ground. Sarah tipped her face upward and watched the snowflakes dance and swirl toward her. Joy bubbled up in her heart. She laughed and stuck out her tongue, but the flakes drifted out of reach.

"I hear you have to hold your breath or you blow them away."

Sarah spun around, afraid her heart was playing cruel tricks on her. But it was no mistake. Justin stood on the sidewalk wearing a heavy navy blue jacket with snowflakes dusting his hair and broad shoulders.

He leaned down and scratched Molly behind her ears. "Hey

there, Miss Molly. Are you giving this lady a hard time?" He looked up and smiled. "Merry Christmas, Sarah."

Tears stung her eyes. "I can't believe you're here."

His smile faded, and his hand dropped from Molly's head. "You want me to leave?"

She sucked in a ragged breath. "No, please don't go." She stepped toward him, her heart pounding in her chest. "I've been praying I'd have a chance to ask you to forgive me for being such a—"

Before she could finish her sentence, he wrapped his arms around her. "Oh, Sarah." He pulled her closer. Seconds ticked by as they clung to each other as if they never wanted to let go.

Finally, Justin leaned back and looked into her eyes. "I'm sorry I wasn't honest with you about my writing. I know relationships need to be built on mutual trust, and I blew it. I guess I was afraid, too, afraid that you wouldn't want to be with someone like me."

She sniffed and smiled up at him. "I'd have to be crazy not to want to be with someone wonderful like you."

Relief flashed in his eyes. His smile spread wider as he ran his gloved finger down the side of her cheek. "Finally, she comes to her senses."

Sarah laughed, her heart overflowing. "There's so much I want to tell you."

Hope shone in his eyes. "Me, too." They linked hands and walked back toward the apartment with Molly trotting beside them.

Sarah spoke first, eager to share what the Lord had been teaching her about understanding her fears and overcoming them through faith and trust in God. Justin listened and then told her how God had also been working in his heart, urging him to come back and work things out with her.

An hour later, after a delicious breakfast of scrambled eggs, cranberry scones, crisp sausage, and orange juice, Justin led Sarah over to the couch in Lillian's living room.

"I think Molly and I will go make some phone calls to the family." Lillian passed them on her way to the hall. "Don't let that mistletoe go to waste." Her eyes twinkled as she pointed to the little bunch she and Sarah had hung in the archway above the couch.

Justin grinned and shook his head. "My grandma's not too subtle, is she?"

Sarah laughed softly and poked his side. "You'd better behave."

"Okay. I'll try." Justin reached into the shopping bag on the floor by his feet and pulled out a small gift. His eyes glowed as he handed it to her. "I got this for you when I was in Toronto."

Sarah smiled as she eagerly unwrapped the box. Inside she found a beautiful vintage pin made of several smaller items put together like a collage. "Oh, this is so pretty." She looked up at him, amazed that he'd chosen such a special gift for her.

"It reminds me of you, because you take all kinds of odds and ends in people's lives, and you organize them to make something beautiful."

Sarah told herself she shouldn't cry, but happy tears came anyway. "Thank you. I love it." She pinned it on her sweater and turned to show him.

A warm look of approval lit his eyes. "Perfect." Then he

reached in the bag and pulled out another gift. "Here you go."

Sarah didn't know what to say, so she tore off the paper and opened the box. Inside she found the red wool hat and scarf she'd tried on at Bryant Park. "Oh, I can't believe you went back and got these for me." She leaned closer and kissed his cheek.

"They were made for you." The affection in his eyes sent her emotions on a dizzying ride.

She slipped the scarf around her neck, enjoying the feel of the soft yarn on her skin. But as she looked at Justin's expectant expression, sadness tugged at her heart. "I wish I had a gift for you."

"Oh, that's okay. I know what you can give me, and it's something no one else can give." He gently pulled the ends of the scarf, bringing her closer.

Her heartbeat sped up, and her cheeks warmed. "What's that?"

The look in his eyes changed from teasing to tender. "I love you, Sarah, and there's nothing I'd like more than the pleasure of your company today, and tomorrow, and the next day, and all the days after that."

Sarah's heart melted, and all of her doubts faded. "I love you, too," she whispered. Their lips met, and they shared a lingering kiss full of sweet promises and love she knew would last for years to come.

CARRIE TURANSKY

Carrie and her husband, Scott, have been married for thirty years and live in central New Jersey. They are blessed with five great kids, a lovely daughter-in-law, and two adorable grandsons. Carrie homeschooled her children for many years, but she recently "graduated" and now has more time for writing and being involved in ministry with her husband. She teaches women's Bible studies, speaks for women's events, and enjoys reading, gardening, and walking around the lake near her home. Carrie and her family spent one year in Kenya as missionaries, giving them a passion for what God is doing around the world. Carrie also is the coauthor of *Wedded Bliss* and *Kiss the Bride* and the author of *Along Came Love*. You may contact her through her Web site, www.carrieturansky.com.

SHOPPING FOR LOVE

by Gail Sattler

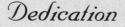

Dedication

To my fellow authors
Vasthi Reyes Acosta, Lynette Sowell, and Carrie Turansky.
Writing this book with you ladies has been a
wonderful experience that I will treasure for a lifetime.

Prologue

P aging passenger Emily Jones. Please report to Gate 27A immediately."

"I've got to go," Emily said into her cell phone, fumbling it as she rose out of the cramped airport chair.

"Wait!" her mother's voice crackled back. "It was a simple misunderstanding. Talk to him. Everything will be fine!"

"A misunderstanding!" Emily sputtered. "He just hoped I wouldn't find out. I'm leaving on the first plane with an empty seat, and I don't care where it's going." Emily snapped the phone shut before her mother could say anything more.

Brian had known what he was doing. He'd lied, tried to cover up his lies, then blamed her when everything went wrong. God was not only telling her it was time to move on; He was also giving her a push to get her started.

Emily hurried to the counter at the boarding gate, pulling her wheeled suitcase and balancing the straps of her purse and laptop case on her shoulder. She slid her ID to the agent. "I'm on standby for this flight. Where is this plane going?"

"Kennedy Airport, New York City." He typed her info into the computer. "Checked luggage?"

"No. All I have are my carry-ons."

He nodded. "You may board now."

Emily was barely seated when the Boeing 757 rolled away from the gate and onto the runway. She smiled, both nervous and excited as she fastened her seat belt. She couldn't have a better destination.

New York City, here I come.

Chapter 1

B ryan Evans pressed his cell phone tightly against his ear, covering his other ear with his opposite hand so he could hear his friend's words in the noisy crowd. "I suppose I can figure something out," he called into the phone.

The man walking next to him turned and stared as if Bryan had been talking to him. Bryan shrugged one shoulder to indicate the phone, then moved to ease out of the moving crowd. He wanted a little privacy to talk to Steve, something impossible in the pre-Christmas rush at Kennedy Airport.

"I'll see you after Christmas," he said into the phone as people bustled around him.

Just as he snapped the phone shut, a mother reaching for her child bumped his elbow.

Bryan's brand-new cell phone flew up in the air, arced gracefully, bounced off someone's shoulder, then crashed to the floor.

"Sorry," he muttered and bent to pick it up. A split second before he would have reached it, contact with a shoe sent it skidding out of his reach.

He cringed. Fortunately, the person hadn't stepped on it. He'd had it less than a week.

He shuffled forward, this time bending lower, intending to be quicker to scoop it up.

As his fingers wrapped firmly around his phone, a shin smacked into his arm.

Someone gasped. The wheel of a suitcase rolled over his foot.

Above him, almost in slow motion, a woman began to flail her arms. Her purse and a laptop case became airborne. Her eyes widened as she began to fall. In light speed, she grabbed for the laptop, pulled it tightly to her chest, and continued downward.

With only a split second to react, Bryan dropped to one knee and twisted to catch her. But between the momentum and the angle, he couldn't catch her properly. He was going down, too.

All he could do was tuck his chin to his chest and brace for impact.

At the same time that he crashed down on his back onto the cold, hard tile floor, the woman bounced on his chest, crushing all of the air out of his lungs.

A tight female voice echoed through his brain. "Are you okay?"

Bryan gasped for air, unable to reply. The woman rolled off him and scrambled to her feet as people slowed and made their way around them. Bryan struggled to get up as quickly as his inability to breathe would allow.

An elderly couple slowed to watch but seemed satisfied that they were getting up on their own and kept walking.

Bryan and the woman recovered their belongings, then maneuvered their way through the crowd toward the wall, out of the way.

Now recovered, Bryan looked down at the woman, who was nearly a foot shorter than him. While she wasn't model thin, she wasn't big, which was a good thing, considering what just happened. She appeared to be close to his own age, probably around twenty-eight. Her shoulder-length brown hair was a mess, but it looked like it had a natural wave. Her cute little nose matched a petite oval face; again, not model gorgeous, but better than average. And most outstanding, she had the greenest eyes he'd ever seen—a mesmerizing sea green.

Bryan cleared his throat. "I'm so sorry. Are you hurt? Can I call a first-aid attendant? I think they have a medical station around here somewhere." He scanned the area for a map of the terminal or, second best, a staff member.

"I'm fine," she muttered. Not looking at him, she pulled her laptop out of the case and began to examine it.

Dollar signs flashed before Bryan's eyes. "If it's damaged, I want to pay for the repairs." He mentally kicked himself for caring about his phone. The cost of repairing the woman's laptop would far exceed the cost of the phone. To say nothing if she were hurt.

She swiped a lock of hair out of her eyes, then turned the laptop upside down. "I had a good grip on it; it should be okay."

"I'm glad for that, but are *you* okay?"

"Don't worry. I'm fine. You?"

"I'm good." However, despite her claim, Bryan was still

worried that a sprain or other injury would catch up with her later, when the shock wore off. "Maybe we should call an attendant anyway. Or how about if we go into the restaurant area and I'll buy you a cup of coffee? We can sit down, away from the crowd, and make sure everything works properly." Meaning her, as well as her computer.

She glanced over his shoulder. "I don't want to make you late if you have a connecting flight or if you're meeting someone."

He sighed. "Not anymore. What about you?"

She opened her mouth, then hesitated. After a few seconds, she said, "I have time. A cup of coffee sounds really good right now. The coffee on the plane was awful." As she spoke, her stomach grumbled. Her cheeks turned an endearing shade of crimson.

She covered her stomach with one hand. "I'm so embarrassed. I didn't have time for lunch, and since my flight was under four hours, I didn't get a meal on the plane."

"Tell you what. Let's grab a couple of burgers. I just have to get my suitcase."

"That's a great idea. Let's go."

❄

As they walked in silence to the baggage pickup area, Emily mentally kicked herself for bringing her laptop. There were a hundred more sensible things she could have taken. In hindsight, when she was already on the plane, she'd thought of all the reasons she shouldn't have brought it—the inconvenience of carrying it, the worry of losing it, the fear of theft if she turned her back for a second. And now, something she hadn't considered, the risk of damaging it.

Not that she could have foreseen falling over a tall, dark, handsome man.

Instead of watching where she was going, she'd been looking up at the posters of the Statue of Liberty and the Empire State Building plastered on the airport walls. It was exciting to be here, but now she was having second thoughts. New York was a big place, and she was all alone.

The tall, handsome man's voice broke into her thoughts. "Where are you coming from? I'm from Seattle."

She didn't want to give any personal information to a stranger, but his question seemed general enough. "Minneapolis."

"Where's home, then—Minneapolis or the Big Apple?"

Emily wasn't sure how to answer. She needed to figure out if it was possible that he planned to mug her outside the airport, knowing she was traveling alone, or if he was simply trying to make idle conversation. She needed to see his face.

When she looked up, he smiled down at her. Emily nearly tripped. Not from anything in front of her, but because he truly was the most handsome man she'd ever seen.

His brown hair was thick and slightly wavy, and so dark it was almost black, making her suspect that his complexion wasn't an out-of-season tan, but his natural coloring. She'd expected dark eyes to match, but instead, they were the color of golden honey, mixed with flecks of olive green. His features were strong, including a nose that on another man might have been too large, but on him, made him that much more masculine. Walking beside him, she guessed that he was six feet tall.

Normally, she liked tall men, but for now, she didn't want

anything to do with any man, tall, short, or anything in between. She just wanted to be left alone and to get lost in a crowd.

"Minneapolis is home," she replied, only because her answer prevented him from asking questions about New York she couldn't answer.

Which was the reason she'd brought her laptop—to research and plan her itinerary, since she didn't know where she was going when she began her journey.

The man pointed to one of the carousels. "There's where the luggage for my flight will be."

The first suitcase reached the top of the conveyor and slid down as they reached it.

"What does yours look like?"

"It's black, just like most of the other ones on this flight. It's got a purple ribbon with a pink pom-pom tied to the handle." He paused, and his ears reddened. "My niece did that so I would recognize it more easily."

They waited only a few minutes, and the suitcase with the telltale markings appeared. "There it is. I'll be right back."

With his suitcase retrieved, they made their way to the food court because it was faster than ordering at one of the restaurants.

When Emily had her burger and fries in front of her, she hesitated. If she had been alone, she would have paused to thank God for a safe journey, silently. If she was with a friend, they would have shared a short prayer, quietly, even in a public place. But she wasn't with a friend. She was with a stranger in a strange land.

She sat without moving, waiting for the man to start eating

so she could sneak in a moment of privacy.

Except the stranger didn't move. His eyes flickered to those around them, then met hers. The fragrant aroma of the grilled burger drifted to her nose, teasing her. Her stomach tightened, about to make more noise if she didn't eat something fast.

Emily gathered her courage. If it was much longer before they started eating, she was going to embarrass herself again. "I know this is a public place, but would you mind if I said grace?"

He blinked, then broke into a wide smile. "I'd like that very much." Without hesitation, he folded his hands on the edge of the small table and bowed his head.

His easy compliance gave her more confidence. She cleared her throat and spoke just barely loud enough for him to hear. "Dear Lord, thank You for our safe flights, and thank You for this food. I pray Your blessings on our time in New York and ask that whatever we do here will be for Your glory. Amen."

"Amen," he answered and raised his head.

Emily dove into her burger before her stomach complained again.

He picked up his burger but didn't immediately bite into it. "Being able to share a prayer in the middle of JKF airport is a pleasant surprise," he said while she had a mouthful.

Being with him did make her feel somewhat safer. All she could do was nod and chew fast enough so she could swallow without choking.

"I don't even know your name. My name's Bryan."

Emily choked anyway. "What?" she sputtered, hoping she'd heard wrong.

"Uh. My name's Bryan. With a *y*. Are you okay?"

"Yes," she said. *No,* she thought.

The reason she'd fled Minneapolis was a man named Brian, but with an *i*. She wondered if this was a sign that she'd been too hasty to leave town. She'd fallen flat on her face professionally because of Brian with an *i*, and in trying to escape, she hadn't even made it out of the airport before she'd fallen on her face physically because of Bryan with a *y*.

"And your name is?"

She swiped at her mouth with her napkin. "Emily."

Bryan studied her for a few seconds without speaking. Before she did or said something else stupid, Emily took another bite of her burger.

The silence didn't last long enough. "Okay, Emily," Bryan said, drawling out her name. "Have you ever been to New York before?"

She shook her head and continued chewing.

"Is this trip for business or pleasure? I see you're packing light. All you have is a carry-on and your laptop."

She finally managed to swallow. "It's a little of both."

"I'm here for both, too."

She doubted it was the same. She was in New York because the business trip she'd been promised, and the promotion that went with it, had been pulled out from under her.

"How long are you staying?" he asked, then finally bit into his burger.

"I'm not sure. I haven't booked a return flight, but I intend to be home for Christmas. You?"

"I've got a flight booked for Christmas Eve." His expression turned serious. "If you haven't booked a flight to go home, I doubt you're going to get one now. How long is your hotel reservation?"

"I haven't got a reservation. I thought I'd book something when I got here."

"You're kidding, right? This is December."

Emily set her burger down on the wrapper, pushed it aside, then brought her laptop to the table. She appreciated his concern, which emphasized the fact that she hadn't fully thought through her decision to take the first plane away from home. "I'll just book something online. They have wireless Internet access here." Her laptop booted up with no problem. "See, I told you it would be fine. Everything works."

She began to search for New York City hotels.

When the list of available rooms appeared, her heart sank. The price for two nights equaled what she spent on an entire month's rent. Including utilities. She'd been prepared to spend hundreds for her accommodations but not thousands.

"Oh," she mumbled, trying to keep the shock out of her voice. "It looks like I'm not going to be here as long as I thought. This probably makes me sound naive, but I wasn't expecting it to be so expensive."

He leaned toward her over the table. "I think I can help you find something you'd feel comfortable with, but it comes with a cost."

"Cost?" Her mind raced. She'd been quick to take the first flight out of Minneapolis. But now that she was in New York City, she had a sinking feeling that getting a flight home, even on standby, would be harder than she thought. Likewise, her chances of securing a hotel at a price that wouldn't put her in debt for the next twenty years weren't encouraging. She began to wonder how many nights she could sleep at the airport before someone noticed. "What kind of cost?"

He smiled and quirked one eyebrow. "Dinner. And. . .the answers to a few questions."

Chapter 2

Now that he finally knew her name, Bryan studied Emily.

He didn't know why he'd asked her to join him for dinner. The reason he was here was to get away from everything and clear his head—he'd been running too long on overload, stretching himself too thin for too many people. Now was not the time to add another relationship into the mix.

But it was just dinner. He'd already asked her, and he couldn't take it back.

Yet he didn't think their time together would be unpleasant. Emily was interesting, and apparently very independent—unlike anyone from back home, which was both good and bad.

But considering that she had been so quick thinking in the way she'd saved her laptop when he accidentally tripped her, he didn't understand why she hadn't thought to have a hotel or her return flight booked. Everyone knew that reservations for Christmastime were next to impossible to make in December. He'd reserved his flight back in October, and already the less expensive hotel rooms had been booked.

She closed her laptop and eyed him stonily. "What do you want to know?"

"Why didn't your employer book your hotel? It seems very odd."

She sighed, and her eyes became unfocused as she stared at something above his head. "I was supposed to go on a business trip, then at the last minute they gave my project, and my promotion, to someone else. We had somewhat of a disagreement over my integrity, and I left town. So I'm here *because* of business, but I'm not actually *on* business."

"When are you going back?"

This time she looked directly at him. "Do you mean back home or back to my job?"

"Both." Something deep inside him told him the answer before she spoke, but he wanted to hear it anyway.

She sighed. "Home, for Christmas. For work, I'm not. I quit."

"Why aren't you looking for another job?"

"Because it's been two years since I've taken any time off." She turned away. "I needed some time for myself to have fun."

Somehow, he didn't think she was having much fun, but he didn't want to point that out. The potential cost of a hotel had definitely burst her bubble.

"I think I can help. The cost of hotels is so expensive, I made a deal with my employer. For less than the amount of money they would have spent on the hotel for one week, I arranged for room and board in a home for a month. The family gets the extra money for Christmas, my boss gets a bargain, and I'm basically staying here for free. Or at least, at no cost to me."

"What does that have to do with me getting a cheaper hotel room?"

"Some families will rent out rooms in their homes for extra money. I set this up through a friend of the friend I was supposed to be meeting today, so maybe you can do the same. The catch is, he recommended me, but I can't recommend you because I don't know you. I can only tell them that you appear sincere in your faith by your actions here at the airport."

She looked down at her laptop. "I wonder if I could use my laptop as collateral. While I'm out sightseeing, they could keep it as a security deposit. Would that help?"

"It might. I can ask." Bryan pulled his PDA out of his pocket, called up the phone number, and dialed. He did his best to answer the person's questions, then snapped the phone shut.

"Well?"

"He's going to make a few calls and phone me back."

She leaned slightly forward over the table, looking at him with big, wide eyes. "How long do you think that will take?"

Bryan stared back, lost in the sea green for a few seconds before he dragged his mind back to where it should have been. "I have no idea."

She sighed, relaxed her posture, and opened the laptop again. "Then I'm going to trust that God will work this out, and I'm going to start planning what I want to see and do." She punched a few keys. "Starting with the Statue of Liberty."

Bryan sat, fascinated, watching her type into her computer. She was remarkably upbeat, while his own mood had continued to spiral downward ever since Steve deserted him.

"Look at this! Double-decker bus tours!" She punched a few more keys. "Look what you can see. The Empire State Building, Greenwich Village, Little Italy, Chinatown, Battery Park, which this says is the departure point for the Statue of Liberty. Also Times Square, Rockefeller Plaza, and a bunch of other stuff. I can even pay with my credit card online. And the Guggenheim Museum. I've heard of that, but I'm not really sure what it is." She looked up at him. "What are you going to do while you're here?"

He shrugged his shoulders. "I was going to make all my plans with Steve once we got together, except he's not coming. Something urgent came up, so he's staying home." The excitement of his vacation was gone. He couldn't picture himself venturing through the attractions of New York alone. After his week of business meetings were finished and he'd done enough sightseeing to satisfy himself, he wondered if there was a possibility of catching a flight on standby, even if it took days of waiting at the airport.

Yet it wouldn't be much fun at home, either. Knowing he was going to be gone for a month, his brother and sister-in-law, their three kids, a family of hamsters, and a bouncy poodle were bunking out in his two-bedroom town house while their house was being renovated. If he went home, either he would end up on the couch in the middle of mayhem for three weeks, or he'd move in with a friend and hurt his brother's feelings.

As he tried to think of other options, Emily returned to the tourist Web sites. He envied her enthusiasm as she hopped from one site to the next.

His cell phone rang while she was oohing and aahing over

pictures of Central Park at different times of the year.

Instead of Steve's friend, the caller was a woman from the same church named Theresa, who was willing to take Emily in.

Rather than be in the middle, Bryan gave Emily the phone.

"Emily Jones," she said, then nodded as if the person could see her. "Yes. Jones, that's my real name. I could give you my address and phone number in Minneapolis, but that won't do much good, because I'm here at the airport. Would you like my pastor's name and number for a reference? No? Okay, but I wouldn't mind."

She laughed heartily, then nodded again, making Bryan wish he'd heard the other half of the conversation. He thought he could use a laugh right now. The more he thought about it, the more he wished he could find a way to go home. Without Steve to share his vacation, he would be going everywhere alone. Three weeks was a long time in an unfamiliar place.

"Wow! Really?" Emily exclaimed. "That would be so nice of you!" She held the phone away from her mouth. "She said she'd take me to her church on Sunday. Isn't that great?"

"Yeah. Great." He'd looked forward to attending services with Steve. Now it looked as if he'd be sitting with a bunch of strangers instead.

Emily listened to the phone, nodding or shaking her head at intervals. "Wait. I'll write this down." Instead of finding a pen and paper, she called up her word processor program and began typing at a speed Bryan had never seen before.

"Yes," she said, nodding again while she hit the SAVE button. "I'll see you soon. Thanks so much!"

She snapped the phone shut and returned it to him. "Thank

you, too. I don't know what I would have done without you."

Bryan simply shrugged. "I'm just happy that you have a safe and affordable place to stay." There were always hostels for less money, but he didn't know if they were advisable for a woman traveling alone. He hadn't spent much time with Emily, yet in the short time since they'd met, he felt a connection. He certainly didn't want to see her taking any risks.

"Now all I have to do is get there. Theresa's brownstone is just blocks away from where you're staying. Would you like to share the cost of the cab?"

"That's mighty generous of you, but I was going to put that on my expense account. So how would you like to share the cost of the cab with me, because half of nothing is still nothing."

She smiled, her excitement growing even more. "I can't say no to that. It's a deal."

Even if he didn't have anyone to share his vacation, he at least could share the cab. He didn't want to dwell on his situation and make himself even more depressed, so he checked his watch. "It's four thirty in Seattle, so that means it's seven thirty here. I would think the rush hour is over."

Her smile dropped. One eye narrowed as she concentrated. "I don't know if the rush hour is ever over in New York City. At least that's what I've heard."

"There's only one way to find out. Let's finish eating and get out of here."

Chapter 3

Emily was more than ready to get on her way. As soon as they were finished, they made their way to the main exit, then stopped near the door to fasten their coats.

"I'm not sure I'm ready for this," Bryan said as began to fasten the buttons on his jacket.

"I doubt riding in a cab in New York for real is like it is in the movies. I'm sure it will be fine."

"Not the cab. I mean that it's so cold out there."

Her brows knotted. "Cold? They announced the weather on my flight. It sounded quite warm for December."

"Maybe for you."

Emily fastened the last button on her knee-length wool coat, flipped her scarf over her head, and pulled her fleece-lined gloves out of her pocket. "It's not bad at all out there."

Bryan did up the last button at his neckline. "When I left Seattle this morning, it was forty-five degrees. The pilot said it was only thirty-four and windy, which would make it feel colder than it actually was. This is a winter coat, but it's made for rain, not wind."

By Emily's definition, he wasn't wearing a winter coat; it was a fall jacket, which didn't look very warm. On his feet were shoes, not boots, like hers. Nor did he have gloves. "When I left Minneapolis, it was eighteen degrees. Believe me, thirty-four degrees isn't cold, even with a wind." She smoothed her hand down her lapel. If they took much longer to get outside, she was going to start to sweat. She'd just seen pictures of a small footbridge, taken in Central Park in the wintertime. The river had been frozen and the ground covered with snow. She was prepared for New York's weather, maybe even a little overprepared.

"Winters are different on the West Coast. Most years we don't get any snow at all, just unbelievable amounts of rain, and there's seldom any wind to speak of. I didn't think about my coat until I started walking through the airport and saw what everyone was wearing. I don't own anything warmer than this. I've never needed to."

"Then it looks like you're going to have to add some shopping to your sightseeing agenda." Her remark was a reminder that she also needed to do some shopping. Besides what she was wearing, she only had two changes of clothes, her toothbrush, a hair dryer, and her bedroom slippers.

"Where should I go?"

"Why do you think I'd know?" she asked as she tugged on her gloves.

"You're a woman. Women instinctively know where to shop."

"Not this woman," she harrumphed, then walked outside.

He followed her to the row of cabs, spoke to the driver of

the one they would be hiring through the window, then turned to her. "He says it will be about forty-five minutes to get there." His voice lowered in volume. "It looks pretty clean inside, so I think we're good to go."

The driver loaded their suitcases in the trunk, Bryan and Emily climbed into the backseat, then the driver edged out of the congestion in the pickup area.

Emily sat with her face almost pushed against the glass as they left the airport grounds and began their journey into New York City. "I wish I could see more, but it's so dark. All I can see is billboards."

"Yeah. Look at that one of the new Honda. I'll have to take one of those for a test drive when I get home."

Emily didn't want to contemplate the remaining life of her ten-year-old car, but her mood improved when Shea Stadium came into view, so brightly lit it nearly glowed. She wasn't a ball fan, but she was still impressed. After that, they passed signs advertising the turnoff for Flushing Meadows Park. She wished she could see the park, but it was so dark, all she could see was that they passed it. She couldn't even look for wildlife. She supposed that any squirrels in the trees had gone to bed for the night, if squirrels were even out in the winter here, which they probably weren't.

"Do you know if squirrels hibernate?" she asked, more to herself than Bryan. "They store nuts and stuff, which makes me wonder if instead of sleeping, they laze around in their dens and eat all winter." That sounded like a good idea if they could add a pile of good books and a big mug of hot chocolate with melted marshmallows on top.

Bryan's voice drifted from across the cab. "I don't know about squirrels. All I do know is that it's cold out there." His voice trailed off. "Driver, do you know the forecast for tomorrow? I have meetings all day, and I have to be in Midtown at 8:00 a.m."

"Temperature is supposed to dip overnight. Maybe snow."

Bryan mumbled something she couldn't hear.

Emily turned her attention away from the window to look at his thin jacket. "It's not even eight o'clock. Surely there's someplace on the way where we could stop and go shopping."

"Probably, but I don't want to pull my suitcase through a crowded mall or store."

"No, you're right." She paused to think. "I know we don't know each other very well, but most men I've known generally don't need a lot of time to pick clothes. Do you?"

"Not usually. Why are you asking?"

"I have an idea." Emily leaned forward in the seat. "Driver, excuse me, but my friend needs to buy a coat. Can we stop someplace where we could run in, just have him try one on, and hurry through the checkout while you waited?"

"I could do that," the driver said over his shoulder. "I can even turn off the meter for you for five minutes, but no more than that, while I run inside for a few minutes, too."

Emily bit back a grin. She'd always wondered what taxi drivers did when the coffee consumption of the day caught up with them. This would work well for all of them. Not that she would have time to shop for herself, but she wasn't the one who was going to freeze to death.

"That would be great. Thank you."

The driver turned his head for a second and nodded.

"Yes," Bryan added. "Thank you."

Emily turned back to watch out the window just as they entered a bridge that spanned some kind of body of water. She couldn't tell if it was a river or an inlet, but once she arrived at her destination, she knew she would go back onto the Internet and find a map. Lights from the city framed the bridge, and more lights reflected on the black water. Tall buildings graced the shoreline, and the combination of moving red taillights and white headlights on the highway bordering the river looked like a diamond and ruby necklace.

"Wow," she muttered. "It's beautiful."

"This is the Triborough Bridge," the driver announced. "This takes us into Manhattan at East 125th Street, then onto the FDR highway. Then we'll be on the west side of the East River, and you can see Yankee Stadium across the river. I'll follow the highway toward Inwood. After that, we'll go to a Target that isn't far from where you're going."

"Great! I think—" She let her words drop, grabbed her purse, yanked the zipper open, and dumped the contents on the seat between herself and Bryan.

"What are you doing?"

"I'm getting my camera." She turned it on, waited for the lens to extend, held her breath, then took a picture out the window just as the stadium came into view. "This is a once-in-a-lifetime trip. I'm going to take as many pictures as my memory card will hold. Look at that!" She wasn't a sports fan, but seeing the famous stadium was still exciting.

"We're moving. That's not going to work."

"Maybe, maybe not. If it does, I'll have a great picture. If it doesn't, I only have to hit DELETE."

She snapped one more. When she turned back to put her camera back in her purse, Bryan wasn't watching out his side of the window. He was staring down at the mess between them.

"What is all this stuff?" He held out his hand to encompass everything. "This looks like you carry your own personal electronics store."

She felt herself blush, making her grateful for the dark interior of the cab. "It's just my PDA, MP3 player, the headset for my cell phone, my flash drive, an extra memory card, and all the accessories that go with everything."

"With extra batteries and a screwdriver, too, I see." He picked up her PalmPilot. "Nice case. These aren't cheap." He opened it to examine the unit. "I've got the same one, just the next model up." He suddenly grinned. "Want to trade some games?"

Emily's heart beat faster. "Yes!" She pressed her hand to her stomach. "Just not right now. I get carsick. I have to look out the window."

She again turned her head, but even the bright city lights blurred in front of her. All she could see was the image of Bryan's smile.

He had a wonderful smile, which made her realize that she hadn't seen it until now.

His words about his friend not being able to join him at the last minute echoed through her head. She'd known from the minute she left home that she would be alone. She hadn't known her final destination until just before takeoff. Bryan, on the other hand, had planned his trip for months.

His vacation had been pulled out from under him, just like her business trip.

She'd quit her job because of it. She didn't want to see him quit his vacation. Up until the last few minutes, he'd seemed sad, as if something was bothering him. She had a feeling that he needed this vacation, just like she did, only for different reasons.

He'd been so nice to her, and that made her want to do something nice in return so he could start his vacation in a good way.

She continued to watch out the window, again becoming more interested in the city lights as they got off the FDR highway. It wasn't long before the driver pulled into the parking lot of a Target.

She crammed everything back into her purse, then slung both her purse and her laptop over her shoulder and exited the cab.

Bryan looked at her with one raised eyebrow.

She patted the strap of her laptop case. "I don't think it's a good idea to leave my laptop in the car. I wouldn't do that at home; I don't think I should do it here, either."

"Smart thinking." He checked his watch. "We have to hurry."

When they got inside the store, they discovered that hurrying wasn't an option.

Emily stared at the long lines at the checkout counters. "We're in trouble."

He pointed to the shortest one. "Quick. You go stand in

line, I'll go find a jacket really fast, and I'll be back before you get to the front."

"But I can't stand in line without anything to buy."

He grabbed a package of gum and handed it to her. "Here. Now go."

He disappeared before she could reply.

Four minutes and thirteen seconds later, he was back, joining her in line with a coat and a new pair of gloves. "Told you I'd be fast," he said. "Do you need anything you can get quickly?"

"What is this? Tag team shopping?"

He grinned again, and it was good to see. "It's something my sister-in-law taught me. That woman knows how to shop. Drives my brother crazy sometimes, but she knows her way in and out of every mall in the Pacific Northwest."

"I hate shopping," Emily grumbled.

He smiled at her, his features softening. "I'm not a big shopper, either."

They stepped forward. Emily looked around. This Target had the same floor plan as the one back home, but she needed more than four minutes.

"If you don't like to shop, what do you like to do?" Bryan asked.

She shrugged her shoulders without looking at him. "Not a lot. I probably spend too much time online. I'm on the worship team at church, so that also means practice time. I used to curl, but the last few years I've been spending more time at work, so I quit the league. I guess I'll be able to rejoin. At this time of year, all I can do is spare, but that's okay."

"What do you do when you're working?"

"I'm an IT support analyst."

"That would explain your purse and why you're so adept with that laptop."

Emily shrugged her shoulders again. "What do you do?"

"I'm an area manager for a national furniture manufacturer. We're setting up some new lines and brainstorming the design ideas that haven't been coming together on the conference calls."

Her stomach knotted. Brainstorming was how Brian-with-an-*i* stole her efficiency programs. When he got her promotion, she'd been accused of being a backstabber and lost her job.

"Emily? Are you okay?"

She wasn't okay, but she was going to make the best of it. She had come to New York to escape and to lick her wounds.

Bryan's fingers brushed her arm. "Is something wrong?"

"What's done is done. I'm here to enjoy myself, and that's what I'm going to do." She forced herself to smile, but she knew it looked fake.

His movements stopped, but his hand didn't leave her arm. His voice lowered in pitch. "I'm a good listener, you know."

She looked down at his hand, still on her arm. Normally, she wasn't a touchy-feely person, but he was gentle and seemed sincere, even concerned that all was not right in her world.

Brian-with-an-*i* had also seemed sincere, then turned the tables when she least expected it. He'd taken advantage of her trust and used her research in his presentation, claiming everything was his own, then became angry when she broke up with him. Brian got the raise and accompanying promotion, and Emily got a reprimand and a broken heart.

Still, she wasn't going to bare her soul to a stranger, especially with another Brian, and she didn't care how he spelled it. Instead, she would be strong and be the woman God wanted her to be. She could be nice to Bryan without getting involved with him. "Thanks for the offer, but there's nothing you can do. Let's just enjoy ourselves while we're here."

"I thought you said you hated shopping."

"Doing it tag team style gives shopping a new meaning." It sounded like a challenge—something she couldn't turn down.

When it was their turn at the cashier, Bryan paid for everything, including the gum. He winked. "Keep it. Consider it a learning experience."

The driver had turned the meter back on by the time they got to the cab, so they resumed their journey and arrived at the home of Emily's hostess very close to the predicted forty-five minutes, plus the ten minutes at Target.

The neighborhood consisted of a mixture of tall apartment buildings and many rows of small but well-kept brownstones. They should have looked boringly similar, but they didn't. Each one had something unique—different window valances, an ornament or flowers by the door or on the steps, colored door coverings, or even a different wood finish on the door. Together, they were an interesting blend, giving the effect of just enough subtle changes but not too much to ruin the atmosphere of consistency. All of the brownstones were three levels high, with the lower level mostly beneath the ground, and steps leading to the doors of the second level. Together, they were quite stately, each unit in each set the same but yet different. She figured that since each was quite narrow, they were probably very long to provide adequate living area.

Bryan, wearing his new jacket, exited the cab with Emily while the driver retrieved her suitcase from the trunk.

He walked with her up the path to the address Theresa had given her.

"You should see how much it costs to buy one of these. Which is probably why the one I'm staying in has a complete suite on the lower level. The family rents it out to tourists to help pay their mortgage."

Emily nodded. "A suite would have been nice, but I'm happy, especially considering the short notice. I'm in the den on the lower level. It's got a futon and a small closet, and she said I can use her washer and dryer when I need to."

"That sounds handy."

It would be, if she had some clothes to wash.

She pressed the doorbell, which made her realize that this was the time to say good-bye. She didn't know why, but regret that their brief acquaintance was over poked at her. She didn't want a relationship, but Bryan would make a good friend. She needed a friend right now, but she didn't want it to be another Brian.

While she waited, she turned her head and looked up at him. "Thanks again for everything. I hope you get whatever you want accomplished at your business meetings this week, and I hope you have a good time on your vacation." She glanced toward the cab. The driver waited patiently on the street, the meter still running. Suddenly, her hopes rose. If her hosts were friends with Bryan's hosts, then maybe she would see Bryan at church on the weekend. She didn't want to like him, but. . .he was very likable, despite his name.

He pulled off one of his new gloves and reached to touch her. Only instead of her arm, this time he gently ran his fingers under her chin. Her breath caught when he began to lower his head.

His soft lips, slightly cold from the wind, brushed her cheek. "I had a great evening," he said softly.

She closed her eyes, thinking that she should have wanted to push him away, but what she really wanted was the opposite. She wanted him to wrap his arms around her and promise that from here on, everything would be fine and the world would be a fair place.

He straightened, then extended his hand to the woman who had answered the door. "You must be Theresa. I'm Bryan. Now that I know Emily is in good hands, I'll be on my way." He paused and looked at Emily. "Remember, you owe me dinner."

He turned, and with a wave of his hand over his shoulder, he was gone.

Chapter 4

Bryan had never been so happy to see a day end. Except, with any luck, the good part was just about to begin.

As expected, he'd been tied up with meetings and brainstorming sessions with the other area managers, designers, and technicians all day.

During their lunch break, those who lived in New York City had told all of the visitors the best places to see, including tips on getting around. They'd ended the day with a supper buffet that provided time to mingle in a more informal atmosphere or, for those who needed it, to break away for some time alone to regroup.

He'd regrouped.

Armed with new information, Bryan had gone to one of the spare computers and done a little surfing of the tourist Web sites, just as Emily had done.

Emily.

He couldn't stop thinking about her, yet he didn't know anything about her. Nor did she know anything about him.

Initially, that was the way he wanted it, but the more he thought about her, the less he was satisfied with that plan.

Automatically, he closed his hand over his cell phone, clipped to his belt.

It felt like a lifeline.

For three more days, brainstorming for his job was supposed to consume every waking minute, both at and away from the office.

But at the close of business on Friday, he would be free.

He'd already escaped from everyone who depended on him at home. He'd even delegated his church obligations. The chance to get away from his hectic life was a gift from God.

Last night he'd prayed about it and finally believed that even without Steve, he was still going to have a good time. There was no better place to get lost in a crowd than New York City at Christmastime—he could simply melt into the pleasant blur of the upcoming celebration of Christ's birth. It didn't matter that he was alone. But was that what was best?

Before he could question himself about wanting some solitary time, he hit the Recall button on his phone. Emily's hostess seemed surprised that Emily was receiving a call but gave her the phone when he identified himself.

"Hi," he said, then cleared his throat when he realized his voice sounded a little huskier than normal. "I was wondering if you wanted to go shopping with me again. I can be there in half an hour."

She hesitated for a few seconds. "I already went shopping this afternoon for a few things I needed, but I do need new clothes. Wait. I thought you hated shopping."

"I thought we could hate it together and do the tag team thing again." That didn't make any sense, because they wouldn't need to hurry, even though he had no intention of taking any longer than necessary.

There was another pause. "Isn't it a little late for shopping?"

"Then we can forget the shopping. Let's go somewhere for coffee and walk around and see some nighttime sights. One of the guys told me about a quaint little coffee shop in an area called Lincoln Center. They have a great Christmas tree and outdoor shows there. He gave me directions. That whole area is supposed to be really spectacular at night in December. People just walk around looking at everything and enjoying the ambiance." He tapped his fingers on the tabletop, starting to get nervous because she was taking too long to respond. "Think of the photo opportunities," he blurted out.

"Uh, okay. . ."

"Great. I'll be there in about half an hour."

Bryan didn't waste time with long good-byes to his coworkers. He would see them all again at 8:00 a.m. sharp the next day. Until then, he had other plans.

Half an hour in a cab had never gone so slowly, but finally he was again standing in front of the brownstone where Emily was staying.

She opened the door as soon as he knocked and accompanied him to the waiting cab.

Compared to the ride from the airport, this one was short, which was good, not because he cared about the cost, but because it was a waste of precious time. He really didn't know her at all, which was probably what made their current arrangement

125

so appealing. She was a stranger, but they'd established enough of a bond to share a safe companionship for a limited time.

But there was more to it than that. Something about her drew him like a moth to a flame, and he couldn't put his finger on it.

But he would.

They ordered a couple of steamy lattes and began to walk with the crowd.

Bryan wrapped his fingers around the paper coffee cup, enjoying the warmth seeping through his new gloves. The beauty of the lights and Christmas decorations dancing around them was even more astounding than described. After walking for a block, his attention wandered from the surroundings and focused on his companion. Emily was spellbound, like a child caught in the rapture of the first time in a big toy store, except this one was outside.

The lights sparkling in her eyes rivaled the twinkling colors above. "Look at the tree! It's magnificent! How did you find out about this?"

"One of the guys at the meeting this morning."

"I wonder if a picture would work."

"It would probably be better than what you tried when we were leaving the airport."

She stuck her tongue out at him. "At least I tried. I'll never look back and regret that I didn't take advantage of an opportunity and lost my only chance."

Lost opportunities.

Bryan nearly missed a step. Maybe that was the reason he'd called Emily and the reason he was with her now. Even though their time together would be short, he didn't want to regret something he hadn't done—and turn his back on what God had for some reason put in his path.

Their initial meeting flashed through his mind. God hadn't exactly put Emily in his path—he'd been in her path, quite literally. Once he got over the shock of knocking down a woman in a public place, he was instantly drawn to her. He wasn't lonely—he was too busy to be lonely—yet he enjoyed Emily's company. Being with her filled a hole. Just as Emily didn't want to lose her photo opportunities, he didn't want to lose her companionship.

Speaking of losing. . . "Squirrels lose 50 percent of what they try to store for the winter," he said.

She looked up at him as they walked. Her mouth hung open for a few seconds, then turned into an adorable grin. "What are you talking about?"

"You asked me about squirrels hibernating yesterday. I didn't know the answer, so I googled it on my break. The answer is that some species of squirrels hibernate, but most don't. They stay pretty inactive in their dens all winter. They only leave if they run out of food, to go find what they've hidden. That led me to discover that they lose about half of what they hide for the winter. I read an estimate that millions of trees in the world are accidentally planted by squirrels who bury nuts and forget where they hid them."

She stared at him as if he'd lost his mind. Maybe he had. But when someone came to him with a need, big or small, he always felt compelled to respond, either by information or by action. For the first time, instead of responding out of necessity, he'd responded simply because the question piqued his curiosity.

And that made him curious about other things. Like why Emily had come to New York alone and unprepared.

Emily guided them out of the flow of pedestrians, stopped, and began to dig through her purse. "Squirrel trivia aside, I want to take a picture of all this."

He held her coffee cup while she snapped a number of pictures, then they resumed their walking tour.

"How would you like to see Herald Square tomorrow?" he asked.

"Don't you have more business meetings tomorrow?"

"Yes, but they're over at the same time they were today, which means I can pick you up at about seven thirty."

"I've done a little online research on Herald Square and Macy's. There's way more there than we can see in a couple of hours. It's also close to Times Square. The ad said it's best to go to Macy's on a weekday before noon. Why don't we do that Monday and make other plans for tomorrow night?"

Bryan found himself smiling. It pleased him that Emily was now the one talking about spending time together. That gave him more confidence to make his next suggestion. "Then how about a dinner cruise? I checked out a Web site that looked perfect. Boarding starts at six thirty, then the boat departs at seven thirty. There's dinner and entertainment, and then we can walk around the boat and enjoy the Manhattan skyline. It's supposed to last three hours. I can do that now with my new, warm jacket."

Emily's pace slowed. "That sounds expensive."

"Moderately. But it's my idea, so I'm paying. I want to do this, but I don't want to do it alone." Bryan bit into his bottom lip. The reason he didn't want to do it alone was because the advertisement had labeled the cruise "romantic." He didn't mind being single among couples, but he hated going to a restaurant, any restaurant, alone. He didn't even go to fast-food places alone.

He quirked one eyebrow, trying to appear nonchalant. The idea of enjoying the colored Christmas lights of the city while walking hand in hand with Emily on the dimly lit deck of a small cruise ship appealed to him more than it should have. "What do you say? Just think, more photo opportunities."

"How can I say no to that?"

He pulled his PalmPilot out of his pocket and opened up the memo file he'd made. "I've got details and directions. Want me to beam it to you?"

Emily pulled out her PalmPilot, and they aimed the two toward each other. "Okay, I'm ready." She grinned up at him. "And what about those games you promised me?"

"Only if you send something else to me."

"Deal. I've got this fantastic Frogger clone. I've also got a great Bible program with a concordance. It would be a trial program. If you like it, you just buy your own CD key. It's very reasonable."

"I'd love that."

Bryan's heart soared as he hit the prompt to send her the files, then received the ones she sent him. Many of his friends had tried to set him up with good, noble, and intelligent professional women. Every one of them left him feeling alone and, unfortunately, bored. His true soul mate would be all of the above, plus someone who understood and embraced the same faith, as well as the same technologies and toys. She would also be someone who didn't need constant approval or help.

He turned the unit off. "I know it's not that late, but I have to be up early tomorrow for the next round of meetings. I have to get back."

"We just passed a subway entrance over there. How would you like to take the subway?"

It would be fun, and a great end to their adventure. But. . . "I'm not sure that's a good idea. I really don't know where to go." He reached to his belt for his cell phone. "I think I'll just call a cab."

Once again, Emily aimed her PalmPilot at his. "I downloaded a map of the New York subway system. There's a stop at West 215th, which is within walking distance of where we're staying. Ya wanna?" She lowered her head and tapped the screen to pull up her file.

She was innovative, prepared, and not afraid to use her newfound knowledge to savor new experiences. All he could do was watch, mesmerized. As they learned more about New York, he was learning more about Emily. And he liked what he saw.

"Got it!" she said. "Are you ready to receive?"

They collaborated over the best route, made their way to the West 66th Street station entrance, paid their fares, then proceeded to the platform to wait.

Emily pointed to the walls. "Wow! Look at that! Those are mosaics."

Bryan looked at the artwork picturing a variety of dancers, singers, and instruments. He could barely believe that all this was underground, but it was.

A rumble in the distance announced the pending arrival of the next train. Before he realized what Emily was doing, she'd pulled out her camera and was busily snapping pictures, first of the walls, then of the train in motion.

"Put that away!" he said in a stage whisper. "Everyone is going to know we're tourists."

"So?" she said as she snapped one more. "We *are* tourists."

He stepped into the train as soon as the doors opened, then gripped a pole. He looked over his shoulder and opened his mouth to speak, to remind Emily to hold on, when a flash lit the car.

"Say cheese," she said as she dropped her camera into her purse. Her hand wrapped around the pole next to her just as the train started to roll.

"Very funny. You caught me with my mouth hanging open. I hope you're going to hit your trusty DELETE button on that one."

"Maybe. Maybe not." Emily grinned, which meant the answer was the one he didn't want.

A couple of teenage boys seated nearby snickered, openly staring at them.

He almost told them to mind their own business, but he couldn't be angry or even annoyed. Her teasing identified them as being together in a fun way—they were simply having fun with no strings attached. He liked it.

"It sure is dark out there," she said, looking through the windows as they sped along their way.

"Well, we are underground."

"I know, but I've never been on a subway before. This is

ordinary to the residents, but I think it's exciting."

He wondered how much longer she would find it exciting. He hadn't thought about it until they were on it, but the train rocked constantly as they moved. Not only did he remember Emily's question about squirrels hibernating, but he also remembered her comment about motion sickness.

"You wouldn't find it exciting if you had to do this every day at rush hour, going from one end of the city to the other, jammed in like a sardine."

"Probably not, but I'm a tourist, and I'm not afraid to act like one."

"Are you calling me afraid?"

"Let me quote you. 'Everyone is going to know we're tourists,' I think you said. That indicates some degree of hesitation."

Bryan centered his weight to counterbalance the movement of the train, let go of the pole, quickly took the two steps toward Emily, and grasped the same pole as her. "I detect a challenge. If that's the way you want it, fine. Starting right now, I'm officially a tourist."

She looked up at him, eyes wide.

He knew she didn't do it on purpose, but her words were exactly what he needed—an open challenge to make this month different from any other time of his life—he had no one to answer to except himself and God. For the first time in his life, he could allow himself to have fun and maybe be a little irresponsible—in a responsible sort of way.

Keeping one hand firmly on the pole, Bryan fumbled to open his jacket with his free hand. He yanked his tie loose, pulled it over his head without undoing the knot, and held it toward Emily. "A tourist would never wear a tie. Consider this the symbol of my surrender."

"You didn't have to do that. I would never have known you were still wearing your tie."

"But I knew. Tomorrow the tie comes off as soon as the last meeting is done, before I leave the building. After Friday, no more ties until I'm back in Seattle."

"Okay. . ." Her voice trailed off, then she gasped. "What's going on? It's getting light!"

One of the teenage boys replied. "We're going out, lady. This line goes up at Dyckman Street. From there, it's aboveground."

"Oh. Thank you." She turned to Bryan. "The map didn't say anything about that. I just assumed the subway was completely underground."

Bryan grinned. "Never assume. It makes. . ." His voice trailed off. He didn't need to finish.

"Har-dee-har," she grumbled, then turned her attention to the window.

Since they were outside and able to see the streets and homes below as they sped along, Bryan also watched as much of the passing scenery as he could see in the dark until they reached their stop.

They stepped out as soon as the doors swooshed open and made their way down.

"Tomorrow marks my first day of becoming an official tourist. I hope you're ready."

Chapter 5

Emily stood at the side of the gangplank. Bryan had e-mailed her the ticket confirmation, but she didn't want to sit at a table alone in a place like this. Instead, while she waited for Bryan outside, she studied the boat.

Except it wasn't really a boat. It was a small cruise ship, luxurious and stately. Strains of soft jazz drifted from within, telling Emily the music wasn't recorded—live musicians were playing, confirming what she already knew. This dinner wasn't going to be cheap.

Emily turned her head as Bryan appeared beside her. "I hope you didn't wait long."

She was barely able to acknowledge his arrival when the horn tooted, signaling everyone that it was almost time to set sail.

While they waited for dinner to be served, Emily checked out the other passengers.

Most appeared to be couples out for a romantic evening, dressed accordingly. Many of the men wore suits, and the women wore cocktail dresses with high heels and accessories to match.

Because she'd left home so quickly, Emily had only brought two mix-and-match outfits and her most practical purse. Fortunately, Theresa had borrowed a beautiful dress in the right size from a friend, so Emily didn't feel underdressed. The skirt was even long enough to hide her boots.

Bryan had come right from his business meetings. His perfectly fitted, custom-tailored suit made him even more dashing and handsome than ever.

But one thing was missing.

She reached to the floor for her purse. "I still have your tie."

He shook his head. "No way. I'm a tourist, remember?"

Before she could argue with him, the boat began to move, signifying that their excursion had begun. Their table gave them an excellent view of the skyline, and they were barely out of the dock when the servers appeared with the passengers' dinners.

Emily had never experienced such a fine meal, even in Minneapolis. The cruise, the dinner, and the live music were designed to be worth the price. The combination was elegant, entertaining, and romantic. Hardly anyone except them was paying much attention to the passing scenery; the other couples were only paying attention to each other, reminding her of what had happened to her life. She'd recently been half of a couple, except in hindsight, she'd been the only one who thought their connection had been for romance.

Brian the Traitor had never taken her to a place like this.

She wondered what he was doing now and how he could live with himself. He'd stolen her work and, with that, her promotion, which ultimately cost her the job she loved. She'd trusted him to do the right thing and confess the truth when confronted. Instead, he lied to the general manager, who didn't believe her when she said the whole proposal had been her own creation and programming, not Brian's, because Brian didn't know enough to make everything come together. He'd even hinted at marriage if she would make it work for him. That wasn't love. His motives were totally self-serving.

So she'd turned the other cheek and taken the first plane out of town.

It wouldn't be long before everyone realized she was right.

The knowledge gave her no satisfaction. Even if they offered her the job back, she wouldn't take it. They'd chosen to take Brian's word over hers, and that had added to the hurt.

One day she would have to go back, but until Christmas, she was in New York to escape. This luxurious dinner cruise with a good Christian man who had nothing to gain was going a long way toward helping her feel better.

It didn't matter that all of the other couples on the cruise were romantically involved. Her fellow tourist was an interesting companion. The only bad things about him were that he was another Brian and another manager. For tonight, if she didn't think too much about his name or his job or the fact that he was there on a business trip and she wasn't, he was fun to be with.

When they'd passed the World Trade Center site, she turned to her fellow tourist, who wasn't behaving like the rest of the men, fawning over their dates. Bryan was reading his PalmPilot.

"We've seen Chelsea Piers and the Empire State Building.

We've just gone past the World Trade Center site and Battery Park City. So that means the next thing we'll see is something called South Street Seaport. It said on the Web site that this was once the gateway to New York City and North America. It's been redeveloped and now is full of shops, restaurants, offices, and a museum. We're going to have to go there during the daytime next week." He looked up and winked. "Think of the photo opportunities."

"I think I've heard that line before. I'm missing those opportunities, by the way, since we're sitting inside."

His smile dropped. "I don't want to miss dessert. After that we can go outside. By then we'll be up to the Brooklyn Bridge, and not long after, we'll pass the Statue of Liberty. In the middle there's a landmark residential district and a historic military post. Just before we dock, we'll pass something called the Colgate Clock. The old Colgate Palmolive plant was demolished, but they kept the clock. Another piece of history. I wrote down the Web site URL if you want to learn more."

Emily was pleased that Bryan enjoyed researching the things they planned to see. She did that, too, and it drove most of her friends crazy; they just wanted to look quickly and move on to the next thing, with Emily usually left behind studying something they considered an insignificant detail. That was why she decided to travel solo, even though she knew it would be lonely. She hadn't known what was in store for her when she arrived in New York. But God knew.

The waiter appeared with their dessert, something called Midnight Mocha Madness, and it was worth the wait. The rich chocolate was a wonderful end to a delectable meal. Still, once they were finished, they wasted no time in making their way to the outer deck.

Bryan pointed to the right. "Let's go over there, away from the main path."

"Sure. That looks like a good place to take pictures."

As she removed her camera from the case, Bryan reached into his pocket and pulled out a state-of-the-art digital camera almost like hers. "Nice," she said.

"Thanks. But I'll bet you can give me some pointers."

She smiled. One day, when she met her Mr. Right, she hoped God would match her with someone who wasn't afraid of technology or of a woman who knew more about it than he did.

While she waited for the lens to extend from her camera, she studied his. "Why didn't I see that before?"

"Yesterday I came straight from my meeting."

"You did today, too."

"Yesterday was a spur-of-the-moment decision. Today was planned, so I'm prepared." He thoughtfully selected his camera's setting. "We'll be at the Brooklyn Bridge soon. The Brooklyn Bridge crossed the most turbulent waters a bridge could at that time. Did you know that technically, this isn't a river—it's a tidal strait? That's why the water moves like this."

Emily also selected her camera settings. "Did you know that they began building it in January 1870, and it wasn't finished and dedicated until May 1883? The monumental construction became a symbol of the greatness of New York and of American ingenuity."

He smiled. "It sounds like you've done your research."

"Of course."

They stood in silence, taking pictures as they the passed the South Street Seaport, then sailed beneath the Brooklyn Bridge. Emily almost forgot to press the button, she was so in awe of the great expanse as they approached it, then went beneath. Once it was behind them, she rested her elbows on the railing in an attempt to steady herself as she took more pictures of the bridge, then of the lights of the city's high-rises glowing in their stately beauty. They passed beneath two other bridges, and the boat began to turn around.

Not many people ventured onto the deck in the cold night air, and fewer actually stopped to view the skyline. No one stayed for very long, no doubt because it was so cold.

Even though Emily was dressed for frigid temperatures, being on the water made it that much colder. Her cheeks tingled, her fingers were stiff, and her teeth were starting to chatter, all of which she had to remedy before they reached the Statue of Liberty. She had to keep the camera still and be able to press the buttons.

Despite her Minneapolis coat, Emily shivered.

Bryan's voice resonated above her. "I know it's cold, but we'll never pass this way again."

Emily tried to repress her shiver and failed miserably. "I feel the same way."

"I know this sounds like a bad pickup line, but if we keep each other warm, we could stay outside a little longer. Let's just step back a bit, where it's more sheltered."

If another man made such a suggestion, Emily would have questioned his motives. But she trusted Bryan. Besides, she wanted to stay outside, too.

As she moved back away from the railing, Bryan stepped behind her. He rested his hands on her shoulders, gently drawing her toward him, nestling her back against his front. When he didn't remove his hands, Emily automatically slipped her hands beneath his. He lowered his head and rested his cheek against her temple.

"I feel better already," he said softly.

Emily didn't know what she felt. She did feel warmer, but it may have been more from the increased tempo of her heart than from the closeness they now shared. Or maybe it was the closeness that made her heart speed up.

She couldn't decide if it made her feel warm, comforted, nervous, or all of the above.

She'd never felt like this with Brian the Traitor. In hindsight, she realized he'd been doing what she expected in an attempt to get what he wanted, which was her knowledge and skill with computers. Maybe that was why she'd felt something was missing from their relationship. There had been no tenderness, only basic contact. They'd never argued, because he was careful to say only what she wanted to hear.

Bryan the Tourist was different. After Bryan positioned her against himself, he'd shuffled his body to make the contact between them a perfect fit. His hands hadn't moved but remained gently on her shoulders. All she had to do was step forward and the contact would be broken.

But she didn't want to break the contact. She wanted to share the warmth, yet there was something else. Pressed together like this, with his face against hers, side by side, the rasp of the day's growth of beard was a startling contrast to his soft lips, also nestled into her cheek.

Their contact was more than simply practical because of the weather—it felt personal, even affectionate. Because of the simplicity of his actions, it was the most romantic thing any man had ever done.

Mostly, he was close enough to kiss. . . .

She wondered if he'd been influenced by some of the romantically inclined couples on the cruise or if his fond gesture had come naturally.

If he did try to kiss her, what would she do?

Emily forced herself to make her voice work. "I don't know how to thank you for this. The cruise isn't even over yet, and already it's been the experience of a lifetime. I wish there was something I could do for you."

"Maybe there is. I can't see the pictures on my view screen with much detail, and I can't download personal pictures onto the company computer. Can I use your laptop to see what we've taken so far?"

"Sure. If you don't have anything planned tomorrow, we could get together."

"Great. Can we meet for supper, close to home? I have to get up extra early Friday for the last of the meetings, and then I'm free until Christmas."

"Deal." Except she'd have to move the one picture she'd taken of Bryan on the subway with his mouth open. She hadn't deleted it like he'd asked, nor would she. She loved that picture. She would keep it forever as a special reminder of how much she enjoyed being a tourist with him.

Before she could move, Bryan slipped around her so he was

now at her front. Keeping one gloved hand on her shoulder, he slid his other arm around her waist. He waited, encouraging her to come to him, but leaving it to be her choice.

Emily didn't want to think about it. She folded her hands under her chin and leaned fully into Bryan's chest as he wrapped his arms around her and pressed his cheek into the top of her head. She sighed and let herself enjoy being cocooned by his size. She probably shouldn't have been doing this, but she trusted him. He had no ulterior motives—he only wanted the same thing she did—to enjoy each other's warmth and company. For the moment, she felt protected, and she didn't want it to end too soon.

After a few short minutes, Bryan spoke softly into her ear. "We should get ready; we're getting close to the Statue of Liberty."

As much as she'd been anticipating taking more pictures, she wasn't ready to let the moment end.

He stepped back before she could think of a reason to stay together, then smiled down at her as he reached into his pocket for his camera. "Are you ready?"

Emily couldn't speak. She'd been ready to kiss him, not take more pictures.

Before she said something stupid, she dug her camera out of her purse and tried to concentrate on the kind of pictures she wanted.

Ready or not, the Statue of Liberty, in all its glory, was upon them.

Emily steadied herself on the railing and began taking pictures of the greatest symbol of American freedom, her torch glowing proudly in the dark sky.

When they were done, Bryan grasped her cold hands, covering them completely with his own. "That was great."

Emily looked up into his eyes, and her breath caught. In the dark, with the colored Christmas lights of the city sparkling across the water, his golden eyes sparkled with the reflections. It was just like a scene in a romantic movie, before the tall, dark, handsome hero kissed his lady and they walked off into the sunset together.

He lowered his head, brushed a kiss against the top of her knuckles, then released her. "Your hands are freezing. We should go in and have some coffee to warm up."

Before she could respond, he led her inside, away from their private hiding spot, and back into the crowd.

Emily didn't know what to think. She'd come to New York to sort herself out. She'd just thought she was going to do it alone.

But tomorrow would bring another day with Bryan.

She wished she knew if that was good or bad.

Chapter 6

Bryan reached toward the door handle of the bistro with one hand, and the other automatically rose to his neck, to the knot of his tie.

It was just an involuntary reaction, because he had no tie. He'd already stripped it off and left it hanging in the coat closet at the office.

He smiled at the thought of the company president's face when he opened the closet in the morning to see a lone tie on a hanger and nothing else.

Bryan ran his fingers through his hair, which made him wish he had a comb after being out in the wind. He hadn't been this nervous last night when he'd taken Emily on what was clearly advertised as a romantic cruise. In fact, he hadn't been this nervous since. . .he didn't know when—high school?

He gave the door a push and stepped in. The whoosh of heat and the aroma of good, strong coffee wafted up at him in greeting.

Emily, with her laptop open in front of her, was the only

one in this cheerful place who was sitting alone.

Guilt roared through him, even though she was early. He nodded to the greeter and made his way to join Emily.

"You beat me," he said as he lowered himself into the chair beside her.

"Only by a few minutes. I haven't even finished booting up yet." While she waited, she looked up at him. "Do you mind if I ask you something?"

"Not at all."

"Do you have anyone special waiting for you when you get back to Seattle?"

Bryan felt his ears heat up. He shook his head. "No. Much to everyone's disappointment."

"Everyone?"

The heat in his ears deepened. "Pretty much. Especially my mother. She keeps introducing me to all her friends' single daughters. My niece has even tried to set me up with her teacher. That was a real disaster."

"I see."

He doubted that she did.

It wasn't as if he was opposed to getting married. He was nearly thirty years old. He'd just never experienced that special connection that made him want to spend the rest of his life with one person.

With Emily, he felt that connection, which of course was just his luck, because after Christmas was over, he would never see her again.

So until then, he had to make the most of every minute, starting right now.

The cruise had been the perfect romantic setting, but it hadn't been right. Emily didn't seem like the romantic type, which was part of her appeal. She spoke her mind and asked nothing of him, which made him want to give more. On the boat, he'd wanted to kiss her so badly it hurt. It had taken all his restraint to hold back when he had the chance, and he'd had many chances. But the moment was never right. He wanted their first real kiss to be special, not because it was almost expected in such a setting.

"Okay," she said, "it's booted up. Can I have your memory card?"

A waitress took their orders while she pushed the card into the slot, then Bryan slid his chair beside Emily's to watch as the pictures were displayed in a slide-show format.

"Turnabout is fair play," he said, trying to sound as though he was just making light conversation, but the possibilities burned in his gut. "What about you? Do you have someone special waiting for you when you get home?"

"No," she mumbled. "To make a long story short, we'll just say that I plan to stay single for a long time. Then it will be someone whose job has nothing to do with computers and who never goes anywhere near an office. Blue-collar only. I'm thinking maybe a plumber or an electrician or someone who works in construction. Something like that."

Bryan wanted to ask why, but her tone told him that she'd been hurt and the subject wasn't open for discussion.

He didn't figure it was the right time to tell her that today he'd been asked to consider a promotion as the Dallas area manager. If he took it, he wouldn't just be working in an office; he'd have an office of his own.

Not that it mattered. When his vacation was over, the only contact they could have would be an occasional phone call or e-mail.

It wasn't enough. In his dreams last night, he'd done what he wanted to do on the boat—he'd held her tight and actually kissed her. When the alarm went off, he'd tried to go back to sleep so he could continue. He'd never hated his snooze setting more than this morning.

To give himself something else to think about, Bryan pulled out his PalmPilot and began making notes of the picture numbers from Emily's camera that he wanted copies of.

"I'm not sure that I'll be able to do anything with you tomorrow," he said as he wrote a number down. "It's the last day of meetings, and I've been warned that we'll be getting out maybe as late as midnight. We have to cover everything that was on the agenda, and they're planning a Christmas party."

"That's okay. I hope you don't think I expected to be with you every day. I came here alone. I was prepared to do everything by myself anyway."

He didn't want to think about that. He forced himself to smile. "It's much more fun to do things with someone else, don't you think?"

"Of course. I just don't want you to feel obligated to bring me along."

Bryan reached to touch her hand, then wrapped his fingers around hers. "That's not how I feel at all. I think we've had a lot of fun so far, and I can hardly wait for Saturday, when I won't have to watch the time. Then Sunday, how would you like to attend church together?"

Her eyes brightened. "I'd like that."

The waitress arrived with their meals then, halting their conversation.

Emily said the prayer of thanks over their food this time. While she thanked God for their time together, Bryan added a silent prayer that they would have a lot more time, even if it meant asking for a miracle.

When they were done eating and all of the pictures had been viewed, Bryan escorted her back to Theresa's brownstone.

She disappeared before he could give her a cursory peck on the cheek, but that was okay. On Saturday they would be sitting side by side on the tour bus most of the day. On Sunday they would go to church to worship together. After lunch they planned to see the Rockefeller Christmas tree and make plans for the rest of the week.

Bryan smiled every step of the three-block walk to his host's home.

❄

Emily grimaced as she slid her credit card across the counter. She'd made more transactions today than she had in the previous six months.

Being in New York was not doing wonders for her charge bill. She couldn't stop buying things, which was strange. She used to hate shopping, but now she loved it. Today they'd been to Herald Square, first at a mall that was at least four stories tall, and now they were at Macy's.

It was like walking through a fantasy. She'd never been to such a place in her life. Even the constant masses of people couldn't tamp her wonderment. There was a huge tree outside, and all of the store windows were decorated in shiny and vivid colors. Yet nothing outside compared to the displays inside. Shimmering lights and decorations hung from the ceiling, and tall trees, brightly decorated, were everywhere throughout the store. The only time in her life she'd ever seen more lights was when they went to Rockefeller Center to see the huge Christmas tree.

She smiled at the memory of Bryan's earlier attempts at skating and how he'd spent more time on his back than on his feet. She hadn't thought about the rink until they got there.

She turned to Bryan. "I'm sorry, I forgot to ask until now. How are you feeling?"

"I'm okay. As long as we don't sit down."

Emily raised her hand in a futile attempt to hide her snicker. She hadn't known that there were no outdoor skating rinks in Seattle. With the temperate climate on the West Coast, it didn't get cold enough in the winter for anything to freeze. The only places to skate were indoors, and open sessions were very limited because most ice time was reserved for hockey. Outdoor rinks were common in Minneapolis. When Emily was a child, one of her neighbors always made a skating rink over their garden, where she'd played hockey with the boys until spring thaw. Therefore, she was a much better skater than Bryan, and most important, through experience, she knew how to fall gracefully. She'd noticed that when they were on the subway, he'd positioned himself very carefully on the hard seats.

"I don't think we're going to be doing a lot of sitting today," she said between her fingers. "There's too much shopping to do."

Bryan stared pointedly at all of the bags in her hand and raised the bags he carried that were hers. "I thought we both agreed that we hated shopping. What happened?"

The clerk slid the charge receipt to her. "You said you hadn't finished your Christmas shopping, either, so quit complaining," she said as she scribbled her signature.

"That would make sense if I didn't know that most of what you bought is for yourself."

Emily tucked the receipt into her wallet and picked up yet another bag. "You're just jealous because I'm more organized than you are."

"You're the one who's jealous because I had most of my shopping done before I left home."

"Watch it, buster. I know too many men who do most of their shopping on Christmas Eve. You're lucky to have me here with you."

Emily waited for his response, enjoying the playful banter. She anticipated his laughter, which would be accompanied by a rascally reply.

Bryan didn't smile. His expression turned serious, and he stepped closer. Slowly, he raised one hand and touched her cheek gently with his fingers. "Yes. I am lucky."

"I. . ." Emily's voice trailed off at his unexpected sober mood. She struggled to get her mind focused. "I feel lucky, too. I'm having a lot of fun today."

He moved even closer, so close that he could kiss her if they weren't still standing beside the busy checkout counter at Macy's. "Me, too," he said, his voice almost a whisper as he ran his thumb softly on the side of her chin.

The temperature in the store seemed suddenly warm. "I think I've had enough shopping for a while. Let's go outside."

"Outside?" His hand dropped, and he blinked. "We can go to that mini Koreatown along 32nd Street between Broadway and Fifth Avenue and get something for supper. Got your camera?"

"Ah, yes. Photo opportunities." Emily gave him a shaky smile, trying to fight the feeling that something had changed, though she didn't know what.

At some point, Bryan had become more to her than simply a fellow tourist. But she didn't want to change the rules of the game. She'd come to New York to escape and make plans and decisions about her future. The only plans she'd made were about where to go—the Empire State Building Observatory with the audio tour, the American Museum of Natural History, and the Rose Center for Earth and Space, plus the Hayden Planetarium. One evening they'd gone to a Broadway show, and she'd had the time of her life, even better than on the cruise, because the theater was warm. The only decisions she'd made were what she'd bought everyone for Christmas.

She patted her purse with her free hand while she tried to push those thoughts to the back of her mind. "I've always got my camera. Let's go."

Chapter 7

W ow. Chinatown isn't like this back home," Emily
muttered as they were jostled once again in the
crowd.

"This is New York City. Everything is bigger here."

"I thought everything was bigger in Texas."

Bryan's heart stopped as Emily looked up at him. Her eyes
glowed, and her breath showed in a white puff. Yesterday, when
they were in Little Italy, it hadn't been as cold or as crowded. The
Chinatown crowd was the worst yet. Still, when she looked
at him like that, Bryan wanted to stop walking, crowd or no
crowd, and kiss her. Instead, he looked forward and kept walking. "I read that New York's Chinatown is the biggest one in
the U.S."

Emily slowed to look at a display of what looked like flat-
tened dried chickens hanging in one of the windows. Bryan
couldn't stop because of the crowd jostling him forward. He
struggled to ease back while she caught up to him. When he
managed to be at her side once again, he reached for her hand

and twined his fingers through hers.

Even through their winter gloves, the contact felt warm and intimate.

He liked it. A lot.

He squeezed her hand gently. "I don't want to lose you today," he said. *Or ever,* he thought.

She squeezed back. "Me, neither."

His heart increased in tempo at her response, even though she could never guess what he'd been thinking.

He had it bad.

She looked up at him again. "I can't phone you like I did at the Radio City Music Hall. I forgot to charge my battery. If we got separated here, we wouldn't find each other until the New Year."

Bryan didn't want to think that far ahead. However, the New Year wasn't so distant anymore. It was less than a week until Christmas. Their time together was nearly at an end. Just thinking about never seeing Emily again ripped his heart in two.

He didn't know when it happened, but he'd fallen in love. He didn't want to let her go, but he didn't know how not to. They had separate lives in separate states half a continent away from each other.

He tried to sound as if he was just making conversation, but his stomach churned and his mind raced as he tried to figure out how to attain the unattainable. "I was wondering if you'd made any decisions about going home. I know we talked about you going home, but you never told me that you booked a flight."

"That's because I haven't. I checked online, and the prices are way too high. I think I'll just hang out at the airport and hope to get something on standby. My mother would understand; she's even cheaper than I am."

"What about Christmas?"

Emily remained silent for a long time. Bryan forced himself to breathe evenly while she was thinking—he bit his lip so he wouldn't blurt out something inappropriate.

"Actually, I'm not in a rush to get back. Everyone I know says that what I did was really stupid." She gave a humorless laugh. "I even got a couple of e-mails from Brian. He chastised me for taking off like that, but in the same message he said that he was sorry, and he wants me to come back and forgive him. He says if I do, he'll tell the boss what really happened, even if he gets fired. He also said he'd get down on his knees in front of everyone and beg me to marry him if that's what it takes. Can you believe it?"

A lump landed in Bryan's stomach. "Yeah. I'd believe it," he muttered to himself. He could see himself doing the exact same thing, except he never would have treated Emily, or anyone, the way Brian had. Bryan had come about his position in his career honestly, through much hard work and dedication. More important, he would rather die than cause something bad to happen to Emily. All he wanted was what was best for her. Even if it meant that what was best for her was to go home without him.

"What did you say? I didn't hear you."

"Nothing important," he mumbled, then cleared his throat. "Have you thought about another job yet?"

Emily sighed. "Sort of. I've prayed about it, and I've gone online to see what's open back home. Nothing seems right. When I left, I really felt this was God's nudge to get a new start. Maybe God just knew how badly I needed a vacation, and that's all this is supposed to be."

"Maybe. Have you given any thought to what church we're going to go to tomorrow?"

"No. Let's figure it out on our way home."

Home.

New York wasn't his home. Every day he spent here, he liked it more and more, but it wasn't home. He didn't want to go to his real home. Emily wasn't there. Even after his brother and entourage moved out of his town house, his home would forever feel empty without Emily nearby. "Speaking of home, I was wondering if I could come and visit you some weekend. It's probably only three hours from Seattle to Minneapolis. You don't have to worry about accommodations or anything awkward like that. I'd get a hotel."

Emily's step faltered for a split second. "Actually, it's three hours and twelve minutes. Or a few minutes less depending on the airline."

Without warning, Bryan pulled her out of the moving crowd to the nearest unoccupied space, which was at a produce market in a gap between the lychee nuts and some kind of leafy vegetables he couldn't identify.

"You mean you've already checked?"

"W—well," she stammered, "yes. Just in case you invited me to come visit you one day. I think it's doable."

Bryan didn't care that they were in the middle of a very

public place. Still holding on to the shopping bags, he slipped his arms around Emily, pulled her close, lowered his head, and kissed her. Not softly, not gently, but with all the love in his heart.

She hesitated for only a second, then her arms came around his waist, and she kissed him right back. She pressed herself against him, making him feel warm from the inside out. Her kiss was electric and sweet—sweeter than the mochas they'd just shared.

Bryan's heart pounded, and his soul sang with joy. Her kiss was better than his dreams. He wanted to make this moment last forever.

A child brushed past them, knocking into one of the bags he held behind Emily's back, a brutal reminder that they were not alone. Bryan pulled away slowly and with much regret.

He slowly straightened Emily's scarf, which was now askew. "I think we should talk," he said, his voice coming out husky. "And pray about this."

"Yes," she replied, her voice not much more than a whisper. "And we should get moving. People are staring."

He didn't care. He could have done cartwheels and danced on the street right now. She was willing to come visit him when their vacation was over. "Let's go into that restaurant over there and get something to eat. I'm starving." In fact, he couldn't remember the last time he'd been so hungry. Maybe it was because, for the first time, all was right with the world.

"Sure. And we can decide what we're going to do tomorrow."

He smiled to himself. He no longer cared about making plans. On the subway ride home, since their situation had changed and their feelings were out in the open, he'd cradle her in his arms and say without words how much he loved her. Nothing else mattered.

And he'd pray harder than he'd ever prayed before that somehow they could make this work.

❄

Emily walked into the church in silence.

This time they'd chosen a church in Midtown, close to Bryant Park, which was where they were going after lunch. They'd been to a different church every Sunday, and each one was special in its own way.

This was the biggest, oldest, and most stately. With its age came the pride of workmanship in the wooden pillars and artwork on the walls that newer buildings didn't have.

The sanctuary was filling fast, with a mixture of young and old, families and singles, different ethnic and economic backgrounds.

Emily liked it. Even though it was much larger than what she was used to, she felt comfortable.

Bryan gave her hand a gentle squeeze. "I like this place," he said.

Her head spun. On the subway, on the way home from Chinatown, he'd held her tenderly, cuddling her as if she were special and treasured. She'd almost pinched herself in case she was dreaming, except if she was, she hadn't wanted to wake up.

Over the past few weeks, Bryan had come to get her sometimes as early as 7:00 a.m. so they could arrive at their chosen destination before the crowds. Then by the time he escorted her home, it was late and she pretty much fell straight into bed. She couldn't remember the last time she actually got eight hours of sleep.

They hadn't known each other for many days, but in hours Emily had spent more time with Bryan than most couples saw of each other in six months. She knew his likes and dislikes. She could often predict what he was thinking and what he was going to say. In many ways, she knew him better than she knew her best friend.

It went both ways. As many times as Emily finished sentences for Bryan, he finished them for her. They also could agree to disagree. The only thing she didn't like about him was his name, which wasn't his fault. She had one Brian too many in her life already; she didn't want to deal with another.

Despite his name, she had a bad feeling that she was falling in love—which was neither right nor smart. Soon they would be leaving to go to their separate homes. Their remaining time together would be bittersweet.

An usher seated them, but she couldn't prepare herself for the service yet.

She turned to Bryan. "We only have a few days left together. What will we do after we leave New York? I don't know if a long-distance relationship will work."

His voice came out in a crackle, low and strained. "Then how can we make it a short-distance relationship?"

Emily bit into her lower lip. "We can't. We both have to go home. And I have to deal with Brian." If she had been a weaker person, she just might have cried. Brian the Traitor would be the first person she'd see when she got off the plane, brought by her mother. She would be forced to argue with him while missing Bryan the Tourist. She couldn't deal with the Brian/Bryan overload.

Bryan turned toward her. "Maybe we could start by changing my name. Maybe Brad. Or Rick. Anything but Bryan, no matter how it's spelled. I can only imagine how strange this is for you. How about a nickname? I don't care what you call me—just don't call me late for dinner."

She tried to smile at his lame joke. It didn't surprise her that he knew what she was thinking. From the first moment they met, they had often thought on the same wavelengths. She'd never believed in soul mates, but she did since she met Bryan. She also wondered why God had given her a soul mate from whom she was destined to be separated.

Emily did the only thing she could do. She turned and took both of Bryan's hands in hers.

He didn't need to be prompted. He knew what they had to do.

They closed their eyes and prayed for guidance and, most of all, for wisdom.

The pastor's voice boomed from the speakers. "Welcome, all! This is our last regular service before Christmas. You're all invited back for our candlelight service on Christmas Eve at six o'clock. Before we break to greet each other, I want to make a short announcement. We're desperately short of volunteers for our annual Christmas Cheer Banquet. For anyone who doesn't know what that is, we open our doors to anyone who is hungry for a free Christmas dinner on Christmas Day. This year one of the local restaurants is donating the desserts, and we've got our committee of gracious volunteers cooking the turkeys and all the trimmings. But we need more volunteers to serve and then help with the cleanup. I'm asking anyone who can donate even just a couple of hours to come. It's a great outreach to those who aren't going to have a very good Christmas. Remember Christ's words—'Whatever you do for the least of these, you do for Me.' Could all of our volunteers please meet in that corner after the service? Now I'd like everyone to greet those around you as we meet in celebration of the birth of our Lord, Jesus Christ."

Emily's heart began to pound. "Did you hear that?"

"Of course I heard it. I'm sitting right here beside you."

"That would be a great way to spend Christmas Day. It would also give us a few more days together. Those strangers need me more than my family does. I don't want to spend Christmas Day arguing with my family about Brian. I finally can forgive him, but I'll never forget what he did, and I'll never trust him."

Bryan's eyes lit up. "My brother and his family are still in my town house because their house isn't ready. They wouldn't mind if I stayed here to do a ministry project on Christmas Day. The service is about to resume. Let's talk about this when it's over."

"Yes, definitely." Emily wanted to jump up and hug him but settled for squeezing his hands again when a few of the people nearby stared at them.

The service was wonderful, and the pastor's words were thought provoking, making Emily want to help people who wouldn't be having a very merry Christmas even more.

When the people around them rose to leave, Bryan and Emily remained seated.

Bryan glanced at where the group of volunteers was starting to gather. "Are you really sure about this?"

"Yes. But I just thought of something. I was going to fly home on standby, so it doesn't matter when I leave. But your company paid for your flight. You can't just cancel."

"Yes, I can. They've got cancellation insurance. They won't mind, especially since I saved them so much money on my accommodations. I just have to tell Ted I need a few more days." He picked up her hands and lightly massaged her wrist with his thumb. "This won't change the fact that we both have to go home, but it delays it, and for now, that's the best we can do. Still, I have to admit that the pastor's message really inspired me to do this. So if we're in agreement, let's join their meeting."

They were quickly welcomed and given instructions. After the small group prayed together, Bryan and Emily were too excited to sit in a restaurant to eat. They went directly to Bryant Park as planned, bought their lunches from a street vendor, and kept walking.

Emily stopped to touch a magnetic beaded bracelet. "This holiday market is fascinating! The European markets are even better than what the tourist Web sites showed."

"Yeah," Bryan said while examining a handmade leather watch strap.

To give him more time, Emily watched the action on the pond. "The skating here is free, you know."

"Forget it," Bryan grumbled. "I learned my lesson last time. But if you really want to skate that bad, fine." He pressed one gloved hand over his heart. "Even if it means risking my life, I'd do that for you."

Emily stared at him with her mouth hanging open. She didn't know whether to laugh or cry, because he looked serious. Extremely serious.

Which led her to believe that he wasn't kidding.

No one had ever said such a thing to her.

His expression softened, and he approached her, brushing his fingers against her cheek as he spoke. "I'm sorry. Not that I didn't mean it, but I think that came out wrong."

"It's okay," she mumbled. "It's too cold to skate anyway. Let's go on the carousel instead."

"Isn't it kind of small? It looks like it's just for kids."

"I've wanted to go on a classic carousel since I was little but never got the chance. There's hardly anyone here. If we ask nicely, maybe he'll let us on anyway."

Emily was thrilled when the attendant did allow them to get on, although it was only because no one else was there except them. Emily insisted on sitting on one of the animals instead of the bench, so Bryan did, too, even though she could tell he felt foolish on the small golden horse.

When the ride was over, Bryan rubbed his reddened nose. "I'm surprised this is open this time of year."

Emily patted her cheeks. "I know. Add the wind to the movement, even though it wasn't fast, and it was awfully nippy."

This time he grinned. "I rode that charging stallion just for you, you know."

"That's mighty gallant of you. You're my hero."

He snorted. "Yeah, right. We're only a few blocks from Times Square. Want to go for a walk?"

"Sure. I haven't done enough shopping today," she said,

adding just a touch of sarcasm to her reply.

"You don't have to buy something just because we're going past those things, you know."

She shrugged her shoulders. "I haven't bought anything today yet. I'm behind on my quota."

Because of Bryan, she'd never feel the same about shopping again. In addition to buying clothing and countless mementos, she'd be going home with something she hadn't planned on acquiring—a heart full of love.

When they stepped into Times Square, Emily's breath caught. Up close the buildings were taller and even more vivid than they appeared on television, and the moving ads were breathtaking. Everything was big and bright and bold. And crowded. "I can't believe so many people squish themselves up to fit in here on one evening. I think they said a million people are here for New Year's Eve every year."

Bryan looked up as they walked. "Yeah. But still, I'd love to be here when the ball drops. The fireworks, the hype, the excitement. I'm not usually a crowd person, but it's something I've always wanted to do. Probably because I knew I never could."

"Maybe. But for now, I'm really excited about Christmas Day. I've donated to missions, but I've never actually done any real work. I think it's kind of humbling."

He gave her hand a gentle squeeze. "I know. But until then, I believe we have more shopping to do."

Chapter 8

Bryan spooned a serving of mashed potatoes onto the pale man's plate. "Would you like gravy with those?"

The man only nodded. Bryan finished and smiled. "I'm glad you came. Have a very merry Christmas."

A flicker of a smile passed over the man's face, then without having said a single word, he walked to one of the banquet tables.

This wasn't like any Christmas Day Bryan had ever experienced before.

He was one of six volunteers who dished out food onto plain Styrofoam plates, while more volunteers walked around the tables set up in the old church basement filling disposable cups or juice glasses and spreading Christ's love as helpers to the poor.

Bryan had seen needy people on the streets, but he'd never been so up close and personal with any of them before.

All kinds of people had come for a free Christmas meal— the elderly, the disabled, alcoholics and drug addicts, entire families on welfare—there were countless people who needed help, for as many different reasons as there were people coming in the door for food served without judgment.

No one was turned away.

A couple of times, he'd caught Emily wiping away a tear.

"Look at that cute little girl," she whispered to him. "She told me how happy she was with her new dress, but when she said that, her mother turned away, embarrassed that it was obviously secondhand. It breaks my heart."

"I know. Earlier a man told me he was a veteran on a disability pension. He was really embarrassed about being here and said he was only here for the music."

A few more people came, halting their conversation. It was Emily's job to serve the vegetables, so she was standing beside him, something he appreciated.

When they'd finished their duties for the current group, he again turned to Emily. "I think a lot of people are taking the free Bibles the church is offering."

Emily nodded. "I wonder how many of them would have heard the real message of Christmas if they hadn't come here today. The only other place they see Christmas is in the malls."

"The only thing they'd see there is Santa. We've been to more malls than I can count, and I only saw a nativity scene in a few."

"I'll never forget this day for the rest of my life."

Bryan pressed the back of his hand to his mouth to hide his yawn. "Same here, but I'm beat. It's been a long day. They're almost ready to close the doors, but there's still the cleanup." Yet as tired as he was, he didn't want the day to end. Tomorrow they were both due to go home. He wasn't ready for that. He loved Emily, and even though he'd only been kidding when he told her that he would die for her, every time he though of living the rest of his life without her, another part of him died inside.

"I know how you feel. My feet are killing me, but I don't mind. I think. . ." Emily's voice trailed off. "I think your cell phone is ringing."

Bryan frowned. "Who would be calling me now? Everyone at home should be in bed. Oh, it's my boss. I have to take this." He looked around for a private spot, but he couldn't leave his post yet. All he could do was turn his back to the banquet room. "Hi, Ted. Yeah, Merry Christmas."

He listened to his boss's words, and the more he heard, the more excited he became.

By the time he flipped the phone closed and turned to Emily, his hands were shaking.

Emily tilted her head and stared at him. "What was that all about? You've got a strange look on your face."

"This isn't the best place, but I can't wait to tell you. Do you remember that my boss asked if I was interested in a transfer, and I turned him down? He's just given me something else to consider. Instead of Dallas, he's asked if I'd like to move here, to New York. The regional manager just quit without notice, and seeing me in action during a week of high-intensity meetings, he said I'd be perfect. The only thing is, I have to take it right away, by the first of the year."

"Wow. . ."

He waited for her to say more. Congratulations, even. But she didn't.

He couldn't wait any longer; he couldn't contain his excitement. "That's not all. During the meetings everyone talked about never having a proper IT department head. Before I knew he was going to offer me the transfer, I told him about a great IT support analyst who was looking for a career jump. He was very interested when I told him where you used to work. If you're interested, he wants to interview you. Not today, of course. Tomorrow. He can't wait to hire someone. If you're willing to move."

Emily blinked a few times, and her eyes glazed over.

A mother and five children approached them with plates needing to be filled, forcing them to move.

When they were taken care of, Emily turned to him. "Do you know what you're saying?"

"Yes. I'm saying that if you're willing, there's a job waiting for you here, in New York City."

"Just like that?"

"It wasn't that fast. Remember, it's been three weeks since I last talked to Ted. He's had a lot of time to check you out. You come highly recommended. He told me he's already talked to your old boss. The interview is just a formality."

"What about you? Us?"

He set the ladle down and cupped her cheeks with his palms. "I'll take the job if you will. I think we'd be a great team. I promise you I won't do anything dirty or underhanded like that other guy whose name I won't mention. In fact, we won't even see each other at the office most days. Unless we do lunch." He lowered his voice. "I love you, Emily. Job or no job, I'd be honored if you'll marry me. Here. In New York City."

"I—uh. . ." Emily's voice dropped to a whisper. "I've been praying about maybe looking for a job in New York. I think God brought me here, so I asked that if it was His will, He would show me a sign. A big one. I'm not too good with subtle hints. This certainly is an answer. I almost don't know what to say."

He brushed a kiss to her lips at the same time a voice announced over the PA system that the banquet was over, along with another wish for everyone to have a merry Christmas. "Say that you'll marry me. That would be the best Christmas present of my life."

"I—uh. . ." She gulped. Her eyes watered, then she blinked back her tears. "But I already got you a present." She fished through her pocket. "I didn't have any paper to wrap it, but I was going to give it to you tonight when we had more time."

She handed him a 1-gig memory card. "This is our combined pictures. I picked out the best ones, touched up the graphics, formatted them all to a size that loads quickly, then put them in order. Merry Christmas."

"Thank you." He was stunned, imagining how many hours she'd sacrificed for such a project. Yet as much as he appreciated her gift, all he could think about was her response to his proposal. He didn't think her reaction was a good sign, especially when she changed the subject so abruptly. But since she'd chosen this moment to give him a gift, this was the time to do the same.

"I have something for you, too." Bryan reached into his pants pocket. "I didn't have wrapping paper, either," he said as he handed her the bag. He held his breath as she reached inside, then pulled out the gold chain with an apple charm hanging from it.

Her small gasp told him she liked it. "It's beautiful. Thank you."

"You didn't give me an answer to my question. I'm starting to feel a little insecure right now. You said you'd take the job, but will you take me, too?"

Before she could reply, one of the other volunteers approached them. "Thanks for helping. If you want to go now, you can, but we'd love it if you could stay and help clean up. That way everyone can get home to their families a little faster."

Emily looked up at him. "I don't mind staying."

Bryan braced himself. Having busy hands would help give Emily more time to think. "I'll stay, too. Just show us what to do."

❄

Emily snapped the lid on the last container of leftovers and began scrubbing the chafing trays.

Most women probably dreamed of the day when the man they loved proposed. She'd had a few white-knight-in-shining-armor fantasies herself.

Bryan's shirt was no longer white. It was splattered with gravy and a few other things she couldn't identify. He hadn't exactly been charging on his mini-stallion on the carousel, either.

Her not-so-white knight appeared at her side. "This wasn't the most romantic setting for a man to ask the woman he loves if she'll marry him. How about if we book another dinner cruise, and I can do it right?"

She'd come to New York alone and depressed, and God had

set everything in order. She'd never been so happy or confident of a good future as she was today. Bryan had done nothing except escort her through the city, being nothing other than the person he truly was, with nothing to gain and nothing to lose. By simply being himself, he'd won her love and her trust.

She rested her palm in the center of his chest.

More than his pounding heart, his eyes showed everything she wanted to know. The tension in his eyes told her that he really wasn't sure of her answer, and his erratic heartbeat told her how much her answer mattered to him. She'd scared him, and she hadn't meant to do that. She loved him so much, but with his fast and unexpected news about the job, she didn't want to make the wrong decision. Brian the Traitor wanted to marry her, too, but for the wrong reasons.

Bryan the Tourist had asked her for the right reasons. He wanted to marry her, job or no job. He loved her, she loved him, and that was all that mattered.

She nestled into his arms, needing to be closer to Bryan. She lowered her voice to a whisper. "What you did came from your heart, so it couldn't be any more right. I love you, too, and I'd move to New York for you, job or no job, although I believe you when you say I've already got it. Yes, I'll marry you."

His heart pounded even more beneath her hand. Gently, he covered her hand with his own. "I don't believe in long engagements. Especially my own."

Emily smiled. "Then how would you like to elope? Maybe we can find the pastor and get married here, in this church. Although first we'll have to check out what we need to get a marriage license online. I hope we don't need blood tests. Needles affect me even worse than motion sickness. Sometimes I faint. Once I—"

Bryan's finger on her lips stopped her. "Shh. Put those thoughts on hold." He plucked the cloth from her hand and dropped it on the table. Then, without releasing her other hand, he waved to get the coordinator's attention. "We'll be right back," he called out and began leading her to the door, speaking over his shoulder. "I want to go outside and, by the lights of the New York skyline, kiss my future bride."

Emily did something that she didn't do often. She felt herself blush. All she could do was giggle and wave as she followed Bryan outside.

She was going to live the rest of her life happily ever after, right here in the Big Apple.

Right after she kissed her future husband.

Gail Sattler

Gail is the author of many heartwarming tales of love and romance mixed with Christian living. When she's not writing, Gail likes to read, knit, and play bass guitar (loud) with the worship team at her church as well as with a local jazz band—and that's loud, too. Gail Sattler lives in Vancouver, BC, where you don't have to shovel rain, with her husband of twenty-eight years, three sons, two dogs, two toads, and a big lizard named Draco, who is quite cuddly for a reptile. You're invited to visit Gail's Web site at www.gailsattler.com.

WHERE THE LOVE LIGHT GLEAMS

by Lynette Sowell

Dedication

This story is dedicated to Mr. Christmas, Santa's nephew.
(But this doesn't mean you can leave
the lights up all year on the house.)
Thanks for always encouraging me.
I love you!

The angel said to them, "Do not be afraid.
I bring you good news of great joy
that will be for all the people."
LUKE 2:10

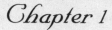

Chapter 1

Gwynn Michaud sighed as she stood in the driveway and watched the last news van leave the snow-crusted street. "That's that."

She hugged her arms around her waist. The raw tree stump made the front yard look desolate. A few weeks earlier, Gwynn had asked the Lord for a change, for something new. And now this. Hal would have flipped if he knew what his family had done. Hal had never been one for changes.

"You okay, Mom?" Staci slipped her arm around Gwynn.

"I'm fine." Gwynn blinked. Who would have guessed the mere cutting down of a tree could bring tears to her eyes?

"Gramma, are you going to plant another tree?" Eight-year-old Jenna hugged Gwynn's other side.

Gwynn smiled at her granddaughter. "Maybe I will next spring." Who could remain wistful standing next to a little angel whose eyes brimmed with expectancy?

"The cookies are done!" Trevor, twelve, bellowed from the side door to the kitchen. Gwynn and his mother had convinced him the news crew didn't want to film him popping wheelies on his bike. When Staci threatened to send him inside to make cookies with his aunt Lisa, he simmered down to watch the crew cut down the massive spruce. The seventy-five-foot tree had been the focus of everyone's attention. Over one hundred residents of Bethlehem, New Hampshire, had shown up with three news crews and two newspaper reporters. Now the onlookers drifted away.

"C'mon, Gramma. . . ." Gwynn let Jenna tug her along, Staci chiding her daughter.

Jenna banged through the door, and Gwynn turned to Staci. "You go ahead. I'll be right in." She nodded at Staci. "I need just a minute."

Staci's forehead wrinkled, but she went inside. The aroma of chocolate chip cookies drifted into the November air.

Gwynn faced the front yard, now missing the elegant spruce. Over forty feet tall when Hal carried Gwynn over the threshold more than thirty years ago, the tree had grown along with their love and the three children God sent their way. And the tree outlived Hal by three years.

She still hadn't figured out what to do about Christmas yet. She probably wouldn't do as much decorating this year. Gwynn usually let Steven decorate the outside of the house, but this year she wouldn't ask him to freeze while putting up the fat bright lights Hal always used. This year maybe she'd put a single white electric candle in each window and hang wreaths on the window boxes. Something tasteful, elegant, uncluttered.

Gwynn shivered inside her calfskin knee-length coat. It was impractical but something she knew would look nice on

TV. She would have preferred being bundled inside thick wool. Lights from inside made faint rectangles on the yard as dusk approached. The early snowfall would be gone in a few days but made it feel like Christmas early.

Hal might have loved this moment, now that Gwynn thought about it some more. She could picture him bursting his buttons while being interviewed, shaking hands with each crew member, wondering aloud if the crane operator had a good hold on the tree once it had been cut. Gwynn smiled. He'd have been proud of his kids' decision. The squeak of the storm door made her turn around.

"Gramma, I saved you some cookies. Everyone's trying to eat them." Jenna's eyes begged her to come in. The child tended to worry too much. Maybe she ought to ask Staci about it sometime, or maybe not. The line of where a grandmother should stop helping wasn't always clearly drawn.

"Thanks. The cookies smell wonderful." Gwynn entered the kitchen, which was brimming with her children and grandchildren.

Lisa wheeled up to the table. She set a gallon of milk next to a plate of cookies, then spun in her chair and glided up to the stove. "Got some real hot chocolate coming up. With marshmallows."

Gwynn hung her coat on the hook behind the door and took an empty chair. "You guys, this is great. The stew should be hot enough to dish up."

Steven saluted her with a spoon. "That's our mom. Planning for a good supper and working a three-ring media circus outside."

"Ha. I'd like to point out that you and your two sisters are responsible for said media circus outside." Gwynn smiled at her eldest. He carried himself like Hal and had settled into his father's construction business as if he'd been born for the job.

"Will the tree be on TV, Gramma?" Jenna asked.

Gwynn nodded. "I still can't believe it. Our tree in Rockefeller Center in New York. At first I wasn't sure it was such a good idea, but your gramps would have been thrilled."

"That's what we thought." Staci glanced at Lisa, who glanced at Steve. Gwynn knew this exchange of glances well. They were up to something.

"Okay." Gwynn grabbed a cookie and bit into the chewy sweetness. "What's going on?"

Lisa twisted in her chair to stir the hot chocolate on the stove. Steve left the room. Jenna giggled, and a grin tugged at the corners of Trevor's mouth as he hunched over his handheld video game. Gwynn crossed her arms. A family secret, of all things.

When Steve returned to the kitchen, he held a small, flat box no larger than a greeting card. "Mom, we're giving you an early Christmas present."

"But it's still November." Gwynn took the box from Steve and ran her fingers over the gold foil embossed with green Christmas trees.

"C'mon, Gramma, open it!" Jenna bounced on her toes, her dark hair swishing on her shoulders.

Inside, Gwynn found an airline itinerary to New York City. For one.

"What about Christmas? Our plans?" Gwynn glanced from

one of her children to the other. "Steve, you need help with the business, and I said I'd pitch in. And, Lisa—"

"Mom, I'll be fine. I can take care of myself. I'll call the van to bring me to physical therapy." Lisa held the pot of hot chocolate in one hand as she glided to the table.

"And, Staci"—Gwynn faced her eldest child—"with Josh working overseas, I'd hate to leave you."

Staci waved the words away. "Mom, we can do for ourselves for ten days. Sometimes I think we ask too much of you."

"But I don't know anyone in New York City." Honestly, these children of hers were impossible. And they got that trait from their father, to be sure.

"I've figured that out." Staci sounded triumphant. "Malina said you could stay with her and her father."

Malina Stellakis, Staci's former college roommate and now a lawyer, lived in Manhattan. Gwynn recalled meeting Malina several times during Staci's college years, and the two women remained close friends. "I see you've figured this all out."

"We have." Lisa poured the hot chocolate, and steam rose from the mugs. "Plus I finagled some tickets to Radio City Music Hall's Christmas Spectacular."

"Oh! The Rockettes!" Gwynn sucked in a breath. She'd always wanted to see them perform, but with Hal's work and their schedules. . .

Staci placed her hand over Gwynn's. "We figured you deserved something special. You'll be there for the tree lighting at Rockefeller Center, and Malina and her father promised to show you the sights. You'll be back in time for Christmas."

Gwynn searched their faces. Trevor and Jenna ran off to

watch TV. "I guess you've settled it, then." She'd prayed for a change, but this sure wasn't the answer she'd expected.

❄

Theophilus Stellakis held his phone closer to his ear. "You what?"

Malina had just said something about a guest. He strode down the street, ignoring the stream of humanity that flowed around him. His last class had gone late, and the nutrition bar he'd consumed two hours ago thumped in his stomach like a brick. Malina undoubtedly would meet him with something healthy for supper, when all he wanted was a strong cup of tea and baklava.

"A guest, Dad."

"That's what I thought you said." Theophilus sidestepped a pile of slush left over from a dusting of snow. "What do you mean?"

"A guest. As in someone staying at our house for a period of time."

"Sarcasm does not become you, young lady."

"Funny, that's what the judge said in court today. Minus the young lady part."

Theophilus sighed. "If your mother could hear you—what's this about a guest? Who's coming? And why didn't you tell me?"

"I told you last week. Gwynn Michaud. My friend Staci's mom."

"When does she arrive?" He glanced for traffic out of habit and kept moving with the stream of pedestrians. Four blocks and dusk would drop upon the city before he arrived home.

"The Tuesday after Thanksgiving..."

Malina launched into an itinerary description, during which space of time Theophilus commenced ruminating about the final exam schedule for the semester. Four classes times four examinations equaled more than 160 chemistry students. His head pounded at the very thought as he paused at the corner newsstand. He could not think about a houseguest underfoot, not at this time of year.

"Dr. S., your newspaper?" Tushar the newsman offered him a folded copy of the news.

Theophilus set down his briefcase, then fished for some change, which he gave to Tushar along with a nod. Tucking the paper under his arm that held the phone, he continued on his way. For more than twenty years, he'd walked this path every day and bought a paper. Tushar had started as a youngster helping his father and now ran the newsstand.

"So is that all right with you?" Malina's question swirled in his brain.

"Er, I..." He'd done it again—let his thoughts carry him away. He had hurt Emma's feelings in the past when he drifted off.

"Never mind, Dad. I'll fill you in over supper." The phone went silent in his ear, so Theophilus snapped it shut.

He didn't blame Malina for hanging up. Her voice hadn't sounded rude, just...disappointed.

The traffic lights changed from green to red. Theophilus waited with the others on their way home from work, shopping, or school. Cabs and cars crisscrossed in front of them. This was his favorite time of night, when the daytime went to sleep and the city lights woke up.

He used to walk for blocks and blocks with Emma, enjoying the lights and walking hand in hand with her, until. . .

The light turned green and the pedestrian sign glowed white, and Theophilus moved with the crowd again. By the time he reached the apartment he shared with Malina, the stars glowed above, somewhere beyond the city lights.

Tonight the six steps up to the apartment door felt like sixty. Theophilus gritted his teeth, climbed in spite of his hip, and reminded himself not to tell Malina. She would fuss and call the doctor.

Christmas music playing full blast greeted him in the entryway, where Theophilus removed his coat and scarf and hung them on the coatrack.

"Dad!" Malina's voice rang out over trumpets blaring "Adeste Fideles." And it wasn't even Thanksgiving yet. Why did people rush into, through, and past the holidays? Barely did Theophilus digest his turkey dinner than the frantic pace of Christmas trappings tried to drag him into the fray. He wouldn't stand for it. That brought him around to the subject of the houseguest.

Theophilus gathered his paper and his briefcase and followed the scent of spices through the swinging door that led into the kitchen. "What's for supper?"

"Takeout from V&T." Malina placed two plates on the table, her glossy dark hair reminding him of Emma. The similarity still made him blink hard sometimes. He laid the newspaper on an empty space of countertop and went to wash his hands. He allowed himself a small smile. Malina never could cook like her mother, but she knew the best restaurants in the neighborhood and how to dial for dinner to carry home.

He shook the excess water from his hands, dried them with a paper towel, and turned to face her. "My dear, as always, you've outdone yourself."

"I slaved all of five minutes over the phone." She took the water pitcher from the refrigerator.

After they settled at the table, Theophilus asked the blessing. Before taking a bite of the warm meal in front of him, he decided to continue their earlier conversation.

"This houseguest—how long will she be here?"

"Just under two weeks."

"That's long enough." He spent ten hours a day, five days a week away from the house, not counting church on Sunday. That left suppers and weekends with the houseguest, and then peace and quiet once again.

"Staci and I got a pair of tickets to Radio City and some museum passes, but with this case at work, I don't think I can make it. The DA wants to get as many cases as possible wrapped up before the winter recess, and I—"

"Say no more." Theophilus tugged at his tie. "Perhaps Rita can take her." The very idea of going to Radio City made him want to hide with a book. He preferred candles, firelight, and the sound of carols by classical guitar in the cathedral. Not glitz and baubles and the sight of bare legs kicking in unison toward the ceiling. He would call his sister in the morning and convince her to bring their guest.

"Dad. Aunt Rita won't go. Besides, I promised Staci her mom would have a good time in New York. It's not good manners for us to shift our houseguest onto someone else."

Theophilus grabbed his fork and waved it before sticking it into a bite of tenderloin. "You've got a point. Why isn't Staci's father coming, as well?"

"He passed away"—Malina's brow furrowed, and she stared at her salad—"a few months after Mom did. I might have mentioned it to you. I—I don't remember right now."

"I still miss her." For some reason his food would not go down. He swallowed again before continuing. "No one can make stuffed grape leaves like she could. I miss the little things."

"Me, too." She took a sip of her water. "I know she'd be aggravated with us for dwelling on this feeling."

"I don't want to forget her." Theophilus pushed away from the table and went to the sink. He found the bottle of ibuprofen on the window ledge and poured three onto his palm. A long day had loosened his tongue, and he wanted to lose himself in a television show for once. He looked out at the rear courtyard they shared with their neighbors.

"And you won't. She'd want us to give Staci's mom a trip she'll never forget. Aunt Rita said she wants her to come to the Stellakis Christmas gathering, but I already told her Mrs. Michaud won't be here that long."

Malina changed the subject then, as he knew she would. Theophilus smiled before he swallowed the pills without water and turned to face Malina. "We'll be good hosts." As far as the Stellakis gathering this year, he knew he wouldn't be there, either. No matter what anyone in the family said. Too much noise, too many verbal missteps, too many offers of blind dates—at his age, even.

"What is it?" Malina wore the penetrating expression she'd

inherited from her mother.

"Nothing." The supper, a nutritional splurge even for Malina, felt worse than the snack he'd had earlier. The ibuprofen probably wouldn't help matters. "I'm just tired tonight."

"Okay." She polished off her last bite of salad. "I need to review some depositions."

"I have papers to grade." Theophilus took a deep breath and released it. He and Malina rattled like a pair of peas in their home, and tonight he was assured of quiet time as they retreated into their professions. He might as well enjoy the silence while it lasted.

Chapter 2

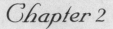

"M"rs. Michaud, would you like to have dinner in or go out?" Malina held the phone and smiled across the kitchen at Gwynn. "You must be tired from your trip."

"I am, just a little." Gwynn shot a look at Dr. Stellakis, who appeared transfixed by the newspaper in front of him. He'd been staring at the front page for ten minutes. "But dinner out sounds like fun. I'm here to see as much as I can, and I'd love to stretch my legs."

Her voice rang out higher than she'd intended, and Dr. Stellakis's brow furrowed.

Well, he didn't have to go. She knew he was a professor, and with final exams looming, he probably preferred to stay home.

"Dinner out it is." Malina set the phone back on the charger. "The Acropolis is a nice place, practically around the corner. We order supper in sometimes because they deliver." Dr. Stellakis met Malina's gaze with an expression Gwynn couldn't discern.

"This is such a cozy neighborhood—in Manhattan, at that." Gwynn shook her head. "I haven't been here in more than thirty years."

Dr. Stellakis's eyebrows shot up. "So you've been to New York before?" He reminded her of Sean Connery, only Greek.

Gwynn tried not to stare too closely into his penetrating dark eyes. "Back in college. I spent my senior year finishing my interior design degree through an exchange program at the Art Institute. I loved it. After college I married Hal, and we pretty much spent our time in New Hampshire." Gwynn made herself stop. The lengthy explanation hadn't been necessary. She'd gotten all keyed up by the trip, and now Malina and her father looked at her as though she was the country bumpkin she felt.

"Wow, interior design." Malina picked up her handbag from the square kitchen table. "When I get a free moment, I love watching design shows. Which isn't often."

"Me, too. I can't believe how many materials and accessories are available now." Gwynn smiled. "Almost makes me want to start my own business."

"I keep saying one of these days I'm going to try retiling the bathroom floor, and then I get busy." Malina shrugged.

"Malina, we can talk on the way to the restaurant." Dr. Stellakis folded his newspaper in half and stood.

"You're right. I'll get my coat."

"I'll get my purse." Gwynn seized the chance to seek refuge in Malina's bedroom upstairs, where Gwynn had put her suitcases.

Once inside with the door shut behind her, she looked out at the city lights spangling the darkened sky. She missed everyone already, even though she'd only been gone a few hours. Gwynn forced herself not to think about what Staci, Steven, and Lisa were doing. They didn't need her, she reminded herself. When Hal was alive, the two of them had never left the children and gone on vacation alone. This was definitely a first, and she wondered if it had been a mistake to come at all. Well intentioned but a mistake—at least to stay with Malina and Dr. Stellakis. Maybe Staci could pick up right where she and Malina left off, but Gwynn felt as if she were imposing. She tried not to decipher the murmur of voices drifting from downstairs.

Gwynn snatched her purse from the bed. The walk sounded like a good idea, and she wanted to move a bit after the drive to the airport in Manchester, the flight to JFK, and then a cab ride into Manhattan—which cost her more than dinner out with her grandkids back in Bethlehem. The delightful driver named Raj, a student at Columbia, had pointed out several sights, even passing by Times Square before heading uptown. When she told Raj about the tree, she'd felt as giddy as a young girl on the first day of school.

Then she arrived at the apartment, where Malina's father met her, and his greeting made her feel as if she'd entered the principal's office. She would do her best not to overwhelm Dr. Stellakis with her enthusiasm and not to let his brooding demeanor dampen her evening.

Gwynn met Malina and Dr. Stellakis in the front hall where they kept their coats.

Dr. Stellakis held up Gwynn's coat with a flourish. "Mrs. Michaud."

The gallant gesture made her pause as she slipped the coat

on, but she smiled. "Please, call me Gwynn."

With a glance at his daughter, Dr. Stellakis offered his arm to Gwynn. "Well then, Gwynn, let's go to supper."

She swallowed hard and took his arm. "Thanks, Dr. Stellakis."

"You may call me Theophilus."

Malina cleared her throat as they started down the steps. "Beautiful night. And that dusting of snow we had a few days ago should make the tree lighting extra special."

"Tomorrow night will definitely be special." Gwynn felt one of her heels skitter on the sidewalk, but Theophilus's gentle pressure on her arm steadied her. "I'm really looking forward to it."

Right now she couldn't think about the tree that once graced her front yard. She couldn't figure out the change in the demeanor of the man walking beside her. It was as if he had stepped into the role of a gentleman and left his prickly manner at the apartment. Like a reverse of Dr. Jekyll and Mr. Hyde, and Gwynn found Mr. Hyde preferable to the doctor. She believed she could stroll like this for hours.

The traffic's din was foreign to her ears, but Gwynn found a rhythm and melody in the sounds. Perhaps the noise wouldn't bother her at night. Malina chattered about planning a trip to the museums one day and how she'd managed to get the tickets for Radio City.

From the corner of Gwynn's eye, she saw a flicker of something on Theophilus's face, like her grandson chomping down on a sourball. Except Theophilus didn't grin, then laugh at the taste. "You don't like shows, Theo?" Oh dear. She hadn't planned on dropping the rest of his name, but four syllables didn't roll off the tongue easily.

He blinked. "I don't like Christmas overdone."

"What do you like, then?"

"To me, our Savior's birth shouldn't be lost in red and green shiny things and loud music that has nothing to do with what Christmas truly means. I like hearing the Christmas story by candlelight. Eating *Christopsomo* bread. Emma always made it." He blinked again, his eyes reflecting the streetlights. "We're nearly there."

Gwynn's heart twinged, and she knew it wasn't from walking. "This has been a nice walk." She glanced away. She understood fighting off an unbidden memory, a sweet yet painful reminder. Moving on was necessary but not easy. Maybe that's what this trip would be about. Gwynn smiled and let herself enjoy the gentle strength of Theo's arm.

❄

The first thing Theophilus had noticed when Gwynn Michaud emerged from the taxi late that afternoon was her eyes. Coffee-colored and shaped like almonds, they took in their surroundings as Gwynn shifted a leather bag onto her shoulder. Her hair curled at the top of her shoulders in waves of dark honey. Then Gwynn gave a slow smile, as if she'd discovered something delightful upon leaving the taxi. Truly, Theo had never seen such a reaction to their modest yet comfortable brownstone.

Now as they stepped into the restaurant's foyer, Gwynn glanced at him with those deep brown eyes that made Theo pause and nearly let the door swing into the faces of patrons entering behind them. Instead of tugging at his tie, he offered to remove her coat.

"Dad, be polite," Malina had said when she chided him earlier.

So Theo had dusted off his manners, and look where it got him. Offering his arm to the elegant Gwynn Michaud, who seemed uncannily at home in her urban surroundings. His gesture had seemed the most natural thing in the world, and now he had the urge to turn around and speed walk back to the apartment. That, and she'd called him Theo. Made him feel twenty again, like a young undergrad with his whole life before him.

"Hey, Dad, Gwynn. Our table's ready."

His arm felt cold without Gwynn's warm hand tucked into the crook of his elbow.

In less than a minute, they were seated in a cushioned booth and hovering over their menus. Theo didn't need his. He always ordered *tzatziki*, a pot of tea, and hearty *moshari yiouvetsi*, so he allowed himself to study Gwynn instead of the menu.

"I'm not sure what to choose."

"Everything here is delicious." Malina smiled and glanced at Theo. "Dad, why don't you recommend something for Gwynn?"

"I'm open to suggestions." Gwynn shifted her gaze from the menu to him.

He named the first entrée he spotted on the page. "If you like pork, I'd recommend the pork kebabs—*souviaki*."

"I think I'll start with the bread and tzatziki dip—the combination of yogurt, cucumber, and garlic sounds delicious. And then the souviaki." Gwynn's skin glowed, and any wrinkles were softened in the lamplight. Then she flushed. "I'm sorry, my appetite sounds ambitious. I'm just in the mood to try things I've never tried before. That, and after traveling for so long, I'm a bit famished. A few weeks ago, I'd never have imagined I'd be here. It's very exciting."

"And I'm excited for you. Staci and I threw the plans together a few days before she sprung the news." Malina sipped her water. "Everything sort of fell into place. So how's Staci?"

"Motherhood is keeping her busy. My son-in-law works for a U.S. contractor in Kuwait, so Staci's been both mom and dad for over six months." Gwynn looked wistful. "I don't know if I would have done as well."

Theo cleared his throat. "Gwynn, I'm sure you'd pull it off like a trouper."

"Why, thank you, Theo." Then she smiled. "I think many times we don't know what we can endure until something happens. Then the Lord comes through and carries us. I know He's carried me."

Theo nodded. "I understand. After Emma, I quite honestly didn't know what to do for quite a long time. Well-meaning friends thought they knew. Perhaps they did. Yet there are some roads only we and the Lord can walk." Theo paused to listen to the soft murmur of voices in the restaurant and the intricate notes of a guitar. He didn't dare glance at Malina. Gwynn's open and frank admissions, plus her zest, had taken him aback at first. Now he found himself mirroring her transparency. And he wasn't used to it.

He and Malina never needed many words, and in the space of less than two hours, they'd exchanged more words with their houseguest than the two of them shared in the space of a day.

Gwynn asked Malina about her work, and as Gwynn moved her hand to brush a curl over her ear, bracelets clinked on her arm. The action entranced Theo. Malina murmured a response, but Theo didn't hear it. Gwynn's presence reminded him of Emma's gentleness, yet her spunky elegance was different. He wanted to know more about her, and that notion made him want to bury himself in exams.

"I'll be glad to escort you to Rockefeller Center tomorrow evening," Theo heard himself say. He didn't recall Gwynn asking for accompaniment, and he tried to ignore the sparkle in Malina's black eyes.

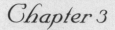

Chapter 3

The crisp night air hummed with electricity, and Gwynn knew it wasn't from the sparkling lights of Rockefeller Center. Her gloved hand was tucked securely in the crook of Theo's elbow, as it had been for the subway ride to Fifth Avenue.

Her tree stood tall as it brooded over Rockefeller Center and its rows of trumpeting figures. No lights glowed on the branches yet, but Gwynn caught a wink here and there of bulbs reflecting the lights around them. The crowd thronged the area, and TV cameras panned while people waved and shouted to friends. The opening music began, and the host spoke to the crowd and to the millions watching the tree at home.

During the first commercial break, the orchestra played. Gwynn's throat swelled at the strains of "O Little Town of Bethlehem." She glanced at Theo, who stood with his eyes closed, his head tilted back slightly as he listened to the music.

After the last notes faded away, the emcee introduced the new young country music sensation Madison Monroe, who'd

won a singing contest on TV. Gwynn recognized her immediately. Staci had played Madison's CD nonstop in her van for
weeks. When the singer belted out "I'll Be Home for Christmas," Gwynn's eyes burned at the emotion in the soprano's
strong voice. She dared not look at Theo, because a wave of
homesickness washed over her. *Where the love light gleams. . .*

She wanted to see Bethlehem's familiar town square; pick
up her grandkids from music lessons and sports practice; have
supper at Napoli's, the best Italian restaurant in Bethlehem; put
electric candles in the window; and hang some garland. She
realized she hadn't thought of having Hal back, though.

*Lord, was this why You helped me come here? To know that
I've moved on? There's a stirring inside. I long, I crave something
new—but I love the old, too. Can I have both?*

"They're getting ready to throw the switch." Theo's voice
snapped her from her thoughts.

Gwynn looked up again at the tree as the crowd hushed
around them. And then, like thousands of diamonds reflecting
the sun, the lights on the tree made the rest of the square seem
dim. A cheer rose into the air and drowned out the orchestra's
fanfare. Gwynn slipped her hand from Theo's protective arm
and clapped.

The tree was still the same as when it grew in their yard, yet
it was so much more when it brought joy to millions. Gwynn
dabbed at a hot tear that tried to escape.

"Theo, it's beautiful. Hal would have. . ." Her voice failed her.

"Yes, a man would be a fool not to like this. It was a good
idea." Theo slipped her hand around his arm again. "And I'm
glad you've come."

"I am, too. When she sang that song. . ."

"You'll be home again before you know it." Then his expression clouded over as his cell phone rang. He removed it from his pocket, and once more Gwynn had her hand free, but she missed the comfort of his arm. "It's Malina."

Gwynn waited as the crowd exited the square, and she and Theo let the river of people stream around them. Malina had come home with a migraine that afternoon, and Gwynn insisted on sending the overworked young attorney to lie down. She had found some frozen chicken in the freezer and started a pot of soup, which should be ready when they returned to the apartment.

"Ah, so you are. All right." Theo closed his phone. "She's feeling better. She said the two aspirin and strong cup of coffee helped. Soup's done, too."

"Good." Gwynn rubbed her arms. "I could look at the tree all night, but this cold is something else!"

"Let's go, then." Theo offered her his arm, and her gloved hand felt warmer again. "Your coat is very elegant but doesn't look well insulated."

They ambled across the plaza and headed for the warmth of the subway station. "No, it's not. But I didn't want a grandma coat that made me feel like a marshmallow."

"You might be a grandma, but I seriously doubt any coat could make you look like a marshmallow."

Gwynn glanced at Theo. She couldn't tell if that was a sparkle in his eyes or a trick of the light. "Well, thank you. I bought this coat at an outlet mall. Regular price over five hundred dollars, and I got it 60 percent off. No sales tax in New Hampshire, either. Hear that, New York?" She grinned at no one in particular, and she doubted anyone was listening.

Theo's courtly attention made her head spin, and here she was, prattling like a teenager about clothes. Theo probably didn't care that her beloved coat was a steal and that there was no sales tax in New Hampshire. Her face flamed at recalling her words. She hadn't meant to sound as if she was bragging. Her earlier homesickness had lifted, and now she knew she'd make the most of the rest of her time in the Big Apple.

"I understand there's good shopping on Fifth Avenue." Theo led her downstairs, and they entered the subway station. A roar echoed off the walls.

"I'd love to come back and explore one day. Not a shopping spree. I want to see those famous animated windows, go through Macy's, *walk* through Saks and cough over a few price tags"—she didn't expect him to catch the humor in that—"and see as much as I can. I'd like to get something special for my grandkids."

"Do they keep you busy?"

"Oh yes. But I love it. I have a nightshirt that I left at home that says 'Grandma's my name, spoiling's my game.' I spoil them, then send them home." No. She didn't just talk about her nightshirt. A train roared up to the platform and glided to a stop, the rush of air cooling Gwynn's hot cheeks.

The doors slid open, and Gwynn lost no time jumping inside and looking for a seat.

❄

With her face flushed and glossy hair bouncing around her

shoulders, Gwynn looked every bit the Manhattan native as she charged onto the wrong train. Theo followed her to the nearest empty seat. She could be quiet but definitely could take charge when the situation demanded. Which it hadn't this time.

"Oh, I'm so glad we made it." Gwynn smiled, and Theo's heart beat a touch faster. "When I first came here as a student eons ago, I used to have nightmares of getting stuck in the train doors when they closed."

"You can move fast. I'm impressed, except. . ." He tucked her hand around his arm again, realizing how nice it felt to have someone by his side.

"Except?"

"My dear, we're on the wrong train."

Her almond eyes rounded. "Oh. Theo. I'm so sorry."

He waved off her apology with his free hand. "No worries. The next stop is coming up, and we can cross over to the right train and be home again in no time."

"All right. Next time I'll let you lead." She squeezed his arm.

Theo tugged on his tie. Normally Theo did not go downtown to bustling places like Rockefeller Center or the shopping district. His life circled around the university, the apartment, his church, a few select stores and restaurants in the neighborhood, and an occasional stroll to the dog walk whenever he contemplated adding a pet to his ordered life.

"I hope you like our church," he said.

"I'm sure I will. As long as you worship the same God I do, I'm okay with that."

"We sing older songs. We have traditions. The younger people have a contemporary service, but I prefer the old ways."

"That doesn't surprise me." Gwynn blushed again. "I didn't mean you—oh dear. I mean, I'm not surprised you prefer classical worship."

He nodded. "I suppose you could call it that. I find comfort and the presence of God in the same patterns of worship that my people have used for hundreds of years. However, if you'd like to go to a contemporary service, Malina will go with you."

"Hmm. . .maybe I'll try both while I'm here. The kids and I go to church together, and then we take turns having lunch at a different home, or we go out to eat."

The lights in the tunnel flicked by as the train zipped along, then the flashes grew slower as the train screeched into the next stop. Gwynn's knuckles whitened as she clutched the seat. Theo smiled. A bit of the college girl still lurked inside her.

"We're here." Theo stood and smiled at the thought. "We can backtrack in no time and make it home at a decent hour."

Back into the bustling station they went, and Gwynn stayed close by his side. Theo's hip complained from hurrying too much. A young couple strolled past them. He could only distinguish who was the female by the long blond hair. At least he hoped he'd guessed right.

". . .and that was how Hal broke his arm the second time in one year."

Theo coughed. He'd done it again, as he had with Emma. "I'm sorry, could you tell me that story again?"

She blinked. "All right. Staci and Steven were young, and Lisa was, well, on the way. We'd just bought the house at Sebec Lake—Maine. The kids went nuts over one tree that was perfect for a tree house. So Hal spent most of our first week there building a fort, and we let them sleep under the stars. One night Hal joined them, and he rolled out of the fort. Broke his arm. Then that November he fell off the ladder while trying to string lights on the big tree. Same arm, too."

"Your family sounds very. . .lively." Theo wasn't sure he'd care to spend a night under the stars like that, but when a man was young. . .

"We always had good times together. Still do." Gwynn bit her lip. "So what about your family?"

Theo chuckled, wondering where to begin. "My family is large and Greek and loud. Emma and I were blessed with Malina. We wanted more children, but evidently that wasn't in the Lord's plans for us. Most of my brothers and sisters live in Astoria, and we gather at my youngest brother, Lukas's, house for holidays."

"How big is your family?"

"I have three brothers, two sisters. And they in turn have children and countless grandchildren. Maybe that's why I enjoy the quiet so much."

"I believe in balance." Gwynn paused. "Too much noise can be stressful, but sometimes too much quiet takes us away from people, and we can end up focusing on ourselves more than anyone else. I don't think God intends for us to be little islands."

Theo thought of students complaining about assignments and the length of exams. Couple that with the inordinate clamor of the Christmas season, and Theo wanted to hibernate. "People, though. . .they can cause many problems. I often prefer the island."

Gwynn's deep eyes made him forget they were ambling

across a crowded subway station. "People do cause problems, don't they? They can also be instruments of God in our lives."

"Ah, here we are. The nice part about transferring is you can ride on the same fare." Theo gestured to the train whose open doors beckoned. "This time we'll be hurrying in the right direction."

They found a pair of seats just as the train's doors closed and it pulled away from the platform.

The idea of people being instruments of God and not sources of irritation clung to Theo's mind. He knew the liturgy backward and forward, loved God with all his heart, and worked to honor Him, but people...

He glanced at Gwynn, who seemed to be studying an ad about a greener, cleaner New York.

"I hope Malina left some of that soup for us." Theo flipped open his phone to see if he could get a signal. "I'll try to call again once we're off the train."

"Malina certainly works hard. She looked ready to collapse into bed and sleep when she arrived home."

"She works *too* hard. Young people. They need to take it easy sometimes. But that's Malina. Driven." Theo shook his head.

"I know. Staci's running herself ragged, chasing the kids, working, taking care of the house." Gwynn sighed. "And I'm away right now. I try to help her, and Lisa, and Steve."

He took one of her hands in his and gave it a reassuring pat. "It sounds like you've done a good job raising them. I imagine they're fine."

"Thanks. I don't know if that's a compliment or if you're

chiding me." A dimple appeared in Gwynn's cheek, and Theo didn't recall seeing it before.

"Both. I'm complimenting you, and I'm telling you to relax and enjoy your vacation. For a week, focus on Gwynn."

"So I'm allowed to be an island, then?"

"No, I'm saying you need some quiet. Here in the city. No one making demands of you or commanding your schedule."

"Is that an order?" The dimple appeared again.

Theo felt a chuckle rise from his chest. Demure Gwynn Michaud was flirting with him. And he realized he liked it. He also realized they'd just glided away from their subway stop.

Chapter 4

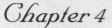

Gwynn paused on the steps of the Metropolitan Museum of Art and glanced over her shoulder. "Until next time."

For the entire morning and for the first part of the afternoon, she'd lost herself in the galleries. Paintings, sculptures, tapestries, relics. Her mind swam at the images and creativity that filled the building behind her.

Made in God's image, man naturally desired to create. Gwynn studied her hands. They showed a few stubborn age spots that persisted despite the cream she rubbed into her skin. God had made her creative, and while she had laid aside a design career, the urge to worship through making things of beauty remained inside her. She rubbed her hands together, then took out her gloves and slipped them on.

Theo was due to meet her at any moment and walk with her to Radio City Music Hall. Ever since the tree lighting, the delightful and courtly Mr. Hyde had made himself known, and Gwynn enjoyed his dry wit.

She turned to face the building and held up her digital camera. She'd promised the kids pictures of everything, and so she'd made good work of adding photos to the memory card.

"Would you like me to take your picture on the steps?" A familiar voice made Gwynn turn.

"Theo! Yes, please." She handed him the camera. "Everyone always complains I'm never in pictures, but someone has to be the family photographer."

He held the camera as if it were a toddler covered with cake frosting. "I'm not quite sure how this works."

"Okay." Gwynn took the camera back and showed him the display screen. "Look here while pressing this button. . .here. And that's that."

She stood with her back to the museum, its gaily colored banners streaming down behind her. A strand of hair wafted in front of her face. "Hang on—"

The camera flashed. "Oh, I'm sorry." Theo looked down at the back of the camera. "Wow, so there's the picture."

Gwynn crossed the few steps between them and looked at the screen. "Delete that one. I look like a fish gasping for breath while I'm touching my hair."

The corners of Theo's mouth twitched. "I'm afraid all I know how to do is shoot the picture. However, I like your hair. You look natural, in motion, as if you didn't know you were being photographed."

"Not at that second, I didn't."

Theo gestured at the museum. "Did you get your fill of art?"

"Most definitely. I feel like picking up a paintbrush and watercolors again."

"You paint?" He moved down the steps toward the sidewalk, and Gwynn remained next to him.

"I love watercolors. Haven't touched them in years. A visit here has inspired me, though." A stray idea tickled her mind. "I wonder if I could go shopping at Pearl Paints."

"Pearl Paints?"

"An artist's paradise and the largest art supply store around. But I only have a few more days left." Gwynn leaned into a gust of wind.

"A few more days." Theo's echoed words made her wonder if he'd be relieved once she was gone. No extra towels in the bathroom, no one to entertain, no more Malina on the fold-out couch. Gwynn could fend for herself, and she didn't want to inconvenience Theo and Malina.

They joined the stream of pedestrians and crossed the street, and a delightful scent wafted on the wind. "Oh, pretzels!" Gwynn wasn't exactly hungry, but the idea of snacking on the warm, salty baked dough made her stomach growl.

She paused at the pretzel stand without asking Theo, and he shook his head at her offer to buy one for him. They continued walking, and Gwynn kept up with the bustling traffic. She was accustomed to covering a route that circled her block four or five times and hoped her stamina had followed her to New York.

Theo seemed off in his own thoughts, so Gwynn let him stay there. Then he took a quick step, as if his knee had locked. Gwynn hesitated for a pace.

"I'm fine. My knee isn't used to going downtown so often."

"I appreciate you coming with me to the show, although

I could have gone on my own."

"Nonsense. You're our guest, and we promised Staci you would have an enjoyable trip."

Theo spoke the word "guest" as if he referred to her as an appointment, a duty, something that must be paid attention to.

"Don't you worry about me." Gwynn tried to quicken her pace, but she'd reached the limit of her stride. "I *am* having a wonderful time so far."

He didn't seem fazed by her reaction and hailed a cab. "We'll get there faster."

By the time they reached Radio City, Gwynn had calmed herself. In less than a week, she would leave New York and the Stellakis family behind. She could picture herself flying home and her own family meeting her at the airport. She would print out the photos on her digital camera. Then Jenna and Trevor would help her make a vacation scrapbook.

She did realize something as she and Theo entered the crimson and gold lobby. Maybe she wasn't in New York only for her own enjoyment. Maybe she was here to help someone else.

Theo appeared to be studying the architecture of the auditorium. The orchestra tuned, with the cacophony at last blending into a harmonious chord. "Beautiful, isn't it?"

Gwynn scanned the hall. "Yes. It's a fabulous hall."

"I meant the sound."

"Oh."

"At first the instruments seemed to clash as they tuned, then somehow the orchestra blended into a unified sound," he said.

"You're right." Gwynn smiled. "Unity with variety. An old

design concept." She hadn't thought of that in years, and now it came back to her.

Her musings came around again to her vacation's purpose. She felt as if her presence at the apartment had caused a disruption in Theo and Malina's carefully choreographed dance. She knew the father and daughter loved each other, but she found little warmth in the home.

At supper the night before, Gwynn had carried the conversation. She didn't fault Malina, though. She seemed to have a lot on her mind, namely, work.

"You're deep in thought."

Gwynn directed her attention back to Theo and the hall around them. "I was thinking about Malina. I hope she doesn't get sick again."

"She's a resilient young woman." Theo focused on the orchestra pit. "Not much of a cook, though. I tell her she should meet a nice man, marry him, and start a family."

"I imagine she doesn't want her father to be alone. I know she doesn't still live at home because she really has to."

Theo waved off the comment. "You're right. I'm fine by myself. But she chooses to stay with me. The city is expensive. She can put more money back for retirement and pay off her student loans faster if she lives with me." His normally well-groomed mustache appeared to bristle.

The house lights dimmed, and Gwynn was forced to end the conversation. Half of her tingled in anticipation of seeing the show, but the other half wanted to find a coffee shop with a cozy corner and talk with Theo for hours.

The more he tried to avoid conversation, the more she

wanted to draw him out. Hal used to tell her she was like a bulldog in cashmere once she got an idea in her head. She resolved to be more patient with Theo and not talk the poor man's ears off and make him want to run away.

Several times during the show, she caught Theo smiling at the antics of some of the dancers. When he caught Gwynn's glance, he coughed and straightened his collar. She didn't know what she could do to get the man to loosen up a little.

Old dogs can't learn new tricks, the old adage taunted in the back of her mind.

Right, and this grandma dog just figured out she could lose her heart again.

❄

The sight of seventy-two legs kicking at the ceiling really wasn't so bad. Theo thought the synchronous maneuvers were truly remarkable. The ability of so many people to perform their steps in the same way at the same time amazed him. He'd never been a "team player," to use one of his students' terms. The costumed and leggy Rockettes had shown Theo he could learn a thing or two.

After the last scene, the live nativity, Theo's heart swelled. He hadn't imagined such a spectacular ending, glorifying Christ. Even here in the glitz, he found an acknowledgment of Jesus' impact on the world. *Amen* would be a fitting end to the show.

He turned to see Gwynn's reaction at the final curtain, before the house lights came on. Her smile lit the space around them. Theo allowed himself to look at her as the auditorium grew brighter to match her smile.

"Enjoyed that, did you?" He stood and took her hand, helping her to her feet.

"Oh *yes*! Thank you, thank you for coming with me." Gwynn squeezed his hand.

His heart leaped. He'd had an echocardiogram as part of his annual physical that year, and her touch also confirmed that his heartbeat was very strong. "I know my sister Rita might have come, but her husband is sick, and Malina's been busy. I'm afraid I'm not the best company," he admitted.

"No, you were the perfect. . .um, person to come with me." Gwynn kept hold of his hand as they entered the aisle. "You didn't talk through the show, and if I was with anyone else, I might have been tempted to chat or comment."

"Well then, I'm glad. . .I think."

They entered the upper lobby, where a Christmas tree reached for the ceiling.

"Theo, could you take my picture in front of the tree?" Gwynn smiled. "I need to get another picture to prove I was here."

He took the camera from her in response and took a few steps back, mindful of the crowd. The image that popped onto the screen was perfect. Gwynn, surrounded by spangles of lights, her bright smile and laughing dark eyes the most beautiful elements of the picture.

"I like it," Gwynn said when she saw the image. "Have you ever thought of being a photographer?"

"Not really."

"That was a joke, Theo." She poked his arm when she took the camera back.

"Photographing you is easy. You lit up that picture more than the tree did."

Gwynn's expression softened. "Why, thank you, Dr. Stellakis." A strand of hair fell across her cheek when she looked at him.

His throat caught, and he stopped himself from brushing the hair away. He cleared his throat, took Gwynn's arm, and whisked her outside the building. He didn't look at her expression as he hailed a cab. Twilight had fallen, and it would be dark soon. He needed to get home to safety, away from honey-colored hair and almond eyes. Exams awaited his attention.

Gwynn snapped pictures as they zigzagged through traffic, not saying anything. Then she checked her phone and started listening to messages, presumably. Theo breathed a bit easier, grateful for the emotional distance.

❅

"Dad, I need to talk to you." Malina stopped him in the hallway when they arrived home. Gwynn retreated to her room, saying she had to call her family.

"Whatever about?" Theo let his daughter lead him into the warm kitchen.

"I know what I want for Christmas."

"Oh? I believe Kris Kringle's already done his shopping." Theo thought of the blue Tiffany box hidden in his sock drawer. The earrings cost a bit more than he usually spent on presents, but Malina deserved something special for her hard work.

"I want Gwynn to stay."

His stomach twisted. "What?"

"I don't mean move in. I mean, I want her to stay for Christmas." Her cheeks looked unusually rosy this evening. "I don't know what it is this year. I. . ."

Theo waited for her to continue, noticing for the first time the pale cast of Malina's skin in the lamplight.

"I miss Mom." Two tears shimmered down her cheeks. "I always have. I'm used to it. This year. . .I don't know." She laid a hand on her forehead. "Gwynn's not Mom, but it's been nice having her around. Oh, I'm too old to act like a baby." Malina gulped and clamped her hand over her mouth.

Theo gulped, too. This was where Emma had been the best. Comforting, doing "momma" type things. He provided security, and Emma provided the nurturing and warmth. He reached for Malina's cheek and found it hot to the touch.

"My dear, I believe you have a fever."

Malina draped herself on Theo's shoulder. "I'm so sorry, Daddy."

He circled her with his arms. "Whatever for?"

"Letting you down," came her muffled reply. "I can't be sick right now. I have to get everything ready, and—"

"No, you do not." Theo grasped her arms and held her away from him. "The first thing you are going to do is get into your pajamas and into bed. I'll—I'll make some tea and get you some pain reliever. You might have the flu." He led her to the stairs and pointed to the second floor.

"You'll talk to Gwynn?" Her eyes pleaded with him as she looked over her shoulder.

Theo put one hand on the railing. "Go get your pajamas,

change, and get into bed. We'll ask her together when she comes downstairs." He couldn't believe he was considering Malina's idea. They'd been fine without anyone else in the house. Just fine.

He went to the kitchen and filled the kettle, then found the acetaminophen. He didn't know whether to laugh or take a pill for the fresh headache he'd earned.

Gwynn, in most respects, had been an ideal guest. No, he corrected himself, in every way. *He* was the problem. And now his heart was in danger.

"Father God, I did not expect this. I am not looking for anyone. I have You. I have Malina. The rest of my family, too. You have blessed my job, given me a good home. I have all I need. Emma is with You." He swallowed hard. "I accept that. I am, as the apostle Paul says, content." A noise in the front hall made him turn around to face the kitchen door.

Gwynn and Malina entered through the swinging door. Gwynn's eyes flashed. "Young lady, you need to lie down. You're positively burning up."

Theo raised a hand to fend off Gwynn's accusing glare. "I'm not the one keeping her out of bed. I'm making her a cup of tea, and I have some medicine right here." He gestured at the medicine bottle on the counter.

"Gwynn, I promise I'll rest." Malina looked ready to slump onto a chair, so Theo put one arm around his daughter and helped her sit.

"Yes, that you will." Theo wondered if Malina would bring up the idea of Gwynn staying. He turned toward the cabinet and searched for the box of Malina's favorite tea bags.

"Dad and I were just talking. . . ." Malina's voice trailed off.

"There's a lot to do this time of year. Right now, I feel like I met up with a subway train and lost. What I'm saying, quite badly, is. . .Dad and I would love for you to stay with us. . .through Christmas."

Chapter 5

"Mom, go ahead, stay." Staci sounded so sure on the other end of the phone. "Change your ticket and take care of Malina. She used to run circles around us in school. Now she needs to put on the brakes."

Gwynn's gaze darted to the front hallway. She sat on the edge of the fold-out sleeper sofa, where she was going to sleep while Malina was sick. "But the baking, and decorating, and shopping. . ."

"You can do those in New York."

"Silly. I meant with you, Lisa, Steve, and the kiddos."

"Christmas is about giving. I think Malina and her father need you more than we do right now." A faint hum of static crossed the phone line. "We always have you, and we know you love us. Think of it as making up for all those getaways you never took when we were growing up."

"I don't know. . ." Gwynn's heart leaped. Christmas. . .New York. . .and she wouldn't need to rush home.

"Until I became a mom, I never knew how much you did.

And you never took much time for yourself." Staci gave a small giggle. "Anyway, New York sounds like it's been good for you. You sound different. Peaceful, rested."

"Did I sound anxious and tired before?" Gwynn teased.

"No, that's not it at all."

Gwynn felt her resolve weakening. "All right. I'll try to get a flight home before New Year's Eve. Malina should be better by then, for sure."

They ended the conversation after Staci shared news from the home front. Gwynn reminded Staci where she'd hidden gifts for Trevor and Jenna. Then she called the airline, trying to get a later return flight. But by this time in December, flights were full. She couldn't stomach paying double the price of a round-trip ticket. Perhaps she could rent a car. She squelched that thought. Battling holiday traffic didn't appeal to her in the least. Frugality won, and Gwynn changed her flight, for a mere hundred-dollar fee, to December twenty-seventh. Now Theo was stuck with her—for three more weeks.

Malina had gone to bed, and since Theo wasn't in the kitchen, Gwynn figured he was in his bedroom, which doubled as an office. She climbed the stairs to the second floor.

Gwynn stood at the door, its patina a rich mahogany. The glass doorknob reflected the hallway light. Courage won, and Gwynn gave a series of short taps on the wood.

"Enter," came Theo's rich baritone from behind the door.

She turned the knob and entered the room, which was larger than she expected. She couldn't make out the details of the room. A desk lamp glowed over the space where Theo worked.

"I spoke with my family, and I've arranged to stay."

"Good, good," Theo said without looking up from his work.

"I also decided to shave my head and get a tattoo in Greenwich village."

"Wonderful." Theo rustled some papers, and Gwynn tried not to laugh.

"I'll let you know when supper's ready." Gwynn didn't wait for a response and closed the door behind her. She shook her head outside in the hallway. Theo was in oblivious professor mode. If she guessed correctly, he'd be involved neck-deep in exams for at least another week.

She peeked in on Malina—still asleep. Those TV commercials about taking medicine and working through the flu lied. People shouldn't medicate themselves and push through their sickness. They needed rest, and that's exactly what Malina would get now that Gwynn was staying. She breathed a prayer for peace and healing before closing Malina's door.

Gwynn returned to the kitchen. She would earn her keep and find her place in this household, temporary though her stay may be. Supper on the table. Cleaning. Christmas.

"What do they need most, Lord?" Gwynn wondered aloud as she rummaged through the freezer. Tonight would be good old American meat loaf, the best she could do on short notice. And au gratin potatoes. She'd toss a spinach salad together.

Dinner for two, she realized, and set to work thawing and seasoning the beef. Malina might not want much to eat, but some chicken soup remained from the other day. Gwynn would toss a few noodles into the broth when she reheated it.

She popped the meat loaf and the pan of potatoes into the

oven and made a pot of coffee before settling at the kitchen table. What now? The sitting room had a floor-to-ceiling bookcase on one wall. She wasn't in the mood to read. Her cell phone's warble called her. Gwynn skittered on the hardwood floors to the front room and fumbled for the phone charging on an end table.

It was the airline, confirming her reservation, reminding her it was a nonrefundable, nontransferable fare. Gwynn hung up, feeling as she had the time she'd ventured onto a roller coaster at Trevor's insistence at Six Flags New England. What had she done?

The squeaking wood of the stairs made her look up. Theo descended, his nose pointed in the air like a dog catching a scent.

"Delicious. I'm amazed you found enough ingredients to prepare a decent meal." Theo stood in the entryway. "I can't recall the last time Malina went by the market."

"It's meat loaf. Nothing fancy, but it'll stick to your ribs." Gwynn tried to smile. Her cheeks felt as if she'd been out walking laps around the block. "The potatoes should be done at any moment. Au gratin."

She rose to enter the hallway, and Theo stepped aside to let her pass. "Were you able to change your flight?"

"I was," she called over her shoulder. He followed her to the kitchen door. "The best deal I got was flying home on the twenty-seventh. More than enough time to make sure Malina rests and gets better."

They moved into the kitchen, now warmed by the oven and smelling of meat, potatoes, and tangy cheese. Gwynn fished through the cabinets until she found a bowl large enough for a tossed salad.

"Well, I wish you the best in getting Malina to be a cooperative patient."

When Gwynn glanced back at him, she caught a twinkle in his eyes. "I'm sure she will. I've tackled the best—Staci and Malina are probably equal in the hardheaded department." Gwynn took out the baby spinach she'd found in the fridge earlier and started washing it for salad. Great. She'd just called Theo's daughter hardheaded.

"I suppose I should turn you loose at the market, that is, if you wouldn't mind picking up a few things." Theo's voice took on a businesslike tone.

"I don't mind." She placed the salad bowl on the table. "Malina probably won't be up to takeout for a while, so I'd like to plan some meals."

"Tomorrow, I'll show you where we shop. D'Agostino's is two blocks over. We have an account there."

Gwynn wasn't so much concerned with groceries. "Let me know when. Except, I was wondering, are there any special traditions you have at Christmas?"

Theo waved off the request and helped himself to a cup of coffee. "Is this the decaffeinated blend?"

"Yes." Gwynn watched him cross the kitchen and take a whiff at the stove. "You didn't answer my question."

"You don't have to go to any trouble for us. Really. We'll be fine. Christmas dinner, if not at Rita's, will be at one of my sisters' homes."

It was Gwynn's turn to wave off his explanation. "I don't

consider it trouble. Not in the least. We could spruce up the whole apartment. No pun intended."

"I. . .I smell burning cheese." Theo looked helplessly at the stove.

"The potatoes!" Gwynn bolted from the chair, nearly upsetting it. Theo moved out of her way as she grabbed a pot holder and yanked open the oven door. A brown crust bubbled on top of the potatoes and cheese. "Oh dear. I'm not the best cook in the world, I've got to warn you. I try to do more than one thing and forget what I'm cooking." And right now Theo's warm, dark eyes had her attention.

"I'm sure your cooking will suffice." Theo picked up his cup of coffee. "Just don't shave your head or get a tattoo in Greenwich village." The corners of his mouth twitched before he spun on a heel and left the kitchen.

❄

Nothing made a man feel as helpless as his child being ill. The thought of Gwynn staying filled Theo with a sense of relief. She would know what to do. No matter that Malina was an adult and had lived through colds and flu before.

Theo climbed the stairs to check on Malina before resuming his exam preparations. He opened her door a crack.

"Hey, Dad." Her voice sounded thin.

"Sleeping okay?"

"I did. That food I smell cooking would be wonderful if I didn't feel like hurling."

"Gwynn is staying."

"Good, because there's something else I want." She fell silent, then continued. "Let Gwynn do Christmas. I can show her Mom's recipes. The Christopsomo bread. Please."

"She burned the potatoes au gratin."

"That doesn't matter to me."

"All right. Show her the recipe box." He didn't let himself sigh.

"Thanks, Dad," Theo heard before he closed the door.

He sat at his desk and tried to complete the final examination for Chemistry C3543. No "multiple guess" exams for these students. Why he'd chosen to rewrite all of his exams this year escaped him now, other than the fact he didn't want any of the questions ending up passed around to the highest bidder.

Manners dictated that he find a present for Gwynn. Something appropriate for her—nothing presuming more of their relationship yet nothing impersonal. Malina would know what to choose. In fact, he'd normally have asked his daughter to shop for him or perhaps go shopping with Gwynn and discover her tastes.

Theo knew what kind of gift would fit Gwynn. Something elegant and practical with a generous dose of fun. Emma would have liked her, despite their outward differences. His wife had been more... His mind groped for the word. *Domestic*, that's what Emma was. Yet both she and Gwynn had nurturing spirits.

His clock glowed seven, and the sounds of clanking dishes filtered up from the kitchen. Dinner for two, Theo suspected. He tugged at his collar. The Christmas bug had infected him as it had his students. He couldn't focus. In about three weeks, Gwynn would be gone. He didn't know if he should feel relieved or prepare himself to let her go.

Theo rubbed his beard. He ought to stop by the barber for a trim. The visit would clear his head. Gwynn making Emma's recipes. Indeed. He understood what Malina wanted. She needed traditions and a little warmth in their home. Theo didn't have time to decorate or embellish, let alone cook. Perhaps the flu had made Malina more vulnerable than usual.

He squinted at the computer screen. Examination questions. One thing at a time. He'd make a list to keep Gwynn occupied, and the days would flash past and he'd have his world back in order again.

Theophilus, methinks thou doth protest too much. Theo brushed the idea aside.

Chapter 6

"You're *not* going all the way to Canal Street by yourself."
Theo's freshly trimmed beard seemed to bristle. He
stood at the coatrack in the apartment entryway.

Gwynn huffed and waved Malina's MetroCard. "I've got
a subway pass and a decent map that I'm not ashamed to use.
Plus my cell phone. And good walking shoes."

"It's—it's quite a distance to travel. What did you say was
there?"

"Pearl Paints," she proclaimed triumphantly, tucking the
card in her coat pocket. "I decided while I'm in New York, I'm
going to do a little painting. Watercolors. The landing halfway
up your staircase has plenty of light and enough room for an
extra kitchen chair. So of course I have to go to Pearl Paints."
Her mouth practically watered at the thought of six floors of
art supplies and the best handmade papers for sale.

"What if Malina needs something?"

"That's a flimsy reason to stay home, and you know it."
Gwynn shook her head. "She sleeps or she sneaks onto her

e-mail and calls the office. I think she'll pull through. Plus I was going to check out some of the street vendors and have a light lunch in Chinatown."

Theo's eyebrows shot to the top of his head as if he'd stuck a finger in a light socket. "You'll. . .get lost. You get uptown, downtown, midtown, east, and west mixed up."

"Theophilus Stellakis, I've never heard you say anything more absurd." Honestly, she only got lost once on the way home from Macy's. "Since you're so outraged, I have an idea."

"And what is that?"

"Come with me. You don't have classes today, and I know your TA is typing your exams."

"I—"

"It'll be *fun*. I haven't had a chance to do anything like this in years, so I'm seizing the moment." Gwynn wrapped her scarf around her neck and let one end dangle over her shoulder. She smiled at him, feeling half her age. So what if she might get lost. She had enough common sense not to get into trouble and to ask for directions.

He appeared to consider her request and studied her face. His gaze made her stomach do flip-flops, something she hadn't felt in years. Maybe she should just stay at the apartment or walk around the neighborhood. Canal Street was blocks and blocks and blocks away. . . .

"I'll go." Theo reached for his coat and hat.

"You can even take a few pictures." Gwynn opened the door, and Theo followed her into the December air.

Once they hopped onto the number 1 subway, Gwynn settled down for the trip. She tried not to stare at her fellow travelers, but she couldn't help but people watch. The kaleido-scope of colors and personalities in New York always fascinated her. Lives intersecting as they traveled together, then diverging again.

Just like her and Theo, who had his nose stuck in the newspaper he'd brought with him. They were together now, and after the twenty-seventh, their paths would veer away from each other. The more Gwynn prayed, the more she believed she wasn't with the Stellakis family just to please herself. Helping care for Malina was one reason. Maybe helping Theo loosen up and enjoy life was another.

For the past week, they'd fallen into a routine. After a quiet breakfast of coffee and toast and fruit, Theo would leave for the university and Gwynn would see to Malina. The flu bug had bitten Malina hard, and Gwynn helped her make phone calls to the law office the first days of her sickness.

Theo folded his paper and tucked it under his arm. "I like what you've done with the banister at home. The greenery and lights are beautiful."

"Thanks. Mr. D'Agostino had a whole box of garland back in the storeroom they didn't use at the store this year. What a nice man to let us use it."

"I don't know why we never thought of pine garland before. It's simple and elegant." Theo stood to allow an elderly woman take his seat, and he grasped the pole across from where Gwynn sat.

"I'm going to look for something special today, too, while we're checking out the street vendors."

"Don't go to too much trouble. In just a couple of weeks—"

Gwynn nodded. "I know. I'll be gone. But I want to do something for you and Malina, to make a difference while I'm here."

"My dear, you've already done that."

She barely caught Theo's words and glanced up. His gaze focused on the platform lights clicking past outside the window as the train rattled on its way. Gwynn hunched forward when the speaker broadcast the next stop, which wasn't Canal Street. She settled back onto the seat.

"Why did you stop painting?" Theo's warm eyes now focused on her, and Gwynn reminded herself to breathe.

"I got busy. Life. Hal. Kids. Church." Gwynn shrugged. "Choices had to be made. I believe when you say yes to something, you're saying no to something else. I didn't stop painting entirely. I'm head of painting and scenery for the local civic theater back home. Twice a year they have productions, and I design the sets. Nothing like Broadway, of course." A wave of homesickness nearly made tears come to her eyes. The nativity play's sets were complete, but she wouldn't be there to add finishing touches. Yet another reason to call Janice, her friend at the theater.

"And it took coming here to get you painting again."

"I suppose it did." Tears stung her eyes anyway. "I know. I could have painted if I wanted to. New Hampshire has art supply stores."

"Are you all right?" The seat beside Gwynn had emptied, so Theo settled next to her.

"I'm—I'm fine." She tried to smile. "I guess I just realized I've been stuck in a rut and didn't even know it."

"Ruts are routines with the purpose drained out of them." Theo took her gloved hand and held it between his. "I know my routines may seem confining to others. But they have purpose. Ruts? Now ruts are entirely different."

"Saying I'm in a rut makes me sound awful, especially since my life revolves around my family." Gwynn slipped her hand from Theo's, then found a tissue in her purse. She scolded herself inwardly for tearing up like a child. "I love my life in New Hampshire. My children, grandchildren, everything we do together. I'm accustomed to life without Hal. I've reached that acceptance stage grief counselors talk about, and I'm okay most of the time. When I was a child and upset over something I couldn't have, I learned to focus on and enjoy what I did have. But now—"

"It's not enough," Theo whispered.

Gwynn nodded. "I'd like to say I'm content. The last few months, I've wanted something more. I've prayed and prayed. . . ." The train lurched.

She couldn't think of anything else to say, and Theo simply squeezed her hand. When she ventured to look into his eyes, she found them full of understanding. Theo *knew*.

And she knew if she let herself, she'd lose her heart to this man. But their worlds were so different, like travelers on a train. What they held in common, this one season, would disappear. Just because she felt she was in a rut didn't mean the answer was falling in love. She was old enough to know that the dizzying sensations of newborn love didn't last, and she wasn't sure if whatever kind of relationship she and Theo had would grow past that new stage. If she allowed herself to love him, of course.

Help, Lord. I didn't ask for this.

❄

Theo rarely dealt in superlatives, but as he stood watching Gwynn in a paper aisle at Pearl Paints, he realized he'd never seen so many different kinds of paper in his whole life. Myriad colors, weights, and textures. Even paper made out of rice, which Theo in his entire realm of experience hadn't imagined.

Gwynn's face glowed as she spoke with the salesclerk. She caressed the sample sheets tenderly. "I'll take a dozen sheets of the 140-pound, six of the 260-pound, and—why not? I'll live a little." Here she tossed a glance in Theo's direction, her dimple flashing. "One sheet of the rice paper. My splurge. I might frame it just because it's so beautiful."

Theo didn't understand what she meant by 140-pound paper. He didn't mind carrying parcels for her in the least but hadn't thought about lugging reams of paper around.

What Gwynn received was a long, narrow tube with the paper wrapped inside sheets of butcher paper. "There." She spun to face him and waved the cardboard tube. "This will be safe on the ride home."

"And now?" Theo was starting to melt inside his long wool overcoat, but he didn't want to rush Gwynn. Her sparkling demeanor had returned, in sharp contrast to her blue mood on the subway.

"Paints and a few brushes." Gwynn tugged on his coat sleeve. "C'mon, Thomas is going to show us to the watercolors." As obedient as one of the dogs he saw at the neighborhood dog walk, Theo followed behind Gwynn and the sales assistant with an eyebrow piercing. Today he felt as if he'd follow Gwynn anywhere—which was probably why he'd trotted to the subway stop with her this morning.

An hour later, Theo's stomach was growling when he received more wrapped packages to carry on Canal Street. Gwynn had exclaimed over a handbag, something she called a "Dooney & Bourke knockoff," that one of her daughters would like. She bought one, as well as a "Prada knockoff," and promptly handed the parcels over to Theo.

"So what if they're not the real thing." Gwynn smiled. "The girls will love them, and I don't think the stitching will come loose anytime soon."

All he could do was nod. This was where she and Emma were most different. Emma didn't fuss about clothes much, but Gwynn—she had a flair.

They continued west on Canal Street, and Gwynn froze in front of a shop selling silk garments, scarves, and belts. The whole thing looked as if a gaily colored parachute had exploded onto the sidewalk. Gwynn fetched a length of red silk, fringed on the ends.

"A scarf." Her gaze devoured the fabric.

"You're quite right." Theo shifted a bag to the other hand. "It's exquisite. You should buy it."

"That's very impulsive of you to say." She looked at the price tag and then at the vendor, a wisp of an Asian man who smiled as if he agreed with Theo's suggestion.

"Treat yourself. You might not come here again." Yet another reminder that Gwynn's time was short. Theo glanced to the next open storefront, where rows of jewelry glinted in the December sunlight.

"May I see that turquoise one?" Gwynn gestured at a display behind the table.

A certain piece of jewelry caught Theo's eye. "My dear, I'll be at the next shop." When she nodded, he stepped a few paces to the jewelry store.

What sparkled so prettily were rows upon rows of brooches and earrings, handcrafted from genuine crystal, or so the handwritten poster-board sign proclaimed. Perhaps they were, although the settings might be vermeil and not fourteen-carat gold. A brooch shaped like a Christmas tree encrusted in multicolored crystals captured Theo's attention. He'd found Gwynn's gift. He glanced in her direction to see the shopkeeper wrapping the crimson scarf. The pin wasn't too extravagant, as he didn't want to presume more of their relationship than he had a right to. But it was an elegant reminder to what had brought Gwynn to New York—and him.

"Genuine Swarovski, that pin is." The woman held the pin up for Theo to examine.

"I'll take it." Theo had enough cash in his wallet and paid the shopkeeper. "Do you have a box?"

"Black velvet. I have a red gift box, too." The saleswoman boxed his purchase in time for Theo to pocket it before Gwynn approached.

"Perfect." Theo sensed Gwynn gliding toward him. He turned to face her. "Did you get your scarf?"

She nodded. "What did you get?"

"A present. For. . .a friend." Now would not be a good time for Gwynn to press him with questions, as she was wont to do, or worse, spend twenty minutes gasping over the jewelry.

Thankfully, Gwynn slipped her arm through his. "I'm famished. And I think I've bought enough for us to carry. I didn't plan to get this much."

Theo chuckled, and he couldn't recall the last time a laugh had felt so free. "With two arms apiece, we'll manage. I'm glad you mentioned lunch. Let's go." They headed deeper into Chinatown, another place Theo hadn't been in countless years.

"What do you want for Christmas, Theo?"

His mind floundered for an answer. Malina usually guessed well, and whatever she bought him, he liked. "Well, I can't really say. I don't know."

"Is there something you really want?" Her breath made puffs in the crisp air.

"I have everything I need."

"I don't mean need. I mean want." They paused at a corner just in time to avoid a bicycle messenger whizzing in an arc as he headed onto the side street. "You don't know when you'll get back here again."

"Touché." A grin tickled the corners of his mouth, something happening a lot more with Gwynn around.

When Gwynn studied his face, Theo wanted very much to kiss her lips, which didn't need those cosmetic injections some women subjected themselves to.

"Hmm. . .you wait, Dr. Stellakis. I'll think of something." With that, she tugged on his arm, and they continued on their way.

Chapter 7

Gwynn, a UPS guy just dropped off an envelope for you." Malina stood in the front doorway, letting blasts of cold air into the apartment.

"Young lady, you need to get out of that doorway. You'll—"

"Catch a cold? Come down with the flu?" Malina's eyes glinted. She looked a little pale, but her mood had improved and she appeared more rested than she had in a few days. In fact, she was starting back to work tomorrow. "Here."

"Ha-ha. Very funny." Gwynn took the envelope. "Lisa overnighted some pictures so I can paint from them."

"Pictures of?"

"Sebec Lake." She handed Malina the stack. "One of these will be your father's Christmas present, once I translate it into a painting."

"He wouldn't tell you what he wanted, would he?"

Gwynn shook her head. "He must be impossible to shop for."

"You have no idea." Malina rolled her eyes.

"Come to the kitchen with me and out of this drafty hallway."

Gwynn headed for the warm kitchen, and Malina followed. The spirited young woman reminded her so much of Staci. God had done a good thing, allowing them to be college roommates. The friendship had blossomed and matured throughout the years, and both families were blessed through their daughters. Gwynn knew she'd been blessed through her time here. Although ever since their trip to Canal Street, Theo had found reasons to stay away from the house on days he didn't have class. In eight days, she'd fly home. Theo would have his space to himself again.

Malina tugged the ends of the belt on her robe. "I love this kitchen. Did you know I grew up in this apartment? My dad did, too."

"That's quite a legacy." Gwynn gazed at the warm walls, the tall windows facing the frosty courtyard in the back. "This building has a lot of history."

"Could you see yourself living somewhere like this?"

"I suppose I could. It's not as large as my home in New Hampshire, but it's cozy and well kept. I have a bad habit of wanting to repaint rooms and rearrange furniture, though." She grinned.

"Do you like New York well enough to live here?" Malina took a plastic box from the shelf next to the oven and sat down at the table.

"Well, Attorney Stellakis, the jury is still out on that idea." Gwynn moved to check the pot of stew that bubbled on the stove.

"So you've thought about it."

Gwynn nodded. "The last time I was in New York, I was twenty-one, and I'd accepted an engagement ring from an amazing man whose love was enough to make me stay in New Hampshire. I'm different now. I'm more set in my ways. I don't know how I'd adapt, and my family isn't here, either. I really miss them."

"Would another man's love make you stay *here*?"

She didn't think she'd been that transparent. During a few idle moments, she'd wondered what life here would be like with Theo. Christmas spangles and decorations didn't stay up year-round, and she had to take the downside of city life along with the attractive parts. Moreover, every day that went by made her miss her children and grandchildren more.

"That depends, Malina. My heart and my feelings aren't the only things I must consider. My family. And. . .someone else's family, someone else's heart." She reached for some index cards that Malina had placed on the table. "What are these?"

"My mother's best holiday recipes." Malina tapped one card. "Her Christopsomo bread, best of all. I asked her to write down the recipe in case one day I'd try to make it myself. She—she died a month later."

"How did she pass away, if you don't mind me asking?"

"I don't mind." Malina blinked three times. "She went to the hospital because of chest pain, and they did a catheterization to check her arteries. They decided to put in a stent, and something went wrong. An artery ruptured. She—we lost her quickly. Internal hemorrhaging. A freakishly horrible complication." She reached for a napkin and dabbed at her eyes.

"I'm so sorry." Gwynn squeezed Malina's hand.

"I know she's with Jesus, but. . ."

"You wouldn't have minded another twenty years with her."

"Exactly." Malina crumpled up the napkin and smoothed over her expression. "Now, if you make anything, you should make the Christopsomo bread. This is a very important part of our tradition, and I would love it if you could bring some to Aunt Rita's on Christmas Day."

"For you, I'll do my best."

"Dad especially likes it." Now Malina's eyes sparkled.

"For him, I'll do my best, too." Gwynn didn't want to tell Malina that she was terrible at baking homemade bread. Some culinary skills she couldn't master. For Theo and Malina, though, she'd try. In honor of Emma Stellakis, who'd nurtured her family so well, she must.

❄

Somehow Theo's resolve to stay neutral yet friendly had crumbled that day on Canal Street. Theo had found reasons to stay at the university every weekday since. Grading papers, entering scores, typing his committee report, cleaning his desk. And now on the Saturday before Christmas, he had nothing more to grade.

He trudged home. From now until after New Year's, his time was free, and he couldn't think of anything else to do to avoid Gwynn. He didn't like the disappointed expression on her face when he retreated to his bedroom after supper.

Wimp. That's what his young students might call him, among other things. Years ago, when he and Emma were introduced, their families had played a big role in matching them together. For most of his adult life, his heart had been solely devoted to one woman.

Now another woman had shown him a possibility he'd never considered. Laughter, warmth, and adventures in the city he loved. He even thought about visiting New Hampshire to see its mountains and winding roads and tucked-away towns such as Gwynn's. That lake in Maine sounded interesting, too, although he'd never fished or camped. With Gwynn, he'd camp in a drafty tent and possibly wear a flannel shirt.

This whole train of thought had troubled his sleep and kept him holed up at the university. He paused at the newsstand for his paper.

Tushar gave him his change. "Dr. S., you been busy?"

"Exams." He nodded and waited before continuing, since Tushar appeared to have something more to say.

"I kept back papers for the days you missed stopping by, this week and last. You're like clockwork, so I thought. . ."

"Thank you, Tushar. That was kind." Theo opened his wallet and pulled out a few bills. "I appreciate the thought."

"You okay, Dr. S.? You look like you got somethin' on your mind."

"I'm trying to make a big decision."

"You taking the plunge?" Tushar's black eyes twinkled, his ample cheeks creasing into a grin.

"What?"

"You getting married again?"

"I'm—I'm not sure." Theo didn't know what advice the man could give him. Not that he was seeking anyone else's opinion.

"I look at it this way." Tushar nodded to a customer and took his change, then focused back on Theo. "Most people get one shot at love. Not the kind that burns out like a firecracker.

The kind that keeps you warm at night and lasts. I say if your God gives you another chance at a good thing, go for it. We only get so many trips around the sun."

Theo stared at Tushar. "Thank you. You're a kind man. Your father would be proud." They had interesting conversations about God sometimes, and Tushar had developed a respect for Theo's faith. Perhaps one day Tushar would embrace God's love for himself.

The tips of Tushar's ears darkened, and although he was around thirty, he looked about ten. "Thank *you*, Dr. S. And merry Christmas."

"Merry Christmas to you." Theo nodded and continued on his way. In the Bible, God had caused a donkey to speak. And now a newspaperman, worth far more to God than a donkey, had acknowledged that God might send Theo another chance at love. Tushar's words reminded him of the verse that says a man who finds a wife finds a good thing and obtains favor from the Lord.

A gaily wrapped Christmas box lay before him, and he'd nearly decided to send it back, unopened. Yet because of Gwynn's close ties to her family, Theo wasn't sure if he could ask her to stay in New York. The thought of her leaving, though, made him think of a cold, empty apartment without her. Gwynn's presence was a tangible reminder of God's love for him, in the little ways she showed she cared without speaking a word. *Lord, I don't want to be wrong. Help me know exactly what to do.*

Chapter 8

Gwynn carried two plastic shopping bags, one in each hand, and left D'Agostino's Market. After two failed attempts, she wasn't going to risk ruining more bread dough. She should have told Malina her baking skills were passable, at best. At worst? The evidence now lined the kitchen trash can at the Stellakis apartment.

She could make a French meat pie so flaky and delicious that Hal's family raved. Even she couldn't mess up refrigerated cookie dough. A gust of wind pressed on her, and its whistling sounded almost like a reprimand. *Yeast killer.*

Malina kept encouraging her from her pile of pillows and blankets, propped up on the fold-out bed in the sitting room. When this last attempt ended in disaster, the determined look on Malina's face gave Gwynn the gumption to head to the store for more ingredients. A trial run of Christopsomo bread before her debut on Christmas Day.

The apartment lay ahead, tucked into the row of nearly identical brownstones on the block. Gwynn couldn't match all of the residents to each apartment, but several knew she was a guest of the Stellakis family.

She climbed the stairs and let the wind blow her inside. "I'm back."

"That didn't take long." Malina had her laptop on the coffee table and files spread out over the afghan.

"What are you doing? You need to rest." Gwynn shook her head.

"I *am* resting. It's Saturday."

"Never mind, I won't nag. I know you're an adult. I'll be making that bread in the kitchen if you need anything." *Young people.* Gwynn continued on to the kitchen, pushing through the swinging door and stopping short. Theo stood at the counter as he poured water from the teakettle into a sturdy mug.

"Good afternoon."

"You're home early." The bags felt like weights hanging from both of her hands.

"I see you've been shopping again." He took his cup to the table with him and sat down.

"Just working on the Christopsomo bread."

"I noticed the trash can."

Gwynn laid the bags on the table with a thump. "Like I said, I'm working on it." Her cheeks flamed, and not from the warm kitchen. "I'm. . .having trouble with the yeast."

"Perhaps I can help."

"You bake?" She hoped she didn't look as incredulous as she sounded.

"My mother taught Rita and me." Here he looked flustered at the admission. "I know, I was different. A young boy, in love with Christmas, eager to learn his way around the kitchen. Especially to make the traditional bread."

"But now. . ."

"I haven't cooked in years. I laid it aside, much like you did your painting." Theo reached across the table for one of the bags. "More flour. Raisins, walnuts. More spices, oranges. Looks like you've picked up everything. Let's get started."

"You're going to show me?"

"I taught Emma. She was twenty when we married, still learning her way around the kitchen." Theo beamed. "On our first Christmas Eve, when I found her in tears over her sagging dough, I stepped in."

"I thought you said she always made the bread."

"Well, almost always." His mustache twitched as he arranged the ingredients on the table. "Now. The yeast."

Gwynn sighed and reached for the glass measuring cup she'd used earlier. "The yeast."

"You can do this, my dear." Theo rolled up his sleeves and scrubbed his hands at the sink. "The secret is the temperature of the water and making sure you let the dough rise long enough. There's no shame in using a thermometer. You can't guess with the water temperature."

"Okay. Not too cold, not too hot." He'd pegged her right, doing her best to guess at the temperature. "My mother told me how to let the water run over my fingers as it heated, but I never learned to guess right."

"See? You can't guess. You must be sure, then act while the water is still hot enough. There's no time to measure the flour and salt while the water cools."

Gwynn nodded, then stood back and watched, not believing what she saw. Theo, in his scholarly clothes, getting his hands covered with flour as he measured and mixed the dough in a large glass bowl.

"Pay attention now." Theo tapped the bowl. "Here's where the beautiful part begins. Pour the warm water and yeast into the well of flour and salt." Gwynn obeyed, and his flour-dusted hand touched her wrist.

"Perfect. Now the liquids." He mixed until a ball of dough formed in the bowl, then gently kneaded. "And we're done. For the moment."

Gwynn nodded. "I got to this part already, when I let the dough rise. Then it always flopped."

Theo found some waxed paper and placed it over the dough, then covered the bowl with a damp towel. "I know. We need to wait, two hours at the most."

"Thank you for helping me. It was. . .quite unexpected." Just when she thought she'd gotten to know Theo, yet another facet of his personality surfaced. "I'll always remember this."

He touched her nose with a flour-covered finger. "Especially when the bread turns out perfect."

Really, his charm made her go soft inside, like the dough now rising in the bowl between them.

❄

Theo normally didn't snoop, but he couldn't resist a peek at the paintings tucked behind the small easel on the landing. Gwynn was on the phone with one of her daughters while the bread dough had its second rising, and Theo stole this chance to see what Gwynn was working on.

He could see a progression in her paintings, the first few with stiff brushstrokes and tentative use of color. Then he guessed her more recent paintings had looser, more deliberate colors in unexpected places. Several renditions of a sparkling lake reflecting green mountains and a blue sky, shadows of deep purple and chestnut. He could almost hear the summer breeze across the lake, smell the fresh air, and feel the warm sun on his skin. It invited him to step into God's natural sanctuary and worship in the quiet.

Gwynn's personality brought passion and life to the picture. She wasn't designed to follow exacting bread recipes but rather to give outlet to creative expression. Yet she tried to give something special to him through baking the Christopsomo bread.

His words came back to him, about being sure of the water temperature and acting while the water was hot. No more shrinking back and hesitating. No hiding at the university, as if he had a choice now that examinations were over. Time to test the waters—for baking bread, for deciding to share his heart with Gwynn. Theo almost cringed at the play on words.

"What are you doing?" Gwynn ascended the stairs and stopped next to him. Red spots shot to her cheeks. "I'm sorry, I didn't mean to sound snippy. I. . ."

"No, I apologize. I was just curious. These are truly excellent. Better than any snapshot." Theo slid the paintings back behind the easel.

"Thanks. I've enjoyed getting the hang of the brushes and paint again."

"From what I can tell, you've picked up your skills quickly."

He wasn't sure how to continue the conversation. Lately, with Gwynn's presence, he'd gotten more practice, but he still found small talk exhausting. "How are your children?"

"They're knee-deep in the frenzy of before-Christmas activities. My daughter Lisa, though. . ." A crease appeared between Gwynn's eyebrows.

"Is she all right?"

"She's fine. She—she said she's getting an apartment with a friend after New Year's." Gwynn rubbed her forehead. "I know, I know. She's twenty-three and an adult, but. . ."

"But what?"

"Lisa was injured in a skiing accident at college the year that Hal. . ." Gwynn blinked. "She's in a wheelchair now, working hard at physical therapy and occupational therapy, and she's been living with me."

Theo grasped her shoulders gently. "You should be proud."

"I know, I know. Lisa's a fighter. She's determined to lead as unrestricted a life as possible. But. . .she's my baby girl." A tear slid down Gwynn's cheek, and she dashed it away. "Even if she could use her legs, I'd still be this upset."

Then Theo surprised himself by drawing Gwynn into his arms and letting her lean her head on his shoulder. "It's the way life is designed. Our Father God entrusts these wonderful children to us, and we raise them as He would see fit, and then He helps us let them go. And one day, we hope He'll tell us, 'Well done, good and faithful servant.'"

"I know what you mean." Gwynn stepped back and brushed at his shoulder. "I'll be fine. Just needed to let it out. I—I dread the thought of being alone in that house."

"Gwynn, you'll never be alone. Of that I'm certain." Theo wanted to touch her silken hair and soothe the ache that only God could heal. He didn't know what to do now. To confess his feelings to her, when her world was rocked once again, might be seen as preying on her vulnerability.

He couldn't very well say, "Well, instead of being alone, be with me." He refused to commit to someone else out of loneliness or expect her to do the same.

"We should probably see about that bread." Gwynn dabbed at the corners of her eyes with her little fingers.

"You're right." He took her by the hand, and they descended the stairs.

Chapter 9

The sound of the organ rippled through the cathedral like a melodious wave, and Gwynn felt the vibrations in her feet. She tried not to look like a tourist, but Gothic architecture was always her favorite, and this church had an exquisite ceiling. She tore her gaze from the Corinthian columns and focused on the altar, decorated with red poinsettias and candles. The minister wore a long scarlet robe in honor of Christmas Eve, and Gwynn wondered if the historical Nicholas had worn such a robe centuries ago as he shepherded God's people.

Theo was right about beauty in traditions. The unfamiliar order of service contained scripture readings that Gwynn knew well. Tonight the sacred words about a young couple seeking lodging in a strange city resounded in her heart.

Gwynn never expected to stay in New York so long, at least not long enough to fall in love. The time she and Theo had shared was deep and meaningful, and a measure of loneliness would follow her back to New Hampshire. And with Lisa moving out, the idea of an empty house made Gwynn sick to her stomach. That idea alone, without Theo added to the mix, was enough to cause Gwynn's eyes to burn with tears.

She saw no easy solution for her and Theo. Their two worlds had converged, and now she must wean herself from this holiday dream and think about real life. Her quiet mountain town would keep her busy enough with family, friends, church, and theater. Theo had responsibilities in New York. Practical Theo probably wouldn't find a reason to venture north to New Hampshire.

Something had happened between them, and Gwynn believed they were both adult enough to withdraw their hearts yet remain friends. She should be content with friendship. Still, she was tempted to offer Theo her heart along with the Christmas present she had for him.

Lord, I need Your guidance. Please reveal Your plans to us. I can be impulsive at times, and I don't want to mistake my emotions or leftover loneliness for true love. Gwynn's friend Janice had been left high and dry by a man she'd met on a whirlwind vacation. The man had drained Janice's bank account well. *Theo would never hurt me like that.*

The reverberations of the organ drifted away, and silence filled the cathedral as the second reader took his place at the podium to continue the next part of the Christmas story.

"And there were shepherds living out in the fields nearby, keeping watch over their flocks at night. An angel of the Lord appeared to them, and the glory of the Lord shone around them, and they were terrified. But the angel said to them, 'Do not be afraid. I bring you good news of great joy that will be for all the people. Today in the town of David a Savior has been born to you; he is Christ the Lord. . . .' Suddenly a great company of the heavenly host appeared with the angel, praising God and saying, 'Glory to God in the highest, and on earth peace to men on whom his favor rests.'"

Peace to men on whom His favor rests. Gwynn believed God had blessed her with peace, even though she didn't have a clear answer about Theo yet. But favor? Favor meant something extra special, not just getting by, not having merely enough. She remembered when Staci, Steven, and Lisa were small. She and Hal delighted in making them smile, bringing them joy, giving them something extra special that let them know they were loved.

Theo knelt next to her in the pew during the prayer, his head bowed. She glanced at his closed eyes, his silent moving lips. His heart and his faith were true. A man like him would be a tremendous example of God's favor. Although her life was full already, her heart spoke of its need to be filled, as well.

Lord, I'm willing. I choose Theo and whatever changes life with him will bring. She prayed Theo would choose her, as well.

❄

All the way to church, the red box had felt as if it burned a hole in Theo's pocket, so he was grateful to remove his coat. Now, during the exquisite and reverent service, Theo knew he should give Gwynn his gift tonight, on this holiest of nights. Tomorrow the annual reverie would ensue at Rita's, and he didn't want family members asking nosy questions or wiggling eyebrows at them both. He wanted to watch Gwynn open his gift without distractions or fanfare. He didn't particularly want Malina watching, either.

Theo wanted to embrace a second chance at love that was a gift from God, as Tushar at the newsstand had referred to it. Not a thoughtless gift that would wear out or come without a receipt, but a gift to last. Tonight, full of its possibilities and re-minders of God's promises, would be a perfect time to share his heart. He wouldn't push if Gwynn was vulnerable, especially with her daughter moving out.

"Dad, we're standing," Malina whispered in his ear. Theo stood, smiling to himself. Tonight would be special for both of them. He'd thought of everything, and Lord willing, it would be a merry Christmas indeed.

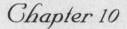

Chapter 10

I'll be home before too long. I promise." Malina wrapped
her scarf around her neck, and Gwynn smiled. "Katie and
Jess are having an open house at Katie's apartment, and I
promised them I'd stop by for a while."

"We're planning to walk home, aren't we?" Theo glanced at
Gwynn.

Her heart beat a little faster. She wanted to tell him how
she felt, even shout it under the Christmas Eve sky. Instead,
Gwynn replied, "Yes, sounds fine to me." Her heart burst with
love, and the tiniest twinge of fear made her tremble inside.
What if the lights and the atmosphere of romance in the city
had her fooled?

"See you later, then." Malina gave a little wave and disappeared into the crowd that milled in the church's entry.

Outside, winter's chill had fallen for the night. Holding
Theo's arm, Gwynn descended the steps of the church, and they
continued in the direction of the apartment. Words failed her
for once. She thanked God inwardly. In the past, many times

she'd spoken before thinking, with less-than-desired results. She dared not mess anything up this time.

"Gwynn. . ." Theo's breath made puffs in the air. "The next day or so will be busy. You'll run the gauntlet of the Stellakis clan before you leave."

She nodded. "I have to admit I'm a little nervous about spending the day with your family tomorrow."

"Don't be. They'll love you. I'm sure of it." A smile teased at his lips. "Especially my great-nieces and great-nephews."

"You're sure, are you?"

He stopped on the sidewalk and took both of her hands. "When I'm sure of something, I'm rarely wrong."

"That's one of the things I like about you. You're determined, decisive. No backing down. Like a rock."

Theo released one of her hands and reached into his overcoat pocket. He held a red square box in his gloved hand. "I'm giving you your Christmas present early."

Gwynn's heart felt as if it had popped into her throat. She swallowed, and it settled in her chest again. "Oh. . .I have to admit, I haven't wrapped yours yet." In fact, she'd snuck away from the apartment earlier that afternoon to pick up her matted and framed watercolor painting of Sebec Lake. It now lay in a flat box underneath the sitting room fold-out sofa.

She opened the box to find a square velvet jewelry case, then opened the case and nearly forgot to breathe.

Multicolored crystals reflected the streetlights. A brooch in the shape of a Christmas tree reminded her of the one in Rockefeller Center. "Theo. . ."

While the pin held her attention, Theo must have removed

one of his gloves, because when she looked up at him, he caressed her cheek and touched her chin with his fingertips. "Gwynn. . ." He leaned closer, eyes closing.

His lips were soft and warm, yet firm, and his beard gently comforting. Gwynn's pulse in her ears drowned out the sounds of the traffic. The kiss wrapped around her heart and seemed to whisper, *I cherish you.*

Then Theo backed away and the cold returned. "Forgive me." He began walking again.

Gwynn closed the velvet box, stuffed it into the red cardboard box, then slipped it into her purse and trotted after Theo. "There's nothing to forgive. I—"

"I shouldn't have presumed." He took her hand. "You're leaving in two days, and I've been fooling myself."

"Well," Gwynn ventured, "then I've been fooling myself, too. But I don't care."

"This is not a decision to be made lightly."

"I've been through this before."

"I know, and I should have considered something else before I. . ." Theo glanced at her, and his eyes were shadowed. "We must both decide if we could ever bear losing someone again. I don't think I could."

❄

He'd made a royal idiot out of himself, but it couldn't be helped. Theo sat in the front room and watched the lights twinkle on the garland-covered banister in the hall. Gwynn was up in Malina's room, wrapping something after she smuggled it upstairs. But he hadn't missed seeing the unshed tears in those beautiful almond eyes. He imagined her tears falling like diamonds as she wrapped his present. If he could, he'd sit next to her with a tissue in hand and coax a smile from those petal-soft lips.

The truth needed to be spoken, and Theo had done so. Marrying meant eventually one of them would lose the other. The idea slammed into him like a punch when he kissed Gwynn. He knew he wanted Gwynn by his side, here in New York. Besides the matter of geography and getting their families used to the arrangement, they couldn't ignore the painful reminder of the past and future. Love meant pain.

The words he used on the way home assaulted him. *When I'm sure of something, I'm rarely wrong.* Spoken like an undergrad with Manhattan-sized bravado. Swept up in holiday romance, Theo had ignored the certainty of what would happen. Quiet words spoken at a hospital bedside, the beeping of a heart monitor. Clasped hands, longing gazes filled with memories, then—

The front door opened, and in came Malina carrying two plastic bags. "Hey, I'm home!" She stood in a halo of light in the entryway and squinted into the front room. "Dad? Why are you sitting in the dark?" She dropped the bags on a chair and turned on the light.

Theo blinked. "I kissed Gwynn." The admission made his cheeks burn and his heart ache.

"Wow." A smile crept across Malina's face as she sat down on her bags. "Oops." She shifted and pulled the bags onto her lap.

"I see I've rendered you speechless. I should tell the judges about my technique."

"Ha. Don't change the subject."

"It was a mistake." Theo closed his eyes for a moment, then opened them again.

"Do you love her?"

"I do, but—"

"Then it's not a mistake. Because I know she loves you." Malina's smile remained, but a few tears sprinkled her cheeks. "Anyone would be blind not to see that. You're both good for each other."

"I was rash. I didn't think everything through before I acted." Theo fumbled for the right words. "One day, one of us will be alone again."

"That's true. But why throw away a blessing from God? Don't be a chicken."

"I'm not. I'm tired of the cycle of pain."

"Is that all you can see? Because do you know what I can see for you?" Malina stood and paced the room. "I see walks in Central Park, summers at the lake she loves so much. Maybe a few messed-up recipes. I see our family growing—I'd have two sisters, a brother, nieces, a nephew. I don't see just pain. And I don't think you should, either."

"So speaks the passion of youth."

"She is a gift to you, Dad. Just in time, I think." Malina sank onto the chair. "Our life is a vapor, as the Bible says. But God has infused that wispy steam with so much abundance, if we only accept it."

"You almost sound like Tushar."

"The newspaper guy?"

Theo nodded. "He said I should, as you younger ones say, 'go for it.'"

"You should." Malina stood, and her gaze swept over him. "I'll go make some decaf." She left for the kitchen, and Theo smiled. A good lawyer always knew when to rest her case.

❄

Gwynn taped the red bow onto the wrapped painting, then touched the glistening brooch on her sweater. She would treasure the gift and try to forget the kiss that had followed it. Several damp tissues made a pile next to the roll of wrapping paper.

She needed some air.

Gwynn put on her coat and new red scarf and slipped downstairs once she'd tidied up Malina's room. She avoided the one creaky stair and paused on the landing. Voices filtered from the kitchen. Malina's laughter rang out.

She'd go to the corner to the dog walk park, probably empty now, and clear her head. If only Theo hadn't kissed her. She could have borne him withdrawing from her, and she would have returned to New Hampshire and added the Stellakis family to her Christmas card list. But the kiss had shown her how he'd felt, and that was much harder to forget.

She closed the front door and descended the stairs to the sidewalk. Home again, day after tomorrow. Normal life, with its changes. Maybe she'd sell the house or lease it and buy a town house. Hal always said real estate was a good investment. Theo would probably say the same thing.

Gwynn quickened her stride, letting her knee and hip joints warm up. She must forget, as much as she could. But that kiss. . .

Christmas Eve traffic crisscrossed in front of Gwynn. Cars full of happy people, either leaving or heading to visit loved ones. Did any cars contain aching hearts?

Gwynn moved with the other pedestrians when the light changed. Under the streetlights, the empty park looked forlorn, its row of benches empty. Gwynn chose one and settled onto its cold wooden seat. She closed her eyes, picturing where each of her children would be at this moment. If her emotions wouldn't have betrayed her, she would have found comfort in talking to them. Gwynn pictured Staci tucking the kids in and "playing Santa" while Josh was overseas. Steven and Lisa would be having coffee before Steven settled into his old bedroom for the night.

She had wanted a change this Christmas. Perhaps the Lord had been preparing her for Lisa moving out. She didn't want to believe she'd been wrong about Theo, though.

Lord, it hurts. . . .

A figure entering through the gate caught her attention. Theo. Puffs of warm breath drifted away from him.

"There you are." He stood on the path, his hat firmly on his head. "You should have seen Malina when she found her bedroom empty."

"I'm sorry. I didn't mean to worry anyone." Gwynn coughed. "I—I needed a few minutes."

"Earlier, on the way home—"

"You don't have to explain." Gwynn held up her hand, fingers numb. She'd forgotten her gloves. "I understand. The idea of losing someone again scares me, too, but. . ."

Theo stepped closer, reached for Gwynn's hand, and pulled

her to her feet. "Your hands are cold."

"Not quite so cold now." She smiled, trying not to hope at the light she saw reflected in his eyes.

He took her other hand and covered both of them with his. "I have been a proud man, Gwynn Michaud. Proud of my intellect, my routines, and my reasoning. But I've been wrong. I left God's provision out of the equation."

"We all fall short, Theophilus. God never expected us to make it on our own."

At that, Theo pulled Gwynn closer and put his arms around her. "That's one of the things I love about you. You remind me of God's grace."

"And you. . .you remind me of how much God cherishes me. I forget that sometimes." Her heart hammered through the front of her coat.

Theo held her gaze. "I love you, Gwynn Michaud. I would rather have twenty wonderful years with you and lose you when we're both much older and grayer than walk away now and be safe."

"I love you, too, Theo." A hot tear rolled down her cheek. "This was unexpected and beautiful and, yes, frightening, too. But I want to give us a chance. I don't want to go home and try to forget you."

"Will you have me, Gwynn, for however long God gives us?"

"Yes, yes, I will!" She found herself swept into Theo's arms again, and then he kissed her, longer than the first time. Hearts were ageless in the glow of new love on Christmas Eve.

"Let's go home and tell Malina and call your children." Arm in arm, they left the park.

"Promise me something?" Gwynn's face hurt from smiling, but she didn't care.

"What's that?"

"We'll spend summers at the lake or in the mountains. And Christmas here. Always here. I can picture the apartment filling up with all the kids. . . ." She glanced at him. "Oh no, I sound like I'm already taking over the place."

"Your family will be my family." Theo's warm, gloved hand squeezed hers as they crossed the street. "One of my long-ago prayers was to fill the house. We can do that for Christmas, anyway. I'm not big on noise, but that's all right."

Gwynn saw the apartment lights ahead of them and began to hum.

Christmas Eve will find me, where the love light gleams. I'll be home for Christmas. . .

"Only," Theo finished, "it's not a dream." And he kissed her again.

LYNETTE SOWELL

Lynette has written four novellas for Barbour, and her first novel for Barbour's Heartsong Presents: Mysteries releases in 2008. She believes stories should take readers on an entertaining ride and offer glimpses of God's truth along the way. Lynette lives in central Texas with her husband, two teenagers, and five cats. She has fond memories of the Big Apple from her college days as an art major and thinks everyone should visit New York City at Christmastime at least once. You can learn more about Lynette and her writing at www.lynettesowell.com.

GIFTS FROM THE MAGI

by Vasthi Reyes Acosta

Dedication

To Rolando Tomas Acosta,
God's precious gift to me.

Trust in the LORD with all your heart
and lean not on your own understanding;
in all your ways acknowledge him,
and he will make your paths straight.
PROVERBS 3:5–6

Chapter 1

Rush hour wouldn't start for another hour. The lack of people made the subway station feel colder than usual. Cecilia tucked her hands in her coat pockets and then heard a *ping*, followed by several musical notes. She turned toward the sound and listened, leaning forward to search the uptown platform. On the other side of the train tracks, a pencil of a man with dreadlocks played "O Come, All Ye Faithful" on a steel drum. A crowd gathered around him: A mother with a folded stroller in one hand and a toddler clutched in the other. Two silver-haired women carrying Macy's shopping bags. And the couple.

They were in love. Cecilia knew from the way his arm wrapped around her waist and the way she leaned into him. The young woman swayed to the music. Her beau kissed the side of her forehead. The kiss seemed to encourage the woman, because she started to sing softly, and the acoustics of the underground tunnel carried her gentle voice, magnifying it.

Cecilia watched the couple, entranced. The two lives intertwined, worshipping the newborn King. Here, in the dungeons of New York City.

To have the freedom to sing from her heart. To have the courage to love like that. To be loved and held. To be a part of two. Her throat closed, and she swallowed hard.

The flash of the arriving train ripped the scene away from her. Just in time. She didn't want to fall through that rabbit hole ever again.

Cecilia stood and joined the rush to enter the subway car. She had to get home. Mamá and Tía Ramona were waiting.

❄

Cecilia stepped off the elevator on the fifth floor and walked to her apartment. She glanced at the wreath hanging on the door and scolded herself for not completing her Christmas shopping. She'd have to do it tomorrow, Christmas Eve. Tonight she needed to get some research done.

Cecilia unlocked the third lock and pushed the door open. The smell of roasted chicken greeted her. Her mouth watered, and her stomach growled.

"Ceci, is that you?" Mamá called from the kitchen.

"Sí, Mamá." Cecilia shrugged off her backpack and let it drop with a thump on the floor. "I'm starving."

Cecilia entered the kitchen and found Mamá at the stove stirring the beans. Tía Ramona sat at the small pine dinette set peeling garlic cloves.

Cecilia kissed Mamá on the cheek while Mamá kept stirring the beans. Then she kissed Tía Ramona's cheek.

"Sit. Sit. We want to know. How was your day?" Tía Ramona motioned for Cecilia to join her at the table.

Cecilia smiled. "I was so nervous before my presentation. My stomach was in knots."

"Did you pray like we told you?" Tía Ramona interrupted.

"In the bathroom, after I splashed some water on my face. I hate public speaking. But then things got worse." Cecilia opened the refrigerator door and stared into its belly.

"What? What?"

"Let the girl breathe, Ramona. She's tired and hungry." Mamá leaned against the counter.

Mamá was an older version of Cecilia—petite, caramel skin, large brown eyes, but with silky, long gray hair fashioned in a bun at the nape of her neck. Tía Ramona was the opposite—soft and round, huggable like a stuffed toy, with dark eyes framed by curly white hair.

Cecilia selected a raspberry yogurt from the back of the refrigerator, then sat across from Tía Ramona. "My thesis proposal is due January seventh. An impossible deadline."

"You work hard. You study. You do what you always do—make us proud." Tía Ramona gathered the garlic cloves with the knife and plopped them into a bowl.

"Ay, Ramona. You don't understand," Mamá chided. "This is terrible. *Mi'ja*, what are you going to do?"

Mamá's kind tone brought tears to her eyes. The tightness in her shoulders threatened a headache. Cecilia lowered her head and focused on stirring her yogurt. No use worrying them.

"Those professors are terrible. Don't they know it is Christmas? *Ateos.* That's what they all are, ateos." Tía Ramona banged the edge of the knife on the cutting board.

"Ya, they can't all be atheists. Some of them must believe in

God, and if they don't, when they read my little girl's paper, they will know the God we serve." Mamá opened the oven door and bent to check the roast chicken.

"Pues, mujer." Tía Ramona motioned with the knife to catch Mamá's attention. "Let's tell Ceci the news."

"What news?" Cecilia looked up.

"Elias Perez is in New York." Tía Ramona exploded with the news.

Cecilia's eyes widened, and the spoon paused on its way to her mouth.

"He's going to be the new youth pastor at church. Isn't that wonderful?" Mamá finished for Tía Ramona, still not looking at Cecilia.

The spoon reached Cecilia's mouth, but she tasted nothing. Elias, her best friend. They had shared everything. When one of them got a dollar, they'd go to the corner grocery store, *bodega*, and splurge on one ice cream pop and bag of chips for each. Elias loved the barbeque-flavored chips, while Cecilia preferred the garlic. Then his mother, running away from the harsh winters, decided to move to Florida when he was ten. Even after the move, they shared phone calls, letters, and e-mails. He knew her better than anyone until the Peter disaster, when she became a fool.

"It's a good job for him. He would know how to comfort others, since he was so sick as a boy." Mamá turned from the oven to look at her.

Cecilia couldn't meet Mamá's gaze. She stared into the yogurt container.

"His asthma was so bad. *Bendito.* It seemed like they lived in the emergency room." Tía Ramona shook her head.

"You remember, Ceci, how you and Elias would read the same book, then spend hours and hours e-mailing about it?" Mamá pointed the spoon at Cecilia.

Cecilia nodded, not trusting her voice to respond.

"It's a miracle he's still alive today. Yes. A miracle," Tía Ramona added.

Cecilia scraped the bottom of the yogurt container and took her last spoonful. Her day had just gone from bad to worse. After what she'd done to Elias, she didn't know how she would face him.

❄

Cecilia held open the heavy metal door for Tía Ramona and Mamá to enter the church. She heard the congregation singing and wished she hadn't taken so long to choose her outfit. Tonight was Christmas Eve. She'd wanted to wear something fancy, festive, while also understated. And that was the problem. Nothing in her wardrobe worked. Cecilia settled on a short black velvet dress with a full skirt and a satin bow at the waist. Tía Ramona and Mamá had waited patiently, watching her with very smug smiles. Yes, they were right. If she had to face Elias, she wanted to look her best. She had changed a lot since the last time he saw her, even more since the last time they'd communicated. She remembered him skinny, with dark circles under his eyes, wayward hair, and an ever-present smile. She wondered how he remembered her: probably selfish, silly, and snobby. Thank goodness she wasn't that girl anymore.

Holding on to all their coats, Cecilia followed Tía Ramona

and Mamá down the aisle toward their favorite seats near the front. The sanctuary was dressed for the holiday. The round steel columns that supported the large open space were wrapped in gold and burgundy rope. Two huge poinsettias sat on the platform, one on each side of the pulpit. A deep burgundy banner embroidered in gold with a crown and cross was draped over the pulpit.

Cecilia sat between Tía Ramona and Mamá and tucked their coats under each chair. She pulled out her hymnal and checked the large screen against the back wall of the platform for the page number of the hymn. She closed her eyes and sang the chorus "O come, let us adore Him" from one of her favorite Christmas carols.

"Have you seen him?" Tía Ramona whispered and nudged Cecilia with her elbow.

She shook her head and wiped her sweaty palms against her skirt.

As the pianist began to play a second hymn, Cecilia scanned the room, trying not to be conspicuous. She couldn't very well keep turning around to search for Elias.

The worship leader asked the congregation to rise for the reading of the Word. Cecilia tried to listen to the familiar Christmas story from the book of Luke, but her mind jumped from thought to thought. Elias a pastor. Still hard for her to accept even though Mamá and Tía Ramona believed he was suited for the role. And he probably was. She'd just never imagined him becoming a spiritual leader. The memories ran like a movie. Elias and her at the cloisters acting out the story of *La Cucarachita Martina*. Elias, pale as flour, tucked in bed and not allowed to play. Cecilia sneaking him a book so he wouldn't be too bored. And the worst memory of all—the day she severed their friendship.

She sat down, and the senior pastor announced that a guest soloist would sing for the offertory. A tall, well-built young man with curly black hair stepped up to the podium, took the microphone, and with confidence, faced the congregation. The recorded music track started, and the young man closed his eyes and sang. He sang about Mary watching over her newborn, angels announcing the birth, and Jesus, the Light of the world. Every note drew Cecilia in. The voice wrapped itself around her heart. She could feel the singer's passion.

Mamá closed her eyes. Tía Ramona's mouth hung open. Cecilia sat transfixed. When the song ended, there was a moment of quiet, and then the congregation burst forth in praise. The young man, with head bowed, put the microphone back in its stand. Pastor Romero stood beside him. "God worked a miracle in this young man's life and has directed his steps to bring him back home." Pastor Romero put his arm over the young man's shoulders. "Let's welcome our new youth pastor, Elias Perez."

Cecilia stopped breathing and watched this strong, vibrant man of God smile. And there was no mistaking him. There stood Elias, the friend she'd rejected.

Chapter 2

The congregation mobbed Elias as soon as the service ended. Everyone wanted to welcome the new, handsome youth pastor. Everyone except Cecilia. With her coat draped over her arm, she turned toward the back of the sanctuary.

Children, free of their mothers' restraint, spread throughout the sanctuary playing hide-and-seek. The girls in their velvet dresses and patent leather Mary Janes. The boys with shirts trailing below their sweater vests and clip-on ties about to drop from their collars. They knew tomorrow was Christmas. Actually, in just a few hours, Christmas Day would dawn.

Cecilia reached the back of the sanctuary and turned to see if she could spot Mamá or Tía Ramona. Fighting not to glance toward the platform, her eyes found Elias anyway. People hadn't even allowed him to reach the first row of chairs before they'd clustered around him like a flock of sheep. He looked so different and yet the same. No longer skinny, he looked as if he had well-developed muscles under his black suit jacket. She recognized the wavy black hair, though not the confident stance.

Hermana Olga, a deaconess in the church since Cecilia could remember, wrapped Elias in a hug that almost toppled him. Cecilia smiled. She knew what that felt like. When Hermana Olga was happy, everyone around got smothered. Elias emerged from the hug laughing out loud. The joyous ring reached her all the way in the back.

Her heart hurt. She'd love to renew their friendship, but she didn't know if that was possible now. She wondered if he'd forgiven her.

Before she turned to pass through the doors out of the sanctuary, she caught a glimpse of Mamá greeting Elias. Cecilia froze, one hand against the door, ready to swing it open, and the other hand strangling her purse.

Elias lifted Mamá up in a bear hug. When he placed her back down, he kissed both of her cheeks. A chuckle slipped out of Cecilia. Her hand dropped from the door.

Mamá swatted Elias's arm and giggled. He must be teasing her. Cecilia took two steps toward them.

Mamá and Elias glanced around the sanctuary as though looking for someone. Cecilia's stomach dropped, and she about-faced like a soldier.

"Where are you going?" Tía Ramona gripped Cecilia's elbow and dragged her toward the platform.

"Tía, ya, ya. *Sueltame.*" Cecilia begged to be released. It wouldn't do to have it look as if Tía Ramona forced her to meet Elias. She tried to walk with her chin up, even while Tía Ramona still held her elbow in a vise grip. As her aunt led her down the aisle, she searched for the right words of greeting.

Please forgive me. I was an infatuated fool. I turned myself inside out for Peter, and you got in the way. Peter didn't like our friendship. And I needed to please him.

They reached the platform. Tía Ramona nudged her forward. Mamá, with a proud smile on her face, drew her close. Dutifully, Cecilia smiled at Elias. His smile lit his eyes. She took one step toward him and found herself in his arms, lifted off the ground.

"Ceci," he whispered in her ear before he settled her back on earth.

Catching her breath proved difficult. But the smile on her face was true.

Tía Ramona wanted to know his plans for tomorrow. *"Muchacho, ¿que haces mañana?"*

"Pues, no se. . ." Elias didn't quite know yet.

"Come over. Evelyn, Sammy, and the boys will be there. It's Christmas; you need to be with family." Tía Ramona and Mamá nodded in agreement.

"Sounds wonderful. I'd love to."

Pastor Romero came up behind Elias. "Sorry, ladies, but I have to steal him away."

Waving Elias and Pastor Romero off, Tía Ramona reminded Elias, "You remember where we live, *¿verdad?*"

Elias graced them with his brilliant smile. *"Hasta mañana."* Then he followed Pastor Romero.

❄

On Christmas morning, Cecilia lay in bed. She stretched her arms above her head, and hit the wall. Someday she'd get herself a real headboard, not one painted on the wall. The coolness of the sheet felt wonderful, and Cecilia burrowed deeper. No use rushing out of bed. The gifts wouldn't be opened until after dinner. She should work on some research now, before the apartment became a madhouse of people. Instead, she covered her head with the comforter.

The slacks and turtleneck would not do for tonight. Too boring. She needed to look festive, casual, and pretty. Last night Elias had felt so strong—his chest hard and muscular when he lifted her up. A delightful surprise.

A shiver ran through her. She threw the comforter aside and sat up in bed. No more silly infatuations that left her hurting and feeling empty. She didn't have time for relationships. She had serious scholarly work to do. Besides, he was just being kind last night. He probably didn't want to have anything to do with her. When he came today, she would act nonchalant. She could play it cool just like him. And for that the slacks and turtleneck were fine.

❄

The smell of fried *alcapurrias* and *empanadas* soaked the air. It wouldn't be Christmas without the dark meat patties made of *güineo* and the light ones made with a flour pastry shell.

"Why does Evelyn always have to be so late?" Cecilia attempted, for the fourth time, to steal an alcapurria from the mound cooling in the colander on the stove.

Mamá swatted her hand away. "Wait for the company."

"I'm starving." Cecilia dropped into a chair.

Tía Ramona bustled into the kitchen. "I can't find anything. We'll have to send Ceci out."

"Ramona, just find something." Mamá wiped her brow with the crook of her arm.

"I've looked everywhere. We only have extra gifts for women, not for a young man. We need something for Elias." Tía Ramona stood at the kitchen door with her hands on her hips. "Ceci, you have to go and get him a gift, right now."

"Give him one of Sammy's gifts." She didn't want to venture out into the neighborhood on Christmas Day. Nothing would be open but the local bodega. And what could she buy there? Soda? Milk? Bread? Great Christmas gifts for the new youth pastor.

"Sammy is twice Elias's size, and all I got him is clothes." Tía Ramona punctuated her sentence with taps on the door frame. "I should have bought cologne. Then I'd have something for Elias."

"Ramona, just find something. I'm hot, and I want to finish all this frying." Mamá wiped the sweat off her brow again and leaned against the stove.

"Don't worry, Mamá. I think I can find a book in my room for him." Cecilia got up from the chair.

"*Eso es.* Perfect idea. You both loved reading when you were young." Tía Ramona stepped back to let Cecilia pass.

The doorbell rang. Cecilia went to open the door, Tía Ramona right behind her.

Evelyn stood at the door, burdened with a diaper bag, three shopping bags brimming with wrapped gifts, and her nine-month-old girl. Her six-year-old son squeezed past his mother and Cecilia, holding on to his little brother's hand. They both wrapped their arms around Tía Ramona's legs. Cecilia took baby Sonia from Evelyn and stepped back to let her enter the apartment.

"My boys. My wonderful boys," Tía Ramona kept repeating as she hugged each of her grandsons.

Evelyn walked into Cecilia's room and dumped her diaper bag on the bed and the shopping bags on the rug. Then she left to hang up her wool coat.

Cecilia laid the baby on the foot of her bed and started to disentangle her from the snowsuit. After adjusting pillows around baby Sonia to protect her from rolling off the bed, Cecilia turned to her bookcase to find a suitable gift for Elias. Her eyes scanned the titles. Most were textbooks; he didn't need those. Others were Spanish titles. She didn't even know if he read Spanish literature. Better to be safe and pick something else. She glanced at her old toy chest at the end of her bed. She should have given it away years ago, but it held her favorite childhood books. Maybe an old favorite of theirs would be appropriate. Something that reminded him of the moments they'd shared when he was too sick to play outside, the moments they'd dreamed they were the characters in the story. Something that reminded him of the time before she told him she loved another.

Yes, she knew just the story she'd give him. They often playacted the scenes in her room, but best were the scenes at the cloisters, where a real courtyard set the stage. She'd give him her treasured copy of *La Cucarachita Martina*. Kneeling before the toy chest, she dug deep to find the picture book by Rosario Ferré. She'd wrap it and tuck it under the tree. The perfect gift.

Cecilia sat on the area rug in the living room with Sonia on her lap. The gifts from Tía Ramona, Mamá, and Cecilia were under the tree, hidden behind Evelyn's shopping bags full of gifts. The lights decorating the fire escape flashed through the window.

Sonia bounced up and down on Cecilia's lap. If Cecilia wasn't careful, she'd soon have a stomachache from the two alcapurrias and three empanadas she'd stuffed herself with. What a glutton she became during the holidays. Still, she looked forward to eating the roast pork, rice with pigeon peas, and pasteles.

The doorbell rang, and Cecilia jumped up, almost dropping Sonia.

"Hey, that's my only daughter you're manhandling there." Evelyn took Sonia from Cecilia's arms. "Who are you waiting for?" She arched an eyebrow.

"No one. Nothing." Flustered, Cecilia stopped one of the boys running past and gave him a hug. He wrestled himself out of her grasp and ran off.

"Yeah, right." Evelyn turned toward the kitchen and yelled, "Mami, who else is coming to dinner?"

Tía Ramona entered the living room, wiping her hands on her apron. "I forgot to tell you, Elias Perez is the new youth pastor at church. You remember him?"

Evelyn glanced back at Cecilia and smiled broadly. "Really? Remind me again, who is he?"

Cecilia sat back down and busied herself rearranging the gifts under the tree.

"You remember, the son of Isabel Perez . . ."

"Who's getting the door?" Cecilia interrupted Tía Ramona.

"Calm down, Professor." Evelyn winked. "Mario went to get it."

Cecilia's hands felt sweaty. She rubbed them against her pants. Everyone trooped out to the front hallway to greet Elias, leaving Cecilia alone in the living room. Cecilia heard his laugh. She got up from the floor and entered the hallway.

The noise level rose a notch higher as the boys chanted, *"Feliz Navidad."* Evelyn yelled for them to be quiet. And Mario bellowed, "Welcome to Christmas in the Montes household!"

She caught a glimpse of curly black hair, and her heart sped up. Within the next minute she found herself in his strong arms again. And it felt wonderful and scary, exciting and painful.

"Ceci, make sure to take Elias's coat." Tía Ramona brought Cecilia back to her senses.

Everyone returned to the living room, leaving them alone in the hallway.

Not trusting herself, Cecilia stepped out of the embrace. "I'll take your coat."

"Ceci, you look twenty times better than I remembered you," Elias said.

Cecilia took his coat, avoiding his gaze. She could feel the red creeping up her neck. Lucky she had worn a turtleneck. Now. She needed to ask for his forgiveness now.

Mamá stepped into the hallway. "Elias, come into the living room."

Without another glance at her, he walked away. When Cecilia returned to the living room, she found Elias with Sonia on his lap, contentedly playing with her feet.

"So Mami tells me you're the new youth pastor. How did that happen?" Evelyn tugged at Sonia's dress.

So the grilling had already begun. Cecilia didn't want to be a part of it. She attempted to leave, but Mario stopped her. "You're not going anywhere," he muttered under his breath. Then, with a hand against her back, he directed her to a seat on the sofa.

"Well, I'd wanted to get back to New York for some time—"

"Really? Why? Didn't Florida appeal to you?" Evelyn interrupted.

"Actually, I missed the hustle and bustle of New York."

"Is that all you missed?"

Sammy entered the room and threw himself on the love seat. "Hey, *El Ratoncito*!"

"I'd forgotten all about that." Tía Ramona followed with Sammy's two-year-old son in hand. She pushed him toward his father. The redheaded boy climbed onto Sammy's lap, kissed his cheek, climbed back down, and ran off.

"Ceci, you used to call Elias, El Ratoncito, from the story. You know the old Puerto Rican folktale. You remember the name of the book?" Tía Ramona yelled to Mamá in the kitchen.

Mamá yelled back, *"La Cucarachita Martina."*

Cecilia swallowed hard; her mouth felt dry.

The book! She couldn't give it to him now. She'd never hear the end of it with this crazy family.

"Elias, did you know we have a college graduate here?" Mario patted Cecilia's shoulder. "She's the first in the family to get a college degree. Do youth pastors have college degrees?"

She jabbed Mario hard with her elbow.

"Not only a college degree, but she's finishing her master's, at Columbia no less. Tell him, mi'ja," Mamá called from the kitchen.

"Cool. I'd love to hear all about it." Elias shifted Sonia from his lap to lean her over his shoulder.

The boys' howling erupted in the hallway. Evelyn didn't move a muscle. Tía Ramona flew out to negotiate peace.

"So—left any girlfriends in Miami?" Evelyn asked.

"Actually, I lived in Orlando, and I only left my mom."

Cecilia tugged her earlobe, trying to calm herself. Earthquakes. Why weren't there any in New York? One about now would be perfect.

She pinched Mario's arm to free herself and got up. "Let me see if Mamá needs some help with dinner."

Evelyn jumped up. "Here. I'll go." She pushed Cecilia down on the sofa near Elias. The minute Sonia saw her, she reached out her tiny arms and whimpered.

"She knows you." Elias passed the baby over. Their hands brushed against each other, and heat rose to her face.

Cecilia hid her face in Sonia's neck and drank in the heavenly scent of baby powder.

"So back to you, Elias. What are your plans?" Sammy asked.

"Well, for the next few days, I'll be running around the city with a group of teenagers, making sure they're busy during the Christmas break and keeping them out of trouble. I need to figure out how we'll get around. The last time I was here, I was ten years old, and I don't remember much—other than dirty subways and slow buses."

"Well, the subways are much better now, but the buses are still slow." Mario laughed.

"I can get you a subway map. That should help," Sammy said.

"*Que* subway map *y* subway map. Cecilia is off from school. She knows how to travel all over the city. She'll help you out. What are friends and family for?" Tía Ramona boomed from the kitchen.

How did Tía Ramona always know every conversation, even when she wasn't in the room? She was supposed to be minding the *loco* tribe of boys.

"Wow." Elias smiled, and a hopeful look shone in his eyes. "That would be such a help. Do you think you could?"

She couldn't deny him. "Sure, why not?"

Evelyn returned to the living room with a tray of alcapurrias. Sammy lunged for it, and she deftly swept it toward Elias. "Guests first."

"Ah—he's no guest; he's just little Elias."

Elias took a napkin from the tray and wrapped the alcapurria in it. Then he closed his eyes as he took a bite. "Mmm. The best in town."

"Cecilia knows how to make them just as good." Evelyn offered a meat patty to her husband.

"Really?" Elias smiled at Cecilia. "Smart *and* she can cook. I'm impressed. Any boyfriends hanging around?"

"Oh, please. Ceci doesn't get her nose out of a book long enough to know there's a world outside." Sammy reached for a second alcapurria. "Hey, weren't you sick all the time?"

"Sammy!" Evelyn knocked him on the head.

"Well, he was, right?" Sammy ducked just in case Evelyn attempted another smack.

Cecilia closed her eyes, tempted to pray for a tornado with big swirling winds and powerful rain to stop the madness and save her.

Elias laughed. "Yeah. I was one sick dude. But God changed all that. I asked Him to heal me, and He did."

Sammy leaned toward Elias. "Just like that. You asked and it happened?"

"Pretty much. I'd been reading my Bible, and I saw how Jesus healed the blind man. And I thought, healing asthma is easier than blindness. So that night, I prayed, and then I went to sleep. When I woke up the next morning, I felt as if my lungs had grown. They felt bigger inside." Elias motioned to his chest. "I took a deep breath." He lowered his head and shook it.

They all focused on Elias. Cecilia's heart swelled, and she sensed the presence of the Holy Spirit.

"I'll never forget how that first deep breath felt. I can't describe it. But I felt free, new, open, strong."

No one moved. The sounds from the street filtered into the room.

"Well, there's no denying, you look like a different man," Sammy admitted.

"Thanks. I think."

Everyone laughed.

❄

The boys gathered in front of the Christmas tree and clamored for their gifts. Little Sonia slept in Cecilia's room. Mamá gave

Cecilia the honor of distributing their gifts. Stepping over the boys carefully, she dug behind Evelyn's shopping bags for her gifts, wrapped in silver and blue. She handed out a gift to each boy and placed Sonia's gift at Evelyn's feet. They watched the boys tear apart the wrapping and exclaim over their gifts.

"Now it's the adults' turn." Evelyn motioned for Cecilia to give out the other gifts.

"Shouldn't Sammy give out his gifts to the boys first? Then we'll do the adults all at once afterward."

Loud protest rose all around.

"Why you changing tradition, Ceci? Give me my gift," Mario shouted over the mayhem.

She didn't know how she'd get away with not giving Elias a gift.

"Evelyn, hope you like it." Resigned, Cecilia handed over a dress box.

"Sammy, tell me if it's the wrong size." She passed him a shirt box, then handed Mario a similar box. "You, too, Mario."

"Tía Ramona. Your gift and Mamá's are connected." She gave Mamá and Tía Ramona an envelope. Inside were tickets for the next premiere at the Sight & Sound Theatre in Lancaster. Cecilia hugged Mamá and then Tía Ramona, hoping no one noticed that Elias hadn't received a gift. She settled herself on the arm of the chair where Sammy sat, then called out, "Mario and Evelyn, you're next."

Mario extricated himself from the sofa and tiptoed over the boys. He reached for a shopping bag, dug in, and came up with Cecilia's gift for Elias. He scrutinized the gift. "Honey, is this ours?"

Evelyn stopped gathering loose wrapping paper from the floor and looked up. "No. Read the label."

Cecilia sat frozen.

"Hey, it's for you, Elias. You are not forgotten." Mario handed the gift to Elias.

With Mamá standing in the door leading to the hallway and Elias by the other door that led to Mamá's bedroom, Cecilia had no escape.

Everyone's attention was on Elias. He unwrapped the gift and burst out laughing. He held the picture book high for everyone to see.

Heat rose from the back of Cecilia's neck and spread all over her face.

The boys caught sight of the book, dropped their toys, and crowded around Elias. Each one demanded to have the book read aloud. Elias assured them he'd read it during dessert. Then he made his way to Mamá and thanked her with a kiss. He did the same to Tía Ramona, and then he stood in front of Cecilia.

He leaned down and kissed her cheek. The boys sent up a loud, "Ooh." No one but Cecilia heard Elias's next words, "*Gracias*, Cucarachita Martina."

Tornado, earthquake, rocket ship—nothing could rock her world more than Elias's tender, whispered words.

Chapter 3

During the entire walk from the subway station to Central Park, Elias had been surrounded by a bevy of teenage girls. Their high-pitched giggles grated on Cecilia's nerves. Once they arrived at the ice-skating rink, she stayed busy getting the group their rented skates.

After helping several novice skaters tie their skates, Cecilia finally tightened the laces of her own. Everyone was on the ice except for the pixie attached to Elias.

"Pastor Perez, come on. I'll help you." The girl couldn't have been more than fifteen years old, but she hadn't left Elias's side.

Well, she'd let Elias extricate himself from the cloying hands of that smart cookie.

Cecilia stepped onto the ice. The fierce wind at her back propelled her, making her feel as if she could fly through the air. Last night had been so much fun. Elias had her whole family wrapped around his pinkie. Even the loco boys fell under his spell and actually acted civilized during dessert. All because Elias promised to read them the picture book she had given him.

As she made the turn and faced the wind, all freedom dissolved. Instead, the wind pressed against her. She wanted to stop and sit right on the ice. Only the thought of losing face in front of all these teenagers kept her skating.

Four spins around the rink and Elias still loitered by the gate with his little admirer right beside him. Cecilia waved as she skated past. Elias lifted his hand as she approached, a pleading look on his face. His waving hand became more vigorous as she passed, and she realized, too late, that he'd probably wanted her to stop.

On the next turn she slowed down. Sure enough, like a drowning man, he waved from the sidelines. Cecilia scraped some ice into the air as she came to a halt in front of them.

"Show-off."

"Who—*moi?*" Cecilia gave him her wide-eyed innocent gaze.

"Why don't you put your skills to good use and teach me how to skate?" He winked.

The pixie next to him grabbed his arm. "But I said I could teach you."

"If I fell, I'd crush you, and your mother would have my neck. So don't worry, Laura. Ms. Cecilia here will take care of me." His eyes pleaded with her. "Won't you?"

Muffling a laugh, Cecilia nodded. Then she turned to look at the skaters in the rink. "Mira, Sara, y Altagracia are in the center making figure eights—why don't you join them?"

With a sad backward glance, Laura skated toward the girls, deftly avoiding crashing into anyone.

"Well. *Pastor* Elias, you certainly seem to have a lot of admirers."

With an arched eyebrow, Elias asked, "Are you one of them?"

Cecilia rolled her eyes. "Please, I knew you when, remember?"

"I'm glad to hear it. Because I definitely remember." His eyes pierced her with their intensity.

The air between them thickened. She didn't want to know what he remembered. Yet she'd missed him—terribly. If there wasn't a broad wooden barrier between them, she wondered if she'd find herself in his arms again.

Then Elias broke the gaze and shrugged. "Are you going to teach me or not?"

"You're kidding, right?" Cecilia tried to match his tone, not letting on how shaken she felt.

"Uh. . .no." Sidestepping, Elias approached the edge of the ice.

He acted as if everything was fine between them. As if she hadn't dropped him like excess baggage just because Peter said so. As if he hadn't warned her that Peter was bad news. And she'd yelled that he was just jealous. Jealous that it wasn't him she was in love with.

But if he wanted to act as if it was all water under the bridge, she would, too.

"Stop. Wait." Cecilia held up her hands. "I'm no bigger than Laura. You could crush me, too, you know."

"Ah, stop stalling, and let's get this show on the road." He stepped onto the ice, wobbled, and grabbed Cecilia's jacket, then they both fell with a thump. Cecilia landed smack across Elias's back. She tried to get her footing, but Elias squirmed.

"Stop moving and let me get up."

"That's what I'm trying to do."

Her skates found sure footing, and she lifted herself up, then bent to help Elias. Between her and the ice-skating rink security guard, they got Elias on his feet and back to the railing.

"That ice is cold."

"No kidding, Sherlock." Cecilia wiped snow off her pants. "Next time wait for me, okay?"

"You slow, you blow."

A laugh burst out of Cecilia. She couldn't help it. This guy was too much. He never let up. "Okay, Scott Hamilton, let's try this."

Holding both of his hands and skating backwards, Cecilia guided Elias through the first spin around the rink, never far from the railing. Both concentrated on not falling again.

As the teens skated past, one laughed and called out, "Gonna hurt in the morning, Pastor." Another said, "Need a paramedic, anyone?" And a third yelled, "How's that back, Ms. Cecilia?"

By the third spin, Elias became bolder and skated along the railing alone. Cecilia trailed right behind him. Then she felt her cell phone vibrate in her coat pocket.

"Elias, I have to stop a minute." She skated to the next gate and stepped out. With careful steps she made her way to a wooden bench and pulled out her cell phone. The caller ID flashed a number she didn't immediately recognize.

Elias followed her out of the rink, and she watched him wobble his way to her.

"Hello." She closed her opposite ear with her finger to better hear the caller.

Elias flopped down on the bench beside her. "My feet are throbbing."

Cecilia tried to concentrate on her call. "Who is this?"

"Andres, your study partner. The one you're meeting tomorrow in the library."

"Tomorrow?"

Elias interjected. "Hey, don't make any plans for tomorrow. You're supposed to go with me and the kids to Riverside Church."

She lifted her hand to make Elias be quiet.

"I'm just saying, you know, you promised," Elias continued.

Cecilia turned away and put her finger in her ear to block out Elias. "Andres, *perdoname*, but I'm helping out with the youth at church, and I just don't see how I can make it tomorrow."

Still she heard Elias's singsong. "Too bad. So sorry, Andres. *Andresito*."

Incorrigible. And he called himself a pastor.

"How about Saturday?" Andres proposed.

Cecilia struggled to hear Andres's voice, but Elias kept humming his too-bad-so-sorry song, distracting her.

"Hey, Cecilia, where are you? It sounds really noisy. Did I catch you at a bad time?"

"Yeah, I'm with these teenagers now."

"So what do you say about Saturday?"

"Yeah, sure, Saturday. See ya." Before she shut the phone, she turned a fierce glare on Elias. "Will you grow up?"

"Who—moi?" Elias feigned innocence.

All she could do was slap his shoulder and grin. "Let's go chaperone these kids."

❄

The hot water soothed her aching feet, the blisters at her ankles a testimony of her ability to ignore pain. Cecilia sat in the kitchen while Mamá prepared her a cup of hot chocolate. Tía Ramona was in Jersey babysitting Evelyn's brood.

"You should have worn double socks," Mamá accused.

"I did."

Mamá sighed as she poured the hot chocolate into a cup and brought it to the table. Gathering her skirt and apron, she sat opposite Cecilia. "How did it go?"

"Not much to tell. The girls have fallen in love with Elias and won't let him breathe. It was really cold and windy, but I think everyone had a good time." She sipped her hot chocolate.

Mamá jumped out of her chair and ran from the room. *"Se me olvido."*

What did she forget? Usually when she dashed like that, it was into the kitchen, not out. Mostly it was because she'd left the oven on or the coffee brewing or the water running.

Mamá walked back into the kitchen with a small FedEx package. "This came for you earlier."

Cecilia frowned. She didn't know who would send her a package. Except for Tío Hiram, Tía Ramona's husband, who lived in Puerto Rico and never remembered to send any gifts, even to his own grandchildren.

Cecilia took another sip of hot chocolate and examined the return address: Mikasa, a Fine China Store.

Mamá handed her a butter knife. The white cardboard box gave nothing away regarding its contents. Cecilia carefully slit the ends of the box open.

"*Ya muchacha, abre.*" Mamá clapped her hands in exasperation. Cecilia took too long to open the surprise gift.

Within the square box stuffed with white tissue paper lay a clear, prism-cut pear and a small card authenticating the contents as quality crystal. No name. No signature.

"*¡Ay que bello!*" Mamá exclaimed at its beauty.

Cecilia lifted the pear from the box and held it up for a closer inspection. Light sparkled off the pear and reflected across the kitchen wall. "Who could have sent this?"

Chapter 4

"Mamá!" Cecilia had been trying all morning to get her computer to boot up with no success. Postponing her research was not an option. She had to get some work done today before she met up with Elias and the youth at Riverside Church.

She slammed the mouse on the table.

"Nice way to treat your things, young lady." Mamá stood at the door.

"Ma, the last time I worked on my computer was Christmas morning, and everything was fine. Now look. Look! The screen is black!"

The sound of the door locks turning announced Tía Ramona's arrival from Jersey.

"Hello, hello." Tía Ramona, still wearing her coat and hat, peeked into the bedroom. "Did anyone miss me?"

Cecilia gave Tía Ramona a peck on the cheek. "How are the loco boys?"

Tía Ramona raised her eyebrows at Mamá as if to say,

What is she talking about? "Oh, by the way, look what I found outside the door when I came in." She opened her gloved hand to reveal a small brown paper bag with Cecilia's name scribbled on it and tied with a thin red ribbon.

Cecilia took the package and turned it over, looking for a return address or any indication of the sender.

"Open it, muchacha." Tía Ramona tapped her elbow.

Cecilia undid the ribbon, unfolded the paper flap, and found two small Dove chocolate candy bars inside. No note. No name.

"I love these!"

"They are hers, Ramona. Don't start salivating for the candy." Mamá pushed past Tía Ramona to exit the room.

Cecilia gave a chocolate bar to Tía Ramona and called after Mamá, "You can have the other one, Mamá."

Down the hallway, Mamá called back, "No, you enjoy it."

Cecilia unwrapped the Dove chocolate bar and bit off a piece.

"Just melts, doesn't it?" Tía Ramona savored her piece. "Well, I'm sweating in this coat. Let me get it off." She walked to her bedroom.

Cecilia turned back into her room and saw that her clock radio flashed 12:19. "Oh no! I'm going to be late for the hand-bell concert."

❄

Cecilia ran up the subway stairs out onto West 116th and Broadway. She waited for the traffic light to change in front of Columbia University. The sight of the gates reminded her of the work she hadn't completed that morning. Her chest tightened. If she didn't get this proposal finished in time, she wouldn't graduate and would disappoint everyone.

Shaking her head, she scolded herself for worrying over the small setback. Tomorrow she'd go to the library and get some work done for sure.

Crossing Claremont Avenue toward Riverside Drive, she glanced at her watch. The handbell concert had already begun, so she picked up her pace. She hoped Elias had managed the group without too much trouble. She rushed past distinguished buildings festooned with evergreen wreaths.

Finally, she saw the Gothic tower with the bell carillon. When those bells pealed, poetry sprang to her mind. Like Tennyson's *Ring out, wild bells, to the wild sky. . . . Ring out the darkness of the land. . . .*

The entrance into the nave always made Cecilia's heart settle down as the sanctity and quiet reverence enveloped her. Arches and flying buttresses and the majestic stained glass windows made her feel as if she'd entered the Holy of Holies. Cecilia took off her coat and tiptoed down the long center aisle. She spotted her group near the front to the left and headed in that direction, hoping to slip in quietly behind them.

The handbells resounded throughout the sanctuary. She spotted Elias's curly black hair and Laura sitting alone in the row behind him. Laura looked different today—shrunken, like a snail hiding inside its shell. Cecilia slipped into the pew beside her.

The unfamiliar music couldn't be Bach or Mozart. The jarring melody confirmed it was a modern piece. Glancing about, she identified her kids, disappointed that only twelve had shown up, but then a handbell concert wasn't as much fun as ice-skating. Yet she agreed with Elias—these kids needed to be exposed to all areas of life.

Laura shivered beside her, even though the room wasn't cold. Cecilia offered Laura her coat, but Laura shook her head, never glancing her way.

Elias turned around and winked. The hairs on her arms stood on end. She rubbed them down.

She was glad he wasn't upset that she'd been late. But she wanted him to know she was responsible and reliable. She'd explain about her computer problem and her need to finish her research later. Then she remembered the anonymous Dove chocolates she'd received that morning.

Toward the end of their relationship, Peter had become almost a stalker. She hoped he didn't intend to come back into her life. She wasn't the same naive girl anymore.

The resounding applause indicated that the concert had ended. Elias gathered the group off to the left side of the church. He stood beside a famous painting by Heinrich Hofmann that depicted Christ in Gethsemane. Elias expounded on the painting, pointing out the agony Christ suffered.

Cecilia's heart grew heavy as she watched Laura hovering at the edge of the group instead of pressing close to Elias as she had yesterday. Something was obviously bothering her. The change from one day to the next was too radical for Cecilia to ignore. She'd have to find out what was going on with her.

❄

"Mamá, did Sammy say he could fix the computer?" Cecilia

handed Mamá a flat bronze platter filled with broken pieces of matzo bread. She was in the church basement kitchen helping Mamá complete the communion preparations for tomorrow's service. She had to get to the library today.

"*Ay. Perdoname.* I forgot to ask him." Mamá put the platter on top of another similarly prepared. "But we can call him now. Get my cell phone."

"There's no reception down here. Let's wait till we get upstairs." Cecilia gathered the extra matzo bread sheets and tucked them into the cardboard box. "Anything left to do?"

Mamá covered the bronze communion set with a delicately embroidered white linen cloth. "No. We're all finished. I know you want to get to the library."

"Here, let me carry that. It's heavy." Cecilia took the tall communion set and turned toward the refrigerator. They'd already filled two hundred tiny communion cups with grape juice.

"Ceci, what was in the bag I found with the morning *Daily News*?" Mamá opened the refrigerator door for Cecilia.

"Three little hens. You know, the ones you find in the ninety-nine-cent store." Cecilia slipped the communion set onto an empty shelf.

"Candy, then hens. What is going on here?" Mamá put the bottle of grape juice in the refrigerator and the box of matzo bread in the cupboard. Then she followed Cecilia up the stairs.

"I think maybe one of the guys in the youth group might have a crush." Cecilia pushed open the door to the foyer. She didn't want to worry Mamá with her real suspicions. Cecilia crossed the foyer, then stopped at the sanctuary doors and peeked through the glass window. She saw streams of sunlight from the side windows puncture the darkness.

"Mamá, the table is bare."

"I'll get the tablecloth." Mamá returned to the basement.

Cecilia entered the sanctuary to rest in a chair. In the dark, empty church, the silence felt like the Gothic reverence of Riverside Church. God's presence permeated her. *Lord, help Laura. Bring someone into her life who will point her to You.*

She heard a soft "Alleluia" followed by a "You are worthy," telling her that someone was in the sanctuary praying. Every muscle tense, so as not to make a sound, Cecilia rose from the chair to give that person the privacy he sought. Her eyes, accustomed to the dark by now, sought out the petitioner. On his knees, head bowed, Bible open at his side, was Elias.

Frozen in place, Cecilia watched. His praise reached her ears, and her heart hungered to join him. Instead, she turned and crept out of the sanctuary.

Mamá emerged from the basement door.

Cecilia blocked her way. "Elias is praying. We shouldn't disturb him."

"I have to set this up now. We'll be quiet." Mamá walked toward the sanctuary. Cecilia followed.

By the time they reached the front of the platform, Elias was on his feet, his back toward them, gathering his Bible from the floor.

"Hey, you can't work here without some lights on. Let me get them." Elias turned to face them, his eyes bloodshot and puffy.

She quickly glanced away, regretting that she'd interrupted such a private moment.

"Muchacho, *no te moleste*. I can manage fine with the sunlight in here." Mamá acted as if nothing was amiss.

"I'm going to call Sammy." Cecilia turned to leave the sanctuary.

"Wait. Help me here first." Mamá struggled to spread the tablecloth over the wide communion table.

"I can help." Elias dropped his Bible on the edge of the platform.

Cecilia rushed ahead of him, up the two steps to her mother's side. "No need." She pulled the tablecloth from the opposite end of the table.

Elias bent to pick up his Bible.

"Maybe Elias can help you, Ceci." Mamá pulled the tablecloth. "Her computer isn't working, and she needs it for school."

"Sure. You mentioned it yesterday. Sammy couldn't fix it?"

Bible tucked under his arm, he looked the full picture of a pastor.

"I forgot to call him. He's not very reliable, even when we can track him down." Mamá smoothed out the top of the tablecloth.

Cecilia had lost her voice. She didn't want to bother him with her small problems. Clearly he had other things on his mind.

"I can try. Let me get my coat, and I'll leave with you right now. They say a big snowstorm is coming. I can't wait. It's been so long since I've seen snow. I hope it doesn't wimp out."

Cecilia appreciated Elias's willingness to help, and she looked forward to spending time with him, but she couldn't help wondering what caused his tears. Her conscience pricked. She needed to set things straight between them.

❄

Mamá and Elias caught up on old family news during the walk from the church to the apartment. Cecilia felt grateful she didn't have to contribute. She needed some time to get herself together.

Inside the apartment, Mamá took Elias's coat and ushered him to the living room. Cecilia hurried to pick up her room. She only had time to dump the last of the clothes onto the closet floor. The piles of books on the floor were too important to her research to move and maybe misplace. At least the computer table looked neat. She could hear Mamá coming down the hallway, and within seconds Elias stood in the doorway.

Cecilia tried to control her blush. "Welcome to my humble abode."

Elias entered her room and leaned against the computer table. "Nothing like I remember. What happened to the balloon wallpaper?"

Mamá laughed. "I think, around twelve or thirteen, she told me she couldn't bear to live in circus land anymore."

Elias glanced her way with an arched eyebrow. She felt no need to defend herself. At twenty-three, she should not have balloons on her walls. "The computer needs help. Not my decor."

"Right. To the task at hand." Amusement lit his eyes as he turned and focused on the computer.

"I'll get some lunch ready." Mamá headed back to the kitchen.

Cecilia turned on the computer and the monitor. "You see, the light shows the computer is on, but the monitor is black."

On his knees, Elias started checking the plugs.

"I did that already." She sat on the edge of the bed.

"Doesn't hurt to check again." He shifted the desk.

Cecilia jumped to catch the monitor that almost toppled. "What are you doing?" Then she saw the flicker and the monitor screen lit.

Careful not to bump his head, Elias emerged from under the desk and shifted it back in place.

Cecilia sat on the edge of her bed. "Thank you, Elias. What did you do?"

He dusted off his jeans. "Be careful with your pencils." Then he flicked a tiny piece of lead onto the desk.

"Where was that?"

"Where it shouldn't have been." Elias held back a grin, then grabbed the half-eaten Dove chocolate bar from her desk. "You know, you keep candy in your room, you're inviting roaches." With one bite the candy bar disappeared.

With her eyes wide open, Cecilia yelled, "That was mine!"

"You snooze, you lose." Turning on his heel, he walked out of the room.

She smiled to herself; some things didn't change. Elias stealing her candy was one of them.

"Ceci, come have lunch," Mamá called.

She could smell the sweet fried plantains. They'd taste great with eggs over easy. She glanced at the clock, grateful she still had an hour before she had to meet Andres.

Cecilia couldn't believe how much Elias ate. Mamá beamed every time he asked for more. This was definitely not the boy she remembered. Her Elias rarely ate, and when he did, it was like a mouse, nibble by nibble.

The phone rang, and Mamá went to answer it. She heard Mamá hang up, then call Elias. *"Ven, muchacho. Mira esto."*

Elias left his seat and went to the living room. Cecilia followed and found both of them gazing out the window. She'd never seen such huge snowflakes. They looked like marshmallows.

"Qué maravilla," Elias whispered. A marvel. He stood behind Mamá, his hands on her shoulders.

Cecilia stood at another window. In just a few minutes, the street had a thin layer of white. The cars driving by left parallel black marks like lines on white paper. The awning of the bodega across the street collected a pile of snow. Pepe, the owner, came out and, using a broom, tapped the awning to empty it of the gathered snow.

"Let's go play." Elias grabbed her hand and pulled her toward the hallway.

Mamá sprang to the closet and pulled out coats, hats, scarves, and gloves. Before she caught her breath, Cecilia found herself wrapped for winter, running down the stairs, holding Elias's hand. Schoolwork would have to wait.

❄

Once out on the street, Cecilia felt awkward. She shook it off. Elias was her good friend, and they were going out to play. Without a word and maybe out of habit, they turned toward High Bridge Park. Elias spread out his arms, lifted his face to the sky, and welcomed the snowflakes.

Cecilia giggled. "You couldn't have missed them that much."

"You have no idea how many things I missed about New York." He sounded wistful.

"Like what?" She watched him try to catch a snowflake with his mouth. "You're going to crash into the lamppost." She pulled his arm to direct him away from the tall metal pole. "So what did you miss?"

They stopped at the corner. He turned his full gaze on her. Her heart raced. The intensity in his eyes made her feel as if he had volumes to tell. Yet he remained silent.

He'd never kissed her, but right now she wanted him to. She leaned closer as if some invisible force pulled her toward him. At the small, almost imperceptible movement, Elias's eyes clouded and he stepped back.

"Let's cross. I'll race you to the hill." Off he ran.

Cecilia ran after him with no intention of beating him. She needed to get her heart in order and exert some control over this body that did things all on its own. *Don't do it again. You don't need this complication. Infatuations are deadly.*

By the time she reached the snow-covered hillside, Elias lay flat on his back making snow angels. She plopped down beside him and made one of her own. "So how old *are* you?"

"Older than you."

"Puh-leeze. Twenty days is not much."

They lay on the ground feeling the fat snowflakes fall on their faces in companionable silence.

Elias spoke first. "Tell me about school."

"The best thing about school is that I'm almost done. All I have left is the thesis."

"What's your topic?"

"Epiphany. I'm documenting how Puerto Ricans carry on their cultural celebrations in the States, using this holiday as an example. The parade on the sixth is the centerpiece of my proposal."

"Do you enjoy the work?"

"I know it sounds real nerdy. But I love it."

His laugh made her tingle inside. She heard him scramble up. But it felt so good to feel the snowflakes grazing her face, she didn't move. Then he stood over her. The sun shone behind him, and he looked like a Latino Superman. *My, what a cutie.*

He bent down, grabbed her hands, and pulled her up. "Let's make the wonderland, remember?"

"Oh yes." Cecilia hopped with excitement.

She felt as if she were living inside a Christmas card as they trudged through the newly fallen snow. They reached the gigantic oak tree, stood right by the trunk, and jumped to jostle a tree branch. As the snow fell around them, they huddled together watching the tumult of flakes encircle them. It had always made her feel as if they'd created a curtain that hid them from the world. Their own private wonderland.

"Let's jump again!" she shouted. In unison they moved to the other side of the tree and jumped again.

"I missed this," Elias whispered.

Cecilia's heart opened and expanded at the words. She threw her arms around him and answered, "Me, too." More than playing in the snow, she missed having a friend and this feeling in her heart. The feeling that anything was possible.

A clump of snow fell right on her ear, and she released Elias to shake it off. Then she realized what she'd done. Thrown herself willy-nilly at the youth pastor, no less. She didn't want to know what he must think of her. To hide her face, she bent and took her time gathering snow into a ball. When she turned to throw it at Elias, it was too late; he'd already gathered an arsenal. Laughing, she raced for cover, dodging the onslaught of snowballs all the way.

Chapter 5

At the underground shopping center beneath the famous Rockefeller Center, Cecilia and Elias watched more than twenty-four teenagers. Cecilia's cell phone buzzed. She pulled it out and chuckled when she saw the picture of a pigeon atop a taxicab. Yesterday, she'd received four such pictures. A pigeon on a window ledge underneath an air conditioner, a pigeon crossing wide Broadway, another perched on top of a fire hydrant, and her favorite, the taxicab. As if the pigeon had decided that walking was passé and riding the true New York way.

She didn't think Peter had sent the pics. He wasn't that creative. Perhaps Andres; he'd been put off when she'd canceled their library date again. Maybe he was letting her know he wasn't angry anymore. Or it could be one of the youth in her group. These guys knew their way around a cell phone.

She answered the phone and heard Gloria Estefan singing about long-lost love. The song was a good one, but she didn't have time to listen. Cecilia noticed Elias calling the group together to go up the escalator into the NBC building and out onto Fifth Avenue.

Cecilia led the way. When almost at the top of the rising escalator, Cecilia looked back. She felt like Moses leading the long line of teenagers out from the dark underground into the bright sunlight. And at the end of the line stood Elias, guarding the rear. She turned back to face the front. She'd developed radar that sought out Elias, a need to know where he was at all times. Not good.

They reached the Rockefeller Center promenade, and Cecilia stepped on top of a bench to be seen above the crowd. Her cell phone buzzed. "Hello."

Luis Miguel crooned about puppy love. Another great song, but she had no time for games. With a flip of her wrist, she cut off the call.

Gathered at her feet, four persons deep, stood the whole youth group. Her eyes sought out Elias standing at the outer edge. All faces turned toward her. Tempted to break out in song, like the one she'd just heard, and do a high kick, Cecilia shook her head. Losing it, she was definitely losing it.

"Okay, guys. Like Pastor Elias told you. If you get separated from the group, call our cell phones or find a cop and have them call us. We're going over to see the *Today Show* window—"

The grumbling and protests interrupted her.

"That's lame."

"What? You think we're from Kansas?"

"Puh-*leeze*. Who needs that?"

"That's for country folk—'Ooh, we're in New York. Ooh, we're on TV.'"

Cecilia lifted her hand. "Okay. Okay. But you know, guys, no one's there now. All the tourists line up early in the morning. By now they're all gone. And all we'll see through the window is the studio itself."

Suddenly, everyone was eager to see it. Go figure. These kids were more fickle than the tabloids. She jumped from the bench.

After stopping by the *Today Show* window, the group crossed the street to see the Rockefeller Center tree. Thousands of colored lights covered the immense evergreen. She'd heard on the news that the tree had been donated by a widow who lived in New Hampshire. She couldn't imagine having that towering tree growing in her front yard.

Cecilia leaned against the railing and watched the ice-skaters gracefully circle the rink below.

"Want to join those skaters?" Elias appeared beside her.

"Nah. Couldn't afford it anyhow."

"You'd look beautiful skating down there. That's a sight worth paying for."

"Beautiful." That's what he said. "Beautiful."

"I, on the other hand, would look like a stumbling clown."

"We can't all be perfect." She winked.

"Ah, so true. But some of us can bask in the glow of those who are."

Laughing, Cecilia smacked Elias's shoulder. "Ya. Enough."

"Hey, I was just following your lead." His eyes teased.

"Sure, blame me." Cecilia lifted her head and checked on the teens.

"Half are shopping along the promenade, and the other group is watching the skaters, like us."

"Shopping? They can't afford anything in those shops."

"Looking never hurt." His eyes scanned her from head to toe.

Daring to play along, Cecilia exaggerated her imitation of his once-over.

Elias laughed. "I knew you had it in you."

The blush that crept into her cheeks betrayed her. She didn't recognize herself. Since when did she flirt? And this was not what she wanted in her life anyway.

"Get any work done yesterday? Tía Ramona invited me to come over for Sunday dinner, but I'd already accepted another invitation from the Morales family."

Cecilia breathed easier now that they were on safer ground. "Part of the job, no? Everybody wants to know the new youth pastor."

"Especially if they have a single daughter," he muttered.

She wasn't sure she'd heard right. Was that a complaint? If so, it was the first she'd heard from his lips.

"Tell me about that. What made you want to be a pastor?"

Elias turned and leaned his back against the brass railing. "I thought I wanted to be a doctor. Spending most of my childhood in and out of hospitals, it seemed the logical choice. Not to mention how pleased Mami would be."

"I know what you mean. Did you see how many times Mamá and Tía Ramona mentioned my college degree?"

"Hey, they're proud of you. I wanted Mami to be proud of me, too."

"She's not proud that you're a pastor?"

"Let's just say she's not happy to be in Florida when I'm here."

"I can understand. I'd miss you, too." The words were out of her mouth before she could take them back.

"Would you?" He stepped closer, the comfortable space between them gone.

"Not that—I meant. . ." She could smell his cologne.

"So what exactly did you mean?" He cupped her elbow with his hand.

Her words tumbled out of her mouth. "As your mother—if I was your mother—any mother. . ." She leaned toward him. The scarf around her neck felt suffocating.

"You are so easy to tease. I love that about you." His hand left her elbow and grazed her cheek.

He said, "I love that about you."

They spied Laura making her way toward them.

He coughed. "Are you free tomorrow?"

"Tomorrow's New Year's Eve. I'll see you at the midnight service." She didn't know how she could sound so cavalier when just a moment ago she'd been a stuttering fool.

"No, I meant during the day. I thought we'd have a picnic at the cloisters, like old times."

"A picnic in winter?" She tried to sound incredulous, not giddy like she felt.

"Sure. Why not? It won't be so cold in our courtyard."

He remembered their courtyard. She couldn't trust her voice, so she nodded yes.

He winked and broke into that smile she treasured.

"I need a bathroom." Laura stood beside her staring at the concrete.

Cecilia remembered how she'd wanted to connect with

Laura and find out if anything was wrong. "Come, I'll take you into Saks."

"Wait. Ceci, maybe others need to go. Let's gather the group and find out."

"I gotta go now," Laura whined.

"Let me take Laura, and you send the rest of the girls after."

When Elias left to gather the group, Cecilia hooked her arm through Laura's, and they crossed Fifth Avenue toward the store entrance. As they passed through the revolving door, Cecilia's cell phone buzzed. This time Cecilia checked the ID. It read PODCAST 103.6 FM. She pressed SEND and heard one of her favorites, Jesus Adrian Romero singing about God's faithfulness. Cecilia listened to the song as they walked through the jewelry department and headed for the elevators. Her thoughts jumping ahead to the picnic with Elias tomorrow, she determined she'd set everything straight between her and Elias. Tomorrow she needed to do the right thing and apologize. When the song ended, she smiled, flipped the phone shut, and pressed the up button of the elevator.

"Your mom?" Laura asked.

"No. Just a message."

"Your mom is cool."

The elevator arrived. They stepped in, and Cecilia pressed the button for the second floor. "Really? You think so?"

"She always talks about your schoolwork and your grades. How you're the first college graduate. How you're so smart. How you're getting a master's, whatever that is."

"All mothers brag."

The elevator doors opened. Cecilia led Laura through the maze of women's accessories. "Everything okay with you?"

"Sure."

Cecilia leaned her shoulder into the bathroom door and glanced back at Laura. A mask had fallen over her features. Laura stared ahead with a blank expression, lips set in a thin line.

"When you finish, I want to show you something," Cecilia said.

They went their separate ways. Cecilia, the first to emerge, stepped over to the window. Looking out, she saw across Fifth Avenue. The angels with their golden trumpets lined the promenade leading toward the majestic Christmas tree. The window looked like a frame around an awe-inspiring vision of Christmas in New York.

"Wow," Laura whispered behind her.

"Pretty cool. Right?" Cecilia moved to give Laura a better view. "It looks even more amazing at night. Then the lights on the angels look as if they are leading you toward the tree."

They stood by the window in comfortable silence, drinking in the sight—until the sound of the door crashing open broke the moment. The girls from the youth group spilled in.

Cecilia's cell phone buzzed two more times that day. Once while they were in line looking at the scenes depicted in each Saks window. And the last time on the subway ride home.

In bed that night, the mystery of the gifts, the cell phone pics, and now the songs perturbed Cecilia. But it was day-dreaming about her date with Elias tomorrow at the cloisters that kept her awake after midnight.

Chapter 6

Cecilia didn't tell Mamá she planned to meet Elias at the cloisters. A twinge of guilt pricked her conscience as she got off the bus. She didn't want to share this yet. The entrance to the museum resembled a medieval monastery. The sun smiled at her. The trees, still laden with snow, welcomed her back. A giggle slipped out.

Maybe Elias was already here. She hurried to cross the cobblestone driveway and entered through the heavy, narrow door. Once inside, she inhaled the cold, musty smell of stone buildings. A small donation, nowhere near the suggested admission fee, garnered her a small metal pin with a huge *M*. The pin also allowed her admission to the Metropolitan Museum of Art downtown. But today was not about gazing at old paintings or sculptures. Today, she hoped, would be about confession, forgiveness, and the start of something wonderful, something new.

Cecilia climbed the steep stone steps to the first floor. Her destination: the courtyard. She walked into the familiar gallery.

The wall-to-wall seventeenth-century tapestries told the story of a unicorn hunt. Once, Cecilia and Elias had given names to the characters who appeared in each tapestry: King Vladimir, Princess Xenia, Lady Costa, Sir Milton. Today she had no time to linger and visit. Elias waited.

A corridor surrounded the courtyard, providing access to different galleries. In the center of the courtyard stood a tall stone fountain. It never sprouted water when they played here as children, but a few summers ago, she'd come to visit and seen the fountain in all its glistening glory. Today there'd be no water, not in winter.

Cecilia searched for Elias as she strolled along the corridor. Instead of hydrangeas and azaleas, dry bushes and hard earth splattered with snow edged the courtyard. She glanced across to the opposite archway and remembered sitting on the ledge acting the part of La Cucarachita Martina.

A diva cockroach named Martina primped and posed by her balcony every day, waiting for her suitors to call. Elias acted the part of each suitor. The frog who professed his love by croaking, the cat who meowed, the rooster who crowed. But it was the suave, gallant mouse of the world, El Ratoncito Perez, who swept the pompous Cucarachita Martina off her feet. Cecilia always wanted to end the playacting with Elias as El Ratoncito Perez professing his love for La Cucarachita Martina. But Elias insisted they finish the story as written. His favorite part was dying in the stew La Cucarachita Martina accidentally cooked him in. A gruesome end every boy loved.

Cecilia realized she'd walked around the whole courtyard and not found Elias. Maybe he'd phoned her. She pulled out her cell phone and checked. No message. She glanced at the time. He was late. She smiled. Now she had something to tease him about. *Mr. Punctuality.*

Ten minutes later, Cecilia still paced the cold corridor waiting for Elias. The silence pressed on her. Too cold to linger outside, she waited in the tapestry gallery.

Forty minutes later, she'd circled the courtyard three times, and her ears hurt from the cold. This was ridiculous. How long did he expect her to wait?

Enough. She was going home. Pulling the scarf off her neck, she wrapped it around her head to cover her frozen ears. Served her right—forfeiting a hat just to look good. And for what? To be jilted.

❄

That night, New Year's Eve, Cecilia slipped into her church sanctuary and glanced around. Most of the congregation knelt praying. Many mothers with sleeping children in their arms sat praying. The hum of the voices raised in prayer gave a sense of reverence. Cecilia scanned the room looking for Mamá and Tía Ramona. They'd have saved a seat for her, she was sure.

Up near the front, as usual, a lone empty chair stood between Mamá and Tía Ramona. Both prayed sitting in their seats. She knew they would have preferred to kneel, but getting up from the cold linoleum floor was difficult for them. A few quick steps and Cecilia eased her way to the empty chair. She sat with her coat still on, trying not to draw attention.

Don't look for him. It doesn't matter where he is. Don't look for him.

"He's in the corner, front row." Mamá startled her with the whisper.

Cecilia schooled her expression, pretending she didn't know what Mamá was talking about. Then she fussed with taking off her coat and tucking it under the chair in front of her.

Mamá hummed softly to herself. Cecilia closed her eyes. *Let them all think I'm praying. I don't want to deal with anything right now.*

"Let's rise and greet this new year with praise to our God." Pastor Romero stood at the pulpit. "Pastor Elias, come lead us."

Elias stepped out from behind the pillar that had hidden him from view and approached the pulpit. The congregation rose.

Elias took the microphone off the stand and strode to the left side of the platform. "We need to be a grateful people. To praise the God who has bestowed upon us this miracle we call life. We have a hope. And this hope gets us through the dark days." He paused, bowed his head, and held the microphone to his chest. The silence in the sanctuary pulsated with expectation.

"When a fifteen-year-old girl attempts suicide, where was her hope? How desperate, how despondent did she feel?" His voice cracked.

No one moved. The swish of the occasional car passing in the street was the only sound she heard.

Elias lifted his head, his eyes glistening with determination. "As the people of God, we must rise up. We must stand in the gap for those suffering and be their champions. For God has been merciful this day and snatched His young daughter from the enemy's grasp. He is worthy to be praised."

On cue, the music began and the congregation broke into

triumphant song. Elias sang as if transported. His face shone as if a light burned within him.

Cecilia lowered her head and clasped her hands tight.

A suicide attempt?

She closed her eyes, and tears slipped out.

Oh no. Please. Not Laura.

Chapter 7

Cecilia spent the night tossing in bed. Dreams about lonely Laura, the cloisters, and Elias tortured her all night. By five in the morning, she gave up, turned on her computer, and began editing the first chapter of her thesis proposal.

The sound of the shower startled her, and she glanced at the clock—7:32 already! At least she'd gotten a lot of work done. She had the first chapter polished and half of the second chapter edited. Now she needed to work at the school library and, most important, experience the Three Kings Day parade firsthand.

Leaning back, she stared at the computer screen. Where was Laura now? She should call her as soon as it was a decent hour and make sure she was okay. She hoped Elias didn't feel responsible for this tragedy. She wondered who comforted the pastors, who held them up in prayer.

Buckle down. No more thoughts about a certain youth pastor. She needed to focus on her studies.

Tía Ramona peeked in the door, her towel-wrapped hair evidence that she'd just stepped out of the shower. "Always studying." She shook her head back and forth. "But you make your mother so proud."

She made it sound as if studying were a vice.

"You going to help us prepare for tonight's dinner?"

Cecilia nodded. "When are Evelyn and the kids arriving?"

"Probably after lunch." Tía Ramona scratched her head and turned to go. "Doesn't that computer screen ruin your eyes?"

Cecilia didn't bother answering but rubbed her eyes.

Elias was coming, and her heart was torn. She wanted to pull him into an embrace. Kiss all his worries away. Help him carry the burdens in his heart. But she had no right. She'd thrown away his love years ago. And hadn't she decided work was enough for her? That relationships only entangled? Look at Tía Ramona, married with a husband who lived far away. That wasn't a marriage. She needed to stay away from any semblance of a love relationship.

She tapped her pencil on the desk. What she needed to do was apologize to Elias. That she had to do. She wished he'd at least called yesterday. She could have helped. Couldn't she? She wanted to. With him beside her, she felt she could. Maybe he didn't want her around in times like this. Maybe he thought she couldn't handle crises.

"Argh!" she yelled and pulled her hair. *Stop this torture.*

❆

Cecilia didn't let Evelyn take off her coat when she arrived but dragged her into her bedroom and closed the door.

"What's up with you?" Evelyn slipped off her coat and draped it on the back of the computer chair.

"I need your help." Cecilia gathered up her gifts from the mystery person.

Evelyn sat on the edge of the bed and pulled off her boots. "Shoot. Tell me."

Cecilia placed the crystal pear in her cousin's hands. "On Christmas, I received this box with my name on it with this in it."

Evelyn turned the pear in her hands, and it reflected the light.

"Then the next day, this bag appeared at our door with two Dove chocolate bars in it," Cecilia continued.

Evelyn shrugged as if to say, *And?*

"Then the following day, these three little hens were left for me."

"I'm picking up a pattern here." Evelyn caressed the hen figurines.

"Wait, I'm not done." Cecilia reached over to her end table and picked up her cell phone. "Look at the pics that I got the following day." Scrolling through her cell phone menu, Cecilia showed Evelyn the four photos of pigeons in different parts of New York.

"How cute—that one of the pigeon on the taxi." Evelyn laughed. "Somebody has a secret admirer."

"I'm not done yet."

"There's more?"

"Oh yeah. After the four calls with birds, I got five with different songs."

"Wait, what did you just say?" Evelyn dumped the objects on the bed, stood up, and paced the room.

"Which part?"

"You said four calls with birds—isn't there a song like that?"

"That's what I'm telling you. I got five songs—"

Evelyn interrupted. She hummed, then sang: "Four calling birds, three French hens, two turtledoves, and a partridge in a pear tree."

Cecilia gasped.

"*Four calling birds.* You got four pigeons as calls on your cell phone, right?" Evelyn picked up the three hen figurines. "Three French hens."

"Two turtledoves. They were two chocolate Dove bars." Cecilia waved the bag.

Evelyn picked up the exquisite pear and danced around the room singing, "And a partridge in a pear tree."

"Wait. Wait." Cecilia stopped Evelyn from dancing. "Then the song goes 'five golden rings.'"

"Well, what came next?" Evelyn shook Cecilia's shoulder.

"I got five cell phone rings with five different songs."

Evelyn marched around the room pumping her arms. "Yes. Yes. Five golden rings—the ringing of the phone with a song."

"But what I got yesterday doesn't fit."

Evelyn stood in front of Cecilia. "What did you get yesterday? This is so romantic."

"Romantic? A flan is not romantic."

"Okay, let me think. How does the song go?" Evelyn dumped herself on the computer chair. She hummed and sang intermittently.

Cecilia finished the song for her. "Six geese a-laying."

They were silent a moment. Then Evelyn jumped up, opened the door, and yelled down the hallway. "Mami, how many eggs does it take to make a flan?"

The answer forced a gasp, and then they burst into laughter. Evelyn closed the door again. "Okay, who is it? This is too much fun."

Cecilia couldn't wrap her mind around all this.

Evelyn shook her shoulders. "Come on, girl. Who has such a crush on you that they'd go to so much trouble? I mean, this is well thought out." She sat beside Cecilia. "Wait. Is today day seven?"

Cecilia nodded.

"So today you are going to get. . ." Evelyn giggled. "Seven swans a-swimming? I can't wait to see that."

Who would do this? This took more effort than she suspected Andres would invest. And one of the teenage boys? They didn't have the ingenuity. It could be Peter, but he'd preferred getting the adulation and attention. Anonymity was not his style. That left just one person. The suspicion left her breathless, made her hug herself. It couldn't be him. Nah. This must be a joke.

"Well, girl? Are you going to spill the beans? Who is the lovesick puppy?"

"I couldn't even guess." Cecilia started picking up the little hens from the bed.

The door opened. Tía Ramona held a crying Sonia. "Someone is hungry."

Evelyn took Sonia from Tía Ramona's arms. "I will get to

the bottom of this," she warned as she followed Tía Ramona to the kitchen.

Cecilia wasn't sure she wanted to get to the bottom of this. If it wasn't Elias, she didn't want to know who it was.

❄

Hearing footsteps near her door, Cecilia, who had hidden in her room all day, saved her thesis file on the computer. A soft knock and the door opened.

Mamá still wore her apron. "Mi'ja, we're going to eat dinner now. Come pray with us."

Cecilia followed her mother down the hall. Mamá stepped into the living room and stood in the center. Cecilia stayed by the entrance. She glanced around the room at her family. Sammy lounged with a son on each knee. Evelyn sat on the edge of the love seat beside her Mario, the boys on the floor at their feet. Tía Ramona sat in the armchair.

Finally, Cecilia allowed her gaze to find Elias. He sat cross-legged on the floor by Tía Ramona, holding a sleeping Sonia in his arms. One look and Cecilia knew she was in trouble. His black turtleneck superbly reflected the color of his hair and eyes, but it also outlined his strong shoulders. She swallowed, preparing to look away, but Elias raised his eyes to meet hers. His searching gaze made her feel as if he wanted to read everything she thought, felt, or dreamed. Or was that the message she sent him with her eyes?

"Elias, could you bless the food?" Mamá bestowed him with the honor.

"*Seguro.*" Elias bowed his head, as did everyone in the room.

"Lord, this new year is a precious gift from Your loving hands. Help us to live it to the fullest, walking in Your truth, doing Your will, bringing glory to Your kingdom. Help us to be bold and unafraid to follow Your lead, to trust You in all things. Thank You for the food we are about to receive and the hands that prepared it. And thank You for the love and warmth of this family. Amen."

After the chorus of amens, Mamá directed, "Cecilia, serve Elias. Then, Evelyn, you can serve the boys and your husband. Ramona, you take care of Sammy."

Evelyn got up and took Sonia from Elias's arms. "Go with Ceci, and tell her what you want to eat."

Cecilia didn't wait for Elias and strode into the kitchen. *Great. Thanks, Evelyn. So thoughtful of you.* She'd avoided Elias all day, her confusion mounting.

In the kitchen the heavenly smells of *arroz con habichuelas* and *pollo asado* made her stomach clench. Because she'd hidden, Cecilia hadn't snacked before dinner.

"I don't want to upset your mom, but I can serve myself and you if you'd like." Elias stood at the door of the kitchen. "I know you've been working very hard all day. You could use a break. So let me serve you."

"My mother would kill me. No man ever serves himself in her home. Women's lib never penetrated her world." She took a dinner plate from the pile on the kitchen table. "Just tell me what you want."

"With your mom's and aunt's cooking, need you ask?"

"A bit of everything."

"*Sí, señorita.*" He stood right behind her as she spooned the white rice onto his plate.

His closeness unnerved her. She could smell his cologne. Calvin Klein One. "Have you seen Laura? I called her house today, but no one answered."

"Today. Before coming here." His voice changed, became deeper, more compassionate.

"It was her, wasn't it?"

"Yeah."

Her hands trembled, and she spilled the red beans onto the stovetop instead of his plate. "How is she?" She attempted to pour another spoonful of red beans over the rice.

"Not good. She asked for you. Can you come with me to see her tomorrow?"

"Sure." The word croaked from her lips. He wanted her to go with him. Laura had asked for her. She felt as if an elephant had sat on her chest. She attempted to breathe. "Want baked chicken?"

"Everything."

Cecilia gave Elias the plate to hold while she opened the oven door, pulled out the roasting pan with the heavily seasoned chicken, and pierced a drumstick. Her eyes watered. Her throat clamped shut.

Now, tell him now. You're sorry. Say it.

She dropped the drumstick on his plate and returned for more.

"Hey, careful with the heat of the oven; you look flushed."

Not trusting her voice, Cecilia nodded while she hunted for another drumstick.

Elias lowered his voice and spoke. "Please forgive me. I

didn't forget about our date. I got the call about Laura. Her family was crazy out of their minds. When I finally got out, I had to get ready for service. I didn't mean to stand you up."

"I know. Part and parcel of your job, right?" The words came out hoarse.

"Serving the Lord isn't always convenient."

Cecilia closed the oven door and took the plate from him. She turned to the kitchen table and added a huge dollop of potato salad to his plate, then turned around and handed it to him. She took a deep breath. The words were right on her lips when Evelyn entered the kitchen. "Whoa, what's going on in here?" Evelyn faked a shiver. "Is this a lovers' quarrel?"

"Shut up, Eve." Cecilia brushed past Evelyn to reach the refrigerator. "What do you want to drink?" She jerked the door open and pulled out a can of diet Coke. "Will this do?"

"Sure." Elias reached beyond Evelyn and took the can from Cecilia.

"Sweetie, whatever you did to upset this one, you'd better fix it."

"Thanks for the advice." Elias met Cecilia's eyes over Evelyn's shoulder. His eyes pleaded for her to understand. A cloud of confusion, guilt, and shame overwhelmed her as she watched him walk back to the living room.

Evelyn grabbed Cecilia's sweater sleeve. "What's up? Is he your secret admirer? Tell me."

"Nothing. No. Just let it be. Please."

Evelyn held on to Cecilia. "You are a beautiful, smart, incredible woman. But sometimes I want to shake you. He's perfect. Don't mess this up."

"You can't mess up what doesn't exist." Cecilia picked up another plate. "And no one's perfect. Want me to serve Junior?"

"Oh, thank you, sweetie. Just give him some rice covered in ketchup. He won't eat anything else." Evelyn finished loading her husband's plate. "Can't wait to see those seven swans a-swimming."

Cecilia watched her cousin leave. Sometimes she loved her family. And sometimes. . .

Chapter 8

Cecilia found herself right next to Elias on the living room floor thanks to Evelyn's maneuvering. A part of Cecilia felt grateful. As they ate, Elias whispered after each bite, "Forgive me." No one else heard him. Not with Sammy's constant yelling at his boys and Evelyn's accompanying corrections.

The words just floated out of his mouth, yet the same words choked her. She needed to ask *his* forgiveness. Still, she dared to smile back and nudged him with her shoulder. He faked a shudder of gratitude and with a luscious smile nudged back.

Junior, Evelyn's eldest, shouted, "Let's see a video!"

Elias moved from his spot and leaned toward the TV. "What's this tape in the VCR?" He turned on the TV and hunted for the VCR remote control.

When he'd moved, she'd wanted to pull him back. Cecilia wrapped her arms around herself and clamped her lips so she wouldn't say, "Don't go. Stay right here beside me."

"Boys, sit still. Pastor Elias put in a tape." Evelyn cuddled with Mario.

"Papi, no gifts?" Sammy's son Tito asked.

Tía Ramona responded, with Mamá echoing her in the kitchen, *"Faltan los Reyes."*

Sammy translated for the boys. "Don't forget Three Kings Day is coming."

Junior shouted, "Yeah!" and all the boys chimed in.

Tito stopped shouting. "What's Three Kings Day?"

Mamá yelled from the kitchen, "Ask Titi Cecilia. She's studying it."

"You're kidding, right?" Sammy leaned forward.

Evelyn left the comfort of her husband's arms to challenge Sammy. "Why, Mr. I've-Never-Been-to-College? You got a problem with that?"

"Let's not get into it." Mario drew his wife back into his arms.

"I'm just saying that school is a lot of money, and aren't there more important things to study?" Sammy sat back.

"Because our culture isn't important? Mr. Gringo." Evelyn pushed forward.

"Don't start calling names. Little Ms. Suburbia."

"Guys. Guys. Let me explain." Cecilia tried to get a word in.

"That's right. Listen to the scholar." Evelyn's lips set into a smug smile.

"I'm trying to document the traditions and customs that Latinos have kept in the diaspora—the holidays they brought from the homeland and still celebrate here in America. Three Kings Day, or Epiphany, is one of them."

"You see. And that's how we keep our culture alive," Evelyn interjected.

"Let me finish." Cecilia addressed the boys, who sat entertained by the adults' banter. "You know when you put out the water and grass?"

"Oh, Mami made me do that. And then there was a gift." Junior rose up on his knees.

"Do you know why you leave water and grass?"

"For the camels?" Junior said.

"Yes, grass for the camels and water for the wise men, who passed your house on their way to worship the newborn King. They were grateful and left you a small gift."

"I got a book." Junior hunched back down.

Tito bounced up and down on his knees. "When do we do this? When do the kings come? When do we get the gifts?"

"You do it on the fifth of January, and by the morning of the sixth, your gift will be there. That should be Monday, five days from today." Cecilia welcomed Sammy's youngest into her lap.

"Maybe the kings will come by here, but out in the Bronx, they might not come," Sammy interjected.

"So let's make sure they do this year." Tía Ramona enunciated every word, making it clear Sammy needed to come through for his boys.

"Movie. Movie," Junior chanted, and soon all the boys followed suit.

Elias pressed PLAY on the remote control.

A home video of trees, a bike path, and a small water inlet came onto the screen. In the far distance, across the Harlem River, they could see the huge blue *C* painted on the cliff. *This must be Inwood Park.* The camera lens zoomed in and focused on the still water of the inlet. Gliding in majestic glory on the water were swans. Seven swans.

Evelyn burst out in laughter, jumped out of her seat, and assaulted Elias. "Where did you get that tape?"

Mamá rushed in from the kitchen. "What happened?"

Sammy and Mario shrugged their shoulders. Cecilia's eyes stayed glued to the TV. The swans glided.

"In the VCR." Elias spread his hands. "I haven't done anything."

Evelyn approached him and stabbed his chest with her finger. "You are guilty until proven innocent."

"Evelyn, ¿qué es esto?" Tía Ramona reproved her daughter.

Cecilia came alive, hearing her aunt's tone of voice. "Nada, Tía. Solo un chiste." She assured her aunt it was just a joke.

Evelyn turned back to stare at her.

Cecilia glared at Evelyn.

Raising her hands up in the air, Evelyn stomped out of the room. "I'm going to the bathroom."

"Well, whatever that is, take it off. It's boring. Put in a good movie." Mario winked at Elias.

Cecilia caught the wink and turned narrow eyes on Elias. His shrugged shoulders and innocent look didn't fool her one bit. But it did send a shiver up her spine.

❄

Elias called Cecilia in the morning to tell her that the policy of the hospital allowed only family and clergy to visit Laura in the psychiatric ward.

Psychiatric ward. The words made her shudder. Cecilia couldn't fathom the thought that Laura was in a locked-down, barred-window facility. Laura probably felt scared, lonely, hopeless.

Cecilia went to school and settled herself in the library, hidden among the stack of books and study cubicles. She tried to lose herself in research. A pile of texts lay before her, Post-it flags sticking out of the pages. Her cell phone vibrated. The ID read ELIAS.

"Hey," she whispered.

"Just wanted to let you know how my visit with Laura went."

"Give me a minute to walk out to the hallway."

"Where are you?"

"Library."

"Don't you ever rest from all that work?"

"Should I ask you the same question?"

Elias's laugh made her think the visit with Laura had gone well. She closed the door behind her and walked to the corner of the hallway opposite the bank of elevators. "How is she?"

Silence. Then, "She asked for you." He said the words as if he didn't want to say others.

"Did you tell her they wouldn't let me in?"

"Yes. As a matter of fact, I used it to motivate her to try to get better."

Silence again. She waited.

"It's not good, Ceci. She has no will to live. Her eyes are dull. If I didn't know she was fifteen, I'd think she was a shrunken old woman." His voice broke.

Cecilia's heart hurt. She felt claustrophobic in the hallway. She walked toward the window and told herself to breathe.

"Let's pray she gets better soon and they move her to the pediatric ward. Then you'll be able to visit." Elias paused as if gathering his strength. "Gotta run. I still have two more visits to make before I get back to church and finish preparing my sermon for Friday. Don't study so hard. And pray for Laura."

"Yes. Of course. Take care." She closed the phone and leaned her forehead against the cold windowpane. *Lord, be with Laura. Be with Elias.*

Behind her, she heard the *ting* of the elevator arriving. Cecilia pulled away from the window, rubbed the cold off her forehead, and returned to the library.

Once at her cubicle, her stomach growled. Only one milk chocolate candy left in the box. This morning the eighth gift waited for her on her bed when she awoke. The song lyrics were "eight maids a-milking," and she'd gotten a box of milk chocolate bars dressed as maidens in colorful aluminum foil. She took the last maiden, unwrapped the red and black foil dress, and popped the chocolate into her mouth.

Trying to loosen her muscles, she raised her arms over her head and twisted her head from side to side. Her shoulders felt like a rock, her neck like a tree that would snap from a single breeze.

She'd make a horrible pastor's wife. She wasn't the "meet and greet" girl. Look where she felt best—in a library, surrounded by books, not people.

And why was she thinking about being a pastor's wife when she chickened out every time and couldn't even confess her own wrongdoings?

❄

Soaking wet from the rain, Cecilia slipped into the apartment. Her boots squished on the hardwood floor, giving her away. Just as she pushed open the door to her bedroom, she heard Tía Ramona.

"Ceci, is that you?"

"Sí, Tía."

"Ven, que llego algo para ti."

Like clockwork, another gift had arrived. Tía Ramona and Mamá probably waited all day for her to get home to see what this gift turned out to be.

"Muchacha. Is it raining that hard?" Mamá grabbed a kitchen towel and wrapped Cecilia's hair. "You could get sick like this. You work too hard, and then you walk around in the rain with no hat, no umbrella. Youth, I tell you, foolish youth. You think you're invincible."

Cecilia allowed Mamá to fuss and followed her to the kitchen.

Tía Ramona put the bowl of raw beans on the table. "She probably hasn't eaten all day, either." She took the plate of food, placed it in the microwave, and pushed the buttons. "They think they can live on air and soda."

Hair wrapped in a towel, Cecilia let her mother guide her to the chair. The microwave beeped. A plate appeared in front of her with a glass of juice.

"Eat. Before you faint."

Mamá picked up the square packet. "Let's see what today's surprise is. May I?" She waited for Cecilia to nod yes, then ripped open the packet. A DVD of the movie *Mad Hot Ballroom*.

"I loved that movie. You know, the children that danced in that movie live right here in Washington Heights." Tía Ramona reached for her bowl of beans. "Someone is going through a lot of trouble to show how much they care."

"Let's watch the movie," Mamá offered.

Nine ladies dancing. A movie about Latino children learning ballroom dancing and winning the championship. He was a hopeless romantic. And she loved him.

❄

Saturday morning arrived, and Cecilia prepared to visit Laura in the hospital. By the time she left the apartment, doubts assaulted her. She had nothing to say to this girl. She didn't know how to treat her. She might say or do the wrong thing. Yet she felt the urgency to go.

All the snow had been washed away by the rain. Now long crystal icicles hung from fire escapes and store awnings. Cecilia picked her way carefully down the street, avoiding any shiny dark patches of black ice.

Once at the hospital, Cecilia approached the visitor reception area and used her most professional voice to ask for Laura Santiago's room. Laura had been moved from psych to pediatrics. Room 436A.

Moved along by the crowd, Cecilia entered the elevator and asked someone to press the fourth floor's button.

Lord, I don't know what I'm doing, but I trust You. Give me the words I need.

Blue walls surrounded the waif wrapped in white sheets

on the hospital bed. Laura's usual shiny light brown hair was matted and tangled. Her eyes closed in sleep, she looked eight years old, not fifteen.

Cecilia moved silently toward the bed. Her hands trembled as she reached out to smooth Laura's hair.

The young girl's eyes fluttered open. "Hey."

"Hey, yourself." Cecilia leaned against the bed. "You scared me."

"Yeah. I know." She closed her eyes for a moment. "I'm better. They don't have me in restraints anymore."

Restraints?

"Hey—take your coat off. There's a chair behind you." Laura pushed herself up on the bed.

Cecilia adjusted a pillow under Laura.

"You not staying?" Laura's eyes reflected defeat.

"Yeah. I'm staying." Cecilia unbuttoned her pea coat and threw it on the chair. "As a matter of fact, I brought a comb to try to do something with that hair of yours." In her purse she found a wide-toothed comb.

"Go for it if you dare." Laura lifted her arms to gather her hair out from under her.

Cecilia took a portion of the dirty hair and, bit by bit, began to pick out the tangles. "Tell me if I hurt you."

"You'd never hurt me. That's for others to do. You and Pastor Elias can't hurt a fly."

"Who hurt you?" It came out like a whisper.

"I told Pastor Elias already."

"You don't have to tell me." Cecilia finished one portion of hair and gathered another one.

"My boyfriend."

Cecilia remained silent, praying Laura would continue.

"When he left me, I thought I was nothing without him, so why live? Pastor Elias says I thought wrong."

"We all think wrong sometimes."

"Yeah. He said that, too. He said he didn't want to live anymore, either, when his asthma got bad. But then God healed him. He says sometimes we need our spirits healed more than our bodies. I get that."

Cecilia bent and kissed Laura on the forehead. Laura reached up and held on to Cecilia in a fierce hug. "I'm glad you came."

Not trusting her voice, Cecilia nodded into Laura's neck. They held each other.

Cecilia settled Laura back on the pillow. "Now let me finish making you beautiful."

Cecilia continued to work on Laura's hair. Because of a broken relationship with her boyfriend, Laura almost died; because of Cecilia's relationship with Peter, she had almost given up her friendship with Elias, and with her God. Yeah, she knew it was true—sometimes we all think wrong and need our spirits healed.

The morning passed as they laughed and joked, watched TV, shared the hospital lunch, and prayed together. By the time Cecilia left, Laura seemed happier and more at peace. Something inside Cecilia shifted.

Chapter 9

T hat night after a hot shower, Cecilia stood before the mirror towel-drying her hair. On top of the computer lay the tenth gift. Ten lords a-leaping turned out to be ten little coquis—Puerto Rican tree frogs—with tiny crowns sitting on a log.

Cecilia laughed at Elias's ingenuity. To compare crowned leaping tree frogs with lords—too much.

Mamá's stern voice surprised her. "Cecilia Maria Montes, *ven aquí.*"

Cecilia wrapped her hair in the towel and rushed to find out why Mamá sounded so upset.

In the living room, Tía Ramona watched TV and Mamá sat on the arm of the love seat, serving spoon still in her hand. Pointing to the TV, Mama said, "A strike. The subways are going on strike."

"No!" Cecilia sat on the sofa and listened to the news anchor. The screen switched to a picture of the mayor announcing alternate travel suggestions in the case of a transit strike. He assured all New Yorkers that negotiations with the Transport Workers Union would go on to resolve the issue. The anchor returned and began to list all the local activities that would be canceled in the event a transit strike occurred. Cecilia listened intently.

The Three Kings Day parade would be among the events canceled. Mamá gasped, and Tía Ramona let out an unexpected word. Cecilia's heart plummeted.

The rush of thoughts tumbling in her mind made her want to scream. She dropped her face into her hands. Wait a whole year to complete her thesis? Impossible! She didn't have the money for that. What was she going to do now?

Cecilia stood and flung her hands up in surrender. "Fine! I'll drop out and work at McDonald's the rest of my life."

Mamá and Tía Ramona exchanged a questioning look.

"Why say that?" Mamá stood up and grabbed Cecilia's hands.

"I'm doomed." Cecilia pulled her hands away and slumped on the sofa.

"You're forgetting about God." Mamá sat next to her.

"Research and studying I know how to do. And then—bang. Life happens." She turned to Mamá. "That's the problem. Life is always going to—bang. And I can't do it."

"*Se ha vuelto loca.*" She's gone crazy. Tía Ramona clasped her hands. Mamá shushed her.

"If I can't even graduate without drama or confront my issues, how am I going to handle being a pastor's wife? They have to take care of everyone. Always knowing the right thing to say. Staying calm in the middle of disaster." She took a breath. "Look at me. I'm falling apart and it's just a stupid thesis. Not someone's life." Silent tears spilled over her cheeks.

Cecilia didn't understand Tía Ramona's smile. She felt as if she'd just emptied out her heart and stood naked before them.

Mamá rubbed her back. *"Una cosa a la vez."* One thing at a time.

Cecilia pulled the towel from her head and used it to wipe her cheeks. Her wet hair fell loose. "Mamá, you know I just wanted to be a college professor. Teach Latin American studies; serve on the occasional committee; present at conferences." Cecilia turned to face Mamá. "Not be responsible for people's spiritual lives. It's too much. I can't do it. I'd disappoint Elias. I'd be a hindrance, not an asset. He needs somebody holy, spiritual, outgoing—you know—not me. And—and. . ."

The tears started again. She couldn't even voice her shame about Peter.

Mamá caressed her arm. "You have it all wrong. And I'm sure Elias will tell you the same thing. Trust in God. He'll give you what you need when you need it. No one is holy and perfect. We are all a mess, struggling in life, leaning on God's strength and understanding. That's what you need to do."

Trust in God. They made it sound so easy. Like turning on a switch. But it wasn't easy—not one bit.

Tía Ramona came to sit on the arm of the sofa. "We pray right now. For strike. For parade. And for. . ." She smiled broadly. "You and Elias. God's will be done. Yes?"

They bowed their heads to pray, then the doorbell rang. Tía Ramona went to answer it and came back into the living room followed by Elias.

Cecilia couldn't believe he was standing before her, like an answer to prayer. It was time to take care of business.

"Mamá, Tía Ramona, can I talk with Elias in private?"

They rushed off to the kitchen on the pretext of fixing something to eat. Elias took off his coat and hung it to dry on the edge of the door, then sat across from her. The tilt of his head and his questioning gaze let her know he had no idea what she was going to say.

Lord, make me brave. Give me the words.

"I need to ask for your forgiveness." Finally, the words were out and her shoulders felt lighter.

"No need."

"Yes, there is. You were a good friend, my best friend. And even when you moved away, you didn't forget me; you still kept in touch. And then with the first boyfriend I got, I threw that friendship away, never understanding how valuable, how precious it really was."

"You were young and in love."

"Love?" Cecilia shook her head. "More like infatuation and immaturity. I lost my way. Did stupid things. Please forgive me." She couldn't look at him any longer. Taking the towel, she dried the ends of her hair.

"You've had my forgiveness for years now." The words were said so softly she wasn't sure she'd heard right. She looked up at Elias and found his eyes clouded, pensive.

He got up, took his coat, and slipped it on. "Well, I'd better go. Tomorrow is Sunday, and I have a lot to prepare."

Before she realized it, Elias had left, even over the protests of Tía Ramona and Mamá. And although she felt released from the guilt and shame, Elias's sudden departure left her feeling uncertain and anxious to see him again.

❄

The sermon on Sunday morning focused on Proverbs 3:5–6. Cecilia felt as if God were using a megaphone to talk to her. *Trust Me. I will show you the path.*

At the end of the powerful sermon, Cecilia bowed her head and laid her heart open to God. *I want to trust You. Help me. Show me how.*

A half hour later, Cecilia waited for Elias in the church foyer. She paced back and forth, then peeked through the door window into the sanctuary. Where was he? He'd asked Mamá permission to walk her home. Mamá readily agreed, and she and Tía Ramona had gone ahead. She checked her reflection in the glass. It would be her first time alone with him since her confession.

"Ready?"

Cecilia spun around. Elias stood by the exit in his coat.

"Sure." She walked toward the door he held open, and they stepped outside.

"Listen. I thought we'd take a small detour before we get to your house."

"Where to?" They stopped at the corner and waited for the light to change.

"A secret place I go to pray and think."

"Not too far, right?"

"Trust me?" Elias's eyes sparkled.

Those words again. *Trust Me.*

Cecilia nodded, and they crossed the street. She wanted to tell him about her visit to see Laura and about the impending transit strike and how it would affect her thesis. Things she hadn't had time to share last night. But he was walking fast, and his strides were much longer than hers. She hurried to keep up.

They crossed two more streets and reached Broadway. Where could he possibly be taking her?

Silent, Elias and Cecilia stared at the traffic signal. Why didn't he say something? The light turned green, and they started to cross. Suddenly a truck turned left onto Broadway and shrieked its brakes. A cab wove around the truck and missed Cecilia by an inch. Elias grabbed Cecilia's hand and pulled her across the street to safety.

Once on the sidewalk, he didn't let go. Instead, he held on tightly as they entered the George Washington Port Authority building and rode up the escalator. And he held her hand even as they walked amid the crowd.

It no longer mattered to Cecilia if they said anything. It felt wonderful to have her hand in his, as if she belonged to him.

But what were they doing in a bus terminal? Maybe they were going to New Jersey. Why would he take her there when he knew Mamá and Tía Ramona were home waiting with supper?

"Elias, we're not going too far. Are we?"

"Shush. We're almost there." He led her through a crowd gathered in front of TV monitors that displayed the buses upon arrival and departure. They went up another escalator and out onto a bus platform. Still pulling her along, Elias led her through the length of the platform to its tip, around the glass partition, and then stopped.

Before them, in all its glory, was the expanse of the George Washington Bridge. The cars going and coming on the bridge made her think of Jacob's ladder, with the angels going up and down. Beneath the bridge lay the Hudson River, a light pristine blue with patches of white ice floating. Behind the bridge, a clear winter sky topped the tree-covered palisades. She'd never seen this view before—New Jersey so close, yet she knew it lay quite far away.

"Doesn't it make you feel as if everything is possible?" Elias interrupted her thoughts.

"Yes. Like Jacob's ladder."

"Exactly!" Elias turned her to face him. "I knew you'd get it." Now he had both of her hands in his. "I feel God's presence here. As if all the things we know we can't achieve—with Him, we can."

Elias pulled Cecilia down with him to sit on the concrete edge of the platform. They sat with their backs against the glass partition, facing the majestic view.

"I never expected to become a pastor. You know I planned on going to medical school." He squeezed her hand. "God had other plans. From the day I left New York and my best friend, I plotted my return. When this opportunity to pastor in my old church came, I knew it was time. Time to renew our friendship and possibly more."

Trust. Cecilia studied the cars fleeing New York toward adventures unknown and the cars speeding safely home.

"I know I can't do all that is before me in my own strength. But with God, I want to try." Elias let go of her hand. Then he pulled out of his coat pocket one, two, three, four, five. . .

Eleven small stick figures made out of orange pipe cleaners. "Eleven pipers piping. I couldn't get pipes—or eleven men for that matter. So here they are. . . ."

Cecilia threw her head back and laughed. Her heart had been right. Elias was her secret admirer. She picked up a figure and then one by one stood the pipers at attention before her on the black asphalt.

"So here's the question, and I don't want an answer right now. I've had a lot of time to think and pray about this. You need the same time." He reached for her hand and looked into her eyes. "Can you see yourself sharing a life with me?"

Her heart screamed yes! Her mind nagged differently. A panic rose in her chest.

She parted her lips. He pressed his finger against them. "Pray. Don't answer until you're absolutely sure."

She nodded, her throat clamped shut.

He gathered the eleven pipe-cleaner figures and handed them to her. Cecilia stuck them in her coat pocket. Then Elias got up and pulled her up after him. "Let's get some supper. I'm famished."

Cecilia tucked her hand in his, her heart pounding like a conga drum. As she left the platform, she caught a quick glimpse of the silver swinging arches of the suspension bridge and sent up a prayer.

Chapter 10

Plastered across the *Daily News* was the headline TRANSIT STRIKE AVERTED! Cecilia hugged the newspaper to her chest. The wind whipped through her hair as she crossed East 106th Street on her way to Fifth Avenue and El Museo del Barrio. She should have worn a hat. But Elias was meeting her for lunch, and she didn't want hat hair. A song bubbled inside her along with the urge to run and skip.

Once inside the museum, Cecilia sought out the parade registration table. She had to wait in line with a mob of people, but at least she was warm. The parade wouldn't start without the half dozen men hovering about the museum lobby dressed in crowns and bejeweled capes. Cecilia fairly hopped from excitement.

Finally, she reached the table and submitted her confirmation form and photography waiver. In turn, she received a ticket to the VIP bleachers on Third Avenue.

Crowds bundled in coats, hats, and scarves lined Third Avenue. Schoolchildren, with their teachers and accompanying parents, sat on the edge of the sidewalk under the police barricades. Many of the spectators wore gold paper crowns in honor of the holiday. A spirit of expectancy and celebration filled the atmosphere. Cecilia needed to write it all down. She didn't want to miss a single detail.

The bleachers faced east on Third Avenue, providing the warmth of the morning sun. Cecilia sat next to a woman in a mink coat and pulled out her notebook and pencil. She scribbled her initial impressions.

"Are you a newspaper reporter?" the woman asked.

Cecilia shook her head.

"So what are you writing?"

Cecilia turned to explain when a wave of excitement spread through the spectators. The parade had begun. The woman in mink lost interest and turned to watch the parade.

Schoolchildren carrying banners marched by dressed like sheep, camels, shepherds, and angels. Floats with mechanical figures of the three wise men drifted down the avenue. Marching bands strode past playing Christmas carols.

Cecilia watched it all and took notes. If only they'd let her film the parade. She took out her camera and snapped pictures of three tall men dressed in flowing royal capes and turbans, each carrying a gift—the gold, myrrh, and frankincense. Although she couldn't see them, she could hear the drums beating out the song "Little Drummer Boy."

The story of a small boy and his simple gift made Cecilia's heart swell with gratitude. No matter what gifts she might bring to the Prince of Peace, she'd never outgive Him. That was true love.

And suddenly she realized that Elias's love was exactly like that—sacrificial, forgiving, generous, and joyful. Not something to be feared and nothing like the possessive immature actions Peter had shown. She could love Elias and have a wonderful life with him because their love was true love. *Trust.* She would trust God to give her exactly what she needed when she needed it in order to be a helpmate to Elias.

The woman in mink exclaimed, "What does that mean?"

Cecilia saw the drum band approach, led by two young men she recognized from her youth group. They carried a banner that read EL RATONCITO PEREZ LOVES LA CUCARACHITA MARTINA.

Beside her, she heard a man explaining to the mink coat lady the details of the well-known Puerto Rican folktale. But the phrase that kept running through her thoughts was "twelve drummers drumming."

And then she heard her name. Elias stood at the foot of the bleachers calling to her. She wanted to fly into his arms and kiss his eyes, his nose, his cheeks—his lips. Laughing, she tripped over a man's briefcase and another's boots on her way down.

When she reached the sidewalk, she threw caution to the wind and flew into Elias's arms.

"You are incredible." She squeezed him tight.

"So you liked my surprise?"

"Liked it? Loved it! How did you manage it?"

"I have my ways. The twelve days of Christmas couldn't finish without a flourish, and especially on your special day." His deep, dark eyes searched hers. "I love you, Cecilia Maria Montes."

Cecilia wanted to laugh and cry and jump and sing. Instead, she hopped and planted a kiss on Elias's cheeks. "I love you, too, Elias Perez." Then she gazed into his chocolate eyes and with a drawn breath announced, "In answer to your question: Elias, I cannot imagine my life *without* you."

The smile began in his eyes, then spread across his face. He grabbed her and lifted her in the air. *"Gracias, Padre."*

Somewhere someone started singing Jose Feliciano's famous song "Feliz Navidad." Elias returned her safely to earth and turned to face the parade with his arms still around her waist and sang along. Cecilia listened to his voice rise in song and took another step of faith and released her own voice. Together, arm in arm, they sang with the crowd. *Feliz Navidad.* It most definitely was a merry Christmas.

Vasthi Reyes Acosta

Vasthi is a native New Yorker. She resides in the Washington Heights/Inwood neighborhood of Manhattan with her husband and two teenaged children. She is excited about writing stories that bring a message of hope through Latino characters. She wants readers to find themselves reflected in her work and to learn about her heritage and her hope, God. She would love to hear from her readers. Contact her through Barbour Publishing.

A Letter to Our Readers

Dear Readers:

In order that we might better contribute to your reading enjoyment, we would appreciate your taking a few minutes to respond to the following questions. When completed, please return to the following: Fiction Editor, Barbour Publishing, Inc., P.O. Box 719, Uhrichsville, OH 44683.

1. Did you enjoy reading *A Big Apple Christmas*?
   ❏ Very much—I would like to see more books like this.
   ❏ Moderately—I would have enjoyed it more if _____
   _____
   _____

2. What influenced your decision to purchase this book?
   (Check those that apply.)
   ❏ Cover   ❏ Back cover copy   ❏ Title   ❏ Price
   ❏ Friends   ❏ Publicity   ❏ Other

3. Which story was your favorite?
   ❏ *Moonlight and Mistletoe*   ❏ *Where the Love Light Gleams*
   ❏ *Shopping for Love*   ❏ *Gifts from the Magi*

4. Please check your age range:
   ❏ Under 18   ❏ 18–24   ❏ 25–34
   ❏ 35–45   ❏ 46–55   ❏ Over 55

5. How many hours per week do you read? _____

Name _____

Occupation _____

Address _____

City_____ State _____ Zip _____

E-mail_____